The Glass Cave

JOHANNA BOETGER

ARCHWAY
PUBLISHING

Cover image by Sherry Arthur First Sight Art Gallery, LLC.

Archway Publishing books may be ordered through booksellers or by contacting:

Archway Publishing
1663 Liberty Drive
Bloomington, IN 47403
www.archwaypublishing.com
1 (888) 242-5904

ISBN: 978-1-4808-3165-0 (sc)
ISBN: 978-1-4808-3166-7 (e)

Library of Congress Control Number: 2016941035

Print information available on the last page.

Archway Publishing rev. date: 05/27/2016

CHAPTER 1

It was a beautiful May evening. The shadows in the woods on both sides of them were just starting to darken. They had found the old logging road off the blacktop secondary highway. Now all they needed to do was to find the red mailbox that marked the turnoff to the cabin. Shelly was tired. The children—Jacob (Jake), eleven, and Amy, nine—had been bickering for the last fifty miles or so, their voices getting louder and angrier. Shelly was on the verge of spouting some useless ultimatum when Jake screamed, "Mom, she broke my nose! She hit me in the nose with her doll, and now it's broken!"

"Did not!" Amy yelled.

"Did so!" Jake yelled. "You hit me in my nose."

"I did not hit you in the nose!" Amy yelled. "I hit you in your eye 'cause you called me a whiny baby."

Shelly was looking in the rearview mirror, trying to see if Jake was bleeding, at the exact moment they drove past a rusted red mailbox that was almost hidden in the over grown weeds. "Oh, come on now, guys," Shelly pleaded. "We are tired, it's getting dark, and I really need your help finding the red mailbox."

"Are we almost there?" Amy asked.

"How far is it? Jake asked.

"I don't know," Shelly told them honestly. "All Daddy said was, 'It's a ways up the logging road, and the logging road is a little rough.'"

Shelly thought about that day, over two years ago, when Doug told her that he had bought a little mountain cabin in the woods. She was so angry. They couldn't afford another bill, but he had been insistent and assured her they could make it. How thrilled he thought she would be when she saw the cabin. He couldn't wait to show it to her. Before they got the chance to go to the cabin, Doug was killed by a drunken driver.

The insurance settlement paid everything off. She intended to sell the cabin but hadn't gotten around to it. Maybe she couldn't bring herself to sell something Doug had been so happy about. "How long are we going to stay in the cabin, Momma?" Amy asked.

"Until the sickness is gone," Jake told her.

"Is that right, Momma?" Amy asked.

"Yes," Shelly said as she thought to herself, "Sickness … right … it's a man-made epidemic started in the Middle East."

At first there had been finger pointing. Some people blamed terrorists, others blamed Israel, and still others blamed the United States. Now it didn't matter. Those that would have known were dead. Now there was just a scramble to stop it and find a cure before the entire human population was wiped out.

As soon as the first case was reported in the United States, Shelly had packed up everything she could think of to survive an extended stay at the cabin and headed out with her family: two children, two dogs, and a cat. Thank heavens the animals had been quiet. Golly was a German shepherd and border collie mix. "By golly," was the first thing Jake said on his eighth birthday, when he opened the box that held the puppy. Amy's dog, Jessie, was a Chihuahua–Maltese mix that had arrived pretty much the same way as Golly on Amy's sixth birthday. Misty, Amy's cat, appeared last year. Running in the back door one rainy night, she decided that Amy belonged to her and that she was now home.

Shelly shook her head, wondering how far they had driven. It was dark, and the logging road had gotten more than just a little rough.

In fact, the road had ended. It was deep woods on three sides from what she could tell. Other than the trees in front of them, lit by the headlights, it was pitch-black outside. "Are we there now?" Amy asked from behind her.

"No, baby, I think we missed the mailbox," Shelly told her. "We are going to have to go back."

When Shelly put the SUV in reverse, the backup lights lit a break in the trees behind the SUV and to her left. "Well, a three-point turn it is," she thought. "Better than trying to back out this SUV."

She eased the SUV back and felt the rear end drop. "Just a bit more and I'll clear that tree," she thought. The SUV went over. Shelly slammed on the brakes, but they kept sliding. She gripped the steering wheel and stood on the brake pedal, Amy started a high-pitched scream that didn't stop. Jacob kept yelling, "Mom, Mom, Mom!" Golly was barking, Jessie was whining, and Misty was howling. Shelly was pleading with God, or Doug, or somebody in the universe to stop the SUV. It seemed to go on forever. The noise inside the car was nothing compared to the sound of tree limbs squealing and breaking along the outside of the vehicle. "Oh, please don't blow up," Shelly thought. "Please don't tip over." She wanted to hold her babies. They came to a stop with a hard bump, and everything was quiet. They were all holding their breath. "Breathe," Shelly said with a gasp. She heard an intake of air from the back. "Is everyone all right?"

"Are we at the cabin now, Momma?" Amy asked as Jake snorted.

Shelly laid her head down on the steering wheel. She was shaking so badly that she couldn't let go of it. "Should we call 911?" Jake asked.

Shelly pulled the phone from the charger and handed it to him. "You do it," she said.

Shelly just didn't have the energy to ponder if there would be a signal this far away from everything. "No signal," Jake reported. He then asked. "Do you think we are at the bottom, or will we fall more?"

"Mommy?" Amy said.

"What is it, baby," Shelly sighed.

"I got to go tinkle," Amy said.

As Shelly was helping Amy, trying to stay patient with the child, who complained about wet shoes and no way to flush, she heard a noise on the other side of the car. "Jake, are you out of the car?" Shelly asked sternly. "Get back in the car, Jake."

"I'm right here, Mom. I just had to ... you know," Jake reported. "And you know, Mom, we hit something."

Shelly ran her fingers through her hair and told Amy to get into the car. Of course they had hit something. They had just rolled who knows how far down a mountside of boulders and trees. "Heck, we could have hit a bigfoot," she thought, feeling her way to the back of the car. Jake was standing on the driver's side of the car with a flashlight shining on what appeared to be a window—a big window. "What is it, Mom?" Jake asked. "Some kind of glass house?"

"I don't know, Jake," Shelly replied. "How far does it go?"

"Can't tell how far," Jake said. "It's past how far the light goes."

Shelly cautiously cupped her hands around her eyes to cut the glare of the light bouncing off the glass and leaned her head forward. "Shine the light over this way, Jake," she instructed. "Maybe I can see what's on the other side."

Jake turned the light toward his mother, making a slow arc of the beam. All she could see was woods. Shelly backed away, thinking to herself, "I sure wouldn't want to be the window washer for this place."

"Let's get back in the car," Shelly said. "I just can't think of anything sensible right now."

"Mom, are we going to drive back up?" Jake asked.

"Not tonight," Shelly replied tiredly. "We'll sleep in the car and then see what it looks like in the daylight."

Shelly sorted out long leashes and tied the animals to small trees. Misty did a couple of flips, trying to slip out of her harness, but she settled soon enough, looking for a place to dig. Shelly dug sandwich makings out of the cooler. Jake and Amy pulled out pillows and blankets from the back, with Amy demanding Jake find her unicorn pillow pet. Shelly wondered what had happened to her sweet baby girl. "When did this little drama queen take over her body?" she thought. "Well, it is going to stop. Not tonight, but soon."

CHAPTER 2

It wasn't the sun, but the birds, that woke them in the morning. It sounded as if each individual bird was trying to be first to announce the day. Shelly scrubbed her eyes. She was tired. She felt as if she hadn't slept. "Too many dreams of too many people," she thought as she eased out of the car. She took in their surroundings and noted they were indeed at the bottom of the mountainside. Her heart fluttered when she looked up and saw how far down they had fallen. She knew they were lucky to be alive. There was no way she was going to be able to drive back up. She wasn't sure if they could even hike back up to the road. Shelly told Jake to find the cereal and milk, and she ignored Amy's demand for a cheese omelet and toast. "Did that child actually stomp her foot?" she thought. "This drama business is going to stop. Not right now, but soon."

Shelly explored the surrounding area, hoping for a road or a trail. Finding none, she went back to examine the strange window. It was surreal, even spooky. She couldn't see a starting or ending point to the glass. She reached out and touched it, and she could have sworn she felt a slight hum. "It doesn't feel like glass or plastic," she thought.

"Mommy," Amy said from behind her.

"In a minute, baby," Shelly said as she pushed on the glass.

"*Mommy*," Amy said, louder and more demanding.

Shelly closed her eyes. "Enough, Amy," she thought, "I have had enough." She turned, ready with a lecture about how all the drama was going to have to stop, but her words erupted as a loud squeak instead.

There were four of them, standing motionless, three males behind a female. They were beautiful, and they were not human. "Jake, Amy, come to me," Shelly called.

She tried to keep the rising panic out of her voice. She saw rapt adoration on Amy's face. "Are they angels, Mommy?" Amy asked.

Shelly understood Amy's connection. They were her height—about five feet six inches tall—and were pale with platinum-blond hair; small, straight noses; and small mouths. It was the eyes—large, wide-spaced, almond-shaped, and the color of aqua—that no human could claim. They were dressed alike in long white tunics and pants of some kind of silk like material, but lighter and airier; and they glowed.

Shelly stepped forward in front of her children as Jake took hold of Amy's hand. Shelly felt her fear rising. She wanted to run—just grab her babies and run. But run to where? Her heart was pounding. She started to shake. Shelly struggled to hold back the scream that was fighting to break loose. "What do you want?" Shelly demanded, her voice strong despite her fear.

The glowing female slowly held out both her hands, palms up. "Do not fear," she said. "We mean you no harm. We are here to help."

The alien voice was soft, melodious. Other than one slow blink, she made no other movement, but waited patiently. Shelly's mind was racing. The whole world was one long nightmare; she lived every day with the fear she had been living with since Doug's death. She had put everything off because of that fear—everything except this mad dash to get her family to the cabin; and look where that had landed them. "What do you want with us?" Shelly asked.

"We want to help you," the female said, gesturing toward the window. "Please come with us. We have prepared you a place."

"Said the spider to the fly," Shelly thought. "But do we really have a choice?" Then Shelly noticed the animals. All of them were sitting quietly, one at the foot of each male. Shelly felt her body start to uncoil. She didn't trust these beings, but she trusted her pets not to cozy up to evil. Jake picked that moment to step from behind her, look straight at the alien group, and ask, "You folks don't have a cookbook, do you?"

Shelly groaned at Jake's reference to an old rerun of *The Twilight Zone* they had watched just the previous week. The beings looked startled for a moment, and then all four of them smiled. "No, young one, we really are here to help," the female said.

One of the males moved slowly around them with Misty at his heels. He stopped at the glass, reached up to touch it, and slid his finger all the way to the ground. A split opened, and he and Misty walked through it. Shelly looked at Jake, who shrugged and nodded. With Shelly guiding her children in front of her, they all turned and stepped through the slit. She looked back as the last male and Golly stopped just inside the opening. The male reached up and slid his finger down the slit, closing it. Shelly felt a moment of trapped panic, and then the female said, "Do not worry. You have stepped through. You can now open and close the barrier the same way we opened it."

Shelly stared at the alien. Had her thoughts shown on her face so plainly? She walked back to the glass, reached up, touched it, and slid her finger to the ground. The slit opened. She reached up and closed it the same way. "Awesome. Can I do it? Jake said.

"Me first," Amy shouted.

Both were running their finger up and down the glass with no result. "You must be an adult for the barrier to respond to you," the female said. "Please come; your people are being gathered and made ready. They will arrive soon, and you have much to learn."

As they walked through the woods, Shelly thought, "My people, gathered, made ready for what?" She wished she could get "cookbook" out of her head. They had hiked some distance when Shelly noticed that though she and the children had been slapping and brushing at biting pesky insects, the glowing beings didn't seem to be bothered by them. The sound of Golly's snapping teeth told her that even the pets were being annoyed. She almost stumbled over Jake when he suddenly stopped. Shelly looked up at Amy's wondrous cry of, "Oh, Mommy!"

Shelly gasped at the beautiful picturesque sight before her. A long, green lush valley spread before them. A wide creek ran the length of it. Cows, sheep, goats, and horses grazed peacefully in scattered groups. In the distance, Shelly could see the mouth of a large cave with more glowing beings around it. "What are they doing?" Jake asked.

"Constructing a door to your cave," the female replied.

Shelly wondered if the males could talk because so far she hadn't heard them say a word. "We speak," the male behind her said.

Shelly whirled to face him. "You're reading my mind," Shelly accused.

"Not reading," he stated. "We hear what you are thinking."

"Well, stop it," Shelly growled.

"Stop thinking so loudly," she heard in her head.

She thought of a huge pillow being pulled around her brain and heard him chuckle behind her. "That will do it," he said.

"Really?" Shelly thought the words. "Just think of a pillow on my head?"

"Yes," she heard him reply in her head.

"Well, it didn't work, because you heard me," she said mentally to him.

"You must learn to think under the pillow" was the silent reply.

Shelly shook her head. "He thinks he's funny," she thought. It was too much. She just couldn't handle any more. "You are stronger than you realize," a feminine voice softly echoed in her mind.

As they approached the cave, Shelly stopped, stunned. There was her car. The glowing beings were unloading it and going through it. "How did that get here, and what are they doing?" Shelly thought. A male turned and held up her tote bag of seeds. Shelly thought of the day she had bought the seeds, selecting vegetables and herbs she and the children especially liked. Then the male jumped on what looked like a Jet Ski and took off up into the air with the bag.

"What was that all about?" Shelly asked the female glow.

"We wished to know what the seeds were. We told them it is food you and the little ones like," the glow answered.

Shelly watched until he was out of sight, turned with a resigned sigh, and silently followed the others into the cave. The entrance hall was wide, and the ceiling was high. Lights were spaced to keep it well lit. "This doesn't feel like a cave," she thought as they proceeded down a wide street-like hallway. There were doors evenly spaced on both sides of the street. Small boxes, about waist high, were attached to the wall next to each door.

Shelly started counting her paces. "Twenty paces between each door," she thought. They had passed at least six doors, but before she could complete the math, they turned a corner to the right. Shelly glanced behind her to see that a left turn would have taken them down another street with the same spaced doors. She looked ahead and saw only an endless street of doors. Then she noticed that there were doors to her left but none to her right. She had just finished counting four doors on the left from the turn when they stopped at the first door on the right. The female waved her hand over the small box and the door slid open. *Star Trek*, Shelly thought. As she stepped into a narrower hallway, Shelly saw a door about four paces to her left. A couple of paces farther, there was a set of double doors on her right. At the far end of the hallway was another door on the left. They stopped at the first door on the left. The female waved her hand in front of the box, and the door slid open. She told Shelly that this was to be their living quarters.

Shelly quickly scanned the layout: open floor plan, living room, dining room, kitchen, and a hallway containing what she assumed were bedroom doors. What she really focused on was the male sitting at a dining room table. The table was loaded with food. He was older—she didn't know how she could tell—and he reminded her of a grandfather. Jake and Amy had already moved to the table. Amy stuffed a strawberry in her mouth. "Please excuse them," Shelly said to the male.

He smiled kindly, lifted his hand, and gestured for her to sit. "Come. You hunger; please eat," he said aloud in a kindly, gentle voice.

Shelly was starving. She had split her supper sandwich with Golly and Jessie the night before. She had skipped eating cereal this morning. And she had just hiked a good seven or more miles to the cave. The meal consisted of various fruits, bread, and cheese. A pitcher of what looked like lemonade with ice in it sat in the middle of the table.

CHAPTER 3

They ate in silence. Shelly noticed that Amy was nodding and shaking her head. "Is she talking to you?" Shelly thought, looking at the female.

"To the other," the female answered.

Shelly wondered if Amy had been afraid when she first heard a voice in her head. "She was not afraid. She adapted quicker than you did."

Shelly knew that the funny male had butted into her thoughts. She could tell by the slight touch of humor she associated with his voice. "So what about Jake?" she silently asked.

There was a long pause. "We cannot hear Jake," the female answered.

Shelly stopped eating and stared at the female. "Why?" she said.

"He has learned to cover his thoughts with a leather jacket," the female voice answered.

Shelly knew the jacket. It was Doug's jacket. She knew that Jake often slept with it, but how had Jake learned to do something that she had just learned was possible? Well, she was going to find out—not now, but soon.

The female stood after all of them had eaten their fill. "Children, would you like to go out and explore the valley with your pets?"

Jake and Amy bounced up, sending their mother pleading looks. Shelly sighed and started to push herself up, but the old male raised his hand. "You stay. We have much to discuss."

Shelly grabbed for her imaginary pillow but then mentally threw it down. She didn't care if they heard what she thought. They weren't going to separate her from her babies; they weren't going to do that. "Who am I kidding," she thought, "they can do as they please." After all, they had powers and technology she couldn't begin to comprehend, but so far they had shown nothing except kindness, generosity, and respect. She slipped back into her chair, looked at both children, looked at the table, and nodded. Jake and Amy understood the unspoken command and immediately started clearing the table. The two children moved everything to the kitchen with the glows jumping in to help. It wasn't long until the door slid closed behind them. Shelly turned her attention to the old one. "You have questions?" her mind heard.

Shelly narrowed her eyes at the power and command of his voice, and she quickly changed her estimation of him from grandfather to general. "Would you be more comfortable if we communicated with spoken words?" The grandfather said aloud.

Shelly was puzzled. The grandfather was back. The other two glows she had mind-spoken with sounded the same in both ears and mind, but this one was different. When he spoke aloud, he sounded like a kindly grandfather, but when he spoke in her mind, he sounded like a general. "We are elder," the grandfather said, as if that explained everything.

Shelly pushed his comment aside. It didn't matter. "All I want to know is what is going on." Shelly said aloud. "About my people getting gathered, about my people being made ready, and about what I must learn."

The old one nodded and said, "Now you are ready to learn what you must learn. As you know, your species developed a biological weapon that was turned loose," he said. "This airborne virus has a one-hundred-percent kill rate for your species, and there is no cure. By the time word of this reached us and we arrived on your world, most of your species was already dead.

"Because your country is separated by ocean and closed its borders to all entry, we concentrated a large effort here to provide a safe haven, and protection, for survivors. Nine days ago, the virus infected your west coast and then appeared on your east coast. We assume the virus traveled by plane. The first death from the virus in your country was three days ago; since then most of your species on both the east and west coasts have died. We had planned to start pickup and were scanning for survivors—a time-consuming process—when you dropped in on us last night. While you slept, we probed your mind for family, friends, and acquaintances. We began the gathering of the living as soon as your probe was complete. As we rescue survivors, some are mind probed, and then our teams are sent in other directions. Soon the first group will complete their exams and medical rehabilitation. They will be placed here in the dormitory to await assignment."

Shelly's head jerked up when she heard "medical rehabilitation." Before she could say anything, the old one sat up straight and the general telepathically said, "Stop. What is wrong?"

A kaleidoscope of Hitler, WWII, and pictures of medical experiments raced through Shelly's mind. The old one sat back staring at her in shock and then with sympathy. "No," the grandfather said quietly. "We heal. Everybody is healed of all traces of injury or malady. Missing teeth are replaced. Eyes are repaired. Unless there is a disfiguring scar, our rehabilitation is limited to the insides of bodies, meaning freckles, birthmarks, and wrinkles will remain. We scan and probe for mental anomalies also, and those deemed evil and dangerous to your society are rejected." The old one rubbed his head, "Your species has promise, but you are too emotional. Your people will awaken in the dormitory," he continued. "They will not remember having seen us or know how they got here. You will be our communications expert, and you will be the only one that will be able to communicate with us. You will be provided with an assignment printout that will show which profession each survivor will start with and which apartment he or she will live in. The assignments are in direct correlation to the information gathered from each mind probe. For a smooth start up of your new society, assignments must be strictly adhered to."

"No," Shelly said. "I won't be thrown into a leadership position. Set up a computer in the dormitory to answer questions, and put the assignment sheets next to the computer. Find the best person to deal with the assignments and answer questions. Call that person the head of personnel. Give me a computer. If I know the answer, good. If not, then I'll contact you. If these people want a leader, they can elect one."

The grandfather studied her for a moment and then nodded. "Any other suggestions?" he asked.

"Is it too late to have at least one window put in the living room of each apartment?" she said with just a touch of sarcasm.

"Come, it is time for the tour," the voice of the general in her mind snapped her to her feet.

They started with the double doors down and across the hall from her apartment. It was a conference room. Shelly eyed the space and then quickly calculated the number of doors on the left she had paced before arriving at the first door on the right. "You have a question?" she heard in her mind.

"Where is the rest of it?" she thought in reply.

She followed him to the back wall and watched as he placed his hand on a slightly discolored spot on the rock. "Place your hand next to mine," she heard.

She did as he instructed, and a door opened. "Oh, *Star Trek* big time," Shelly thought.

It was a huge room wrapped in what resembled computers. In the middle of the room was what looked like a tall, tricked-out barber's chair facing a screen. "This is the heart of your caves system," he silently told her. "From here all of what you call electricity, water, heating, cooling, and waste is controlled. Every aspect of what runs your cave system is run from here. This is also where you will be able to contact us. Touch nothing without first contacting us."

"Touch it," Shelly thought, "I'm scared just looking at it."

"We will come back here later, and we will show you how to use the contact chair," the elder said, ignoring her comment. "You are the only one who will be able to open this door. Allow no one else in here."

Shelly edged back toward the door. She didn't like this room. There was too much here. They left the conference room and headed toward the door at the far end of the hall. The general, as Shelly had been thinking of him since they left the table, waved open the door. They entered a long, narrow hall, and the only door Shelly could see was the one at the very end. When the general opened it, she saw it was the dormitory. There were hundreds of beds, not much bigger than cots, all made up with sheets, blankets, and pillows. At the far end was what looked like a nurse's station with an office behind it. There were several glows working around it. Before they reached the station, the glows picked up their tools and left. As they got closer, Shelly noticed the lettering over the office. She stopped and stared. "Powers I can't even start to comprehend," she thought.

"Head of Personnel" in block letters was printed on a sign hanging above the office entrance. She walked into a nice-sized office. There was a desk; an overstuffed desk chair; a computer on the desk, with sheets of paper stacked neatly beside it; two comfy-looking chairs in front of the desk; and a short sofa along the wall. Then she noticed the name plaque on the front of the desk: "Roberta Black." Shelly knew Roberta, but not well. She was a friend of a friend who worked in Protocol at a military base, and she acted a little pushy and uppity. Shelly shrugged. The woman had been probed, and the glows seemed to know what they were doing.

Shelly turned and followed the general out a door next to the office and into a huge cafeteria with seating for what looked like hundreds. Four large restaurant-size stoves, a group of ovens, several walk-in refrigerators, sinks, and dishwashers had been set up along the back wall. Food prep tables were spaced strategically in front of cooking stations. Everything was set up behind the long serving line. The kitchen looked to be well stocked. Shelly looked around the room again and noticed a stage. "Well," she thought, "every society needs a stage." Then she thought of school plays and dance recitals. Yes, they would need a stage.

They left the restaurant and entered a large plaza. In the middle of the street, just to the left of the restaurant, was a fountain with seating around it. Up and down both sides of the street were shops. The glows were painting names on the windows of the shops in block letters. Shelly took a moment to read some of the names that were finished: Cake Shop, Music Shop, Cobbler Shop, Card Shop, Toy Shop, and Book Shop. She smiled and wondered how long it would take the new proprietors to change the names. As they walked past the shop windows, she glanced inside, noticing that all shops came filled with stock. "How long have you been working on all this?" she thought.

"The main cave system has been here a very long time. We have been putting the finishing touches on it for a little over seven days," he thought back.

As they left the shopping district, the general stopped, and a moment later a small car pulled up. A female glow climbed out of the front seat, nodded to the general, and then walked off. The car looked like a bullet with a seat in front and a seat in back. "This will save time," he thought at her, settling into the front seat.

Shelly eased into the back, looking around for the seat belt. "No seat belts," she concluded, and the bullet sped down the street.

CHAPTER 4

Shelly was just starting to enjoy the ride when she saw a set of closed double doors rapidly approaching, and the bullet car was not slowing down. She grabbed her mental pillow and imagined herself screaming under it. Just at that moment, both doors opened, and they sped into what looked like a farmer's field. She closed her eyes when she felt the bullet rise from the floor of the cave high into the air. Opening her eyes, she saw they had entered another cavern still inside the massive cave complex. High above the floor of the cave, she looked down upon a panorama of divided fields, barns, and other structures. Shelly was amazed at what was being produced inside the cave. She could distinguish fields of wheat, corn, oats, cotton, and vegetables ready for harvest, but there were also fields at different stages of growth. "How can all this grow inside?" Shelly thought to the general.

"A form of hydroponics," the general answered in thought.

"How did you know what to plant?" she asked.

"Most of what you see is what humans have eaten or used for hundreds, even thousands, of years. The seeds found in your vehicle helped, and mind probes gave us much information."

"Hydroponics," Shelly thought, trying to remember what she knew of it. "Plants grown in water with stuff added to the water," she thought.

"You are correct," the general sent. "Plants are grown in water. Nutrient solutions are added to the water to feed the plants. We have installed nutrient dispensers in each field. As long as your farmers keep the same plants in the same fields and follow instruction manuals, these fields should last your people a very long time."

As they reached the end of the fields, the bullet lowered back to ground level and Shelly found herself looking at fencing. They got out of the bullet and walked toward an enclosure. "This is where your large animals will be housed and cared for," he thought at her. "Our probes received conflicting information about the living arrangements from those in the professions of farming and animal husbandry. Some of your species desire to live very close to their crops and animals, while others of you prefer to live away from them. These are the only professions whose workers will be given a choice of residence."

"You have thought of everything, haven't you?" she asked in her mind.

"No, we only reproduced what was heard in the minds of your people." The general halted and turned to her. "The last of the living have been picked up." There seemed to be a hint of sadness in his thought.

Suddenly, for the first time since they had left the dining table, he changed back into the grandfather, smiled, and spoke to her aloud. "They have babies. The staff at a large hospital barricaded themselves in a nursery, allowing no one access. The air in the nursery was filtered. They rescued forty-two babies along with the nursing staff."

He turned and marched back to the bullet. "Come; there is much to be done." Shelly heard in her mind that the general was back.

They were once again in the air, flying over the fields. Shelly could barely make out the long, low troughs filled with water. "What are those troughs for?" she sent.

"For fish farming," he sent back.

She looked up for the first time. "What kind of lights are those?" she asked of the huge, flat round lights hanging from the ceiling of the cavern.

"Grow lights for the fields," he responded as the car dropped to reenter the living area.

Shelly saw the double doors approaching. She closed her eyes, knowing in her mind that they would open, but her body braced for the impact. Inside the living area, the bullet zipped along new streets, not returning them by the same path they had left. "I am going to need a map of this place," Shelly thought.

"Noted," the general replied, his voice loud in her mind.

As they pulled to a stop in front of the short hall leading to her apartment, Shelly was astonished to see a large window. Not only had one been installed for her, but identical windows had been installed in all the apartments she saw along the street. She rushed over to inspect her window, thinking, "Oh boy, now I can get curtains."

"Curtains—why?" the general asked.

Shelly turned to him, saying aloud, "Well, so no one can see in, of course. Does it open?" The general stared at her for a long moment. Shelly grabbed her imaginary pillow, pulled it over her mind, and then thought, "Did his eyes just narrow at me? I didn't know they could do that."

"The others will be here momentarily with your children," the general thought at her. "We shall return later." He turned and stalked off without a backward glance.

Shelly had just waved open the short hallway door when she heard Amy's laughter as the group came around the corner. "Mommy, I have flowers for our new home," Amy squealed. Holding her shirt filled with flowers out in front of her, she broke into a run toward her mother. "And I got a rock collection, and Jake caught fish for supper."

Jake held up a stringer of fish with a grin. Shelly could see his face shining with happiness. She looked at Amy and saw twinkling eyes and a smile that showed all her teeth. Shelly felt a pang of guilt. When was the last time she had seen her babies this happy? How could she have been so self-absorbed in her own grief not to have seen how unhappy her children were? "My, how productive you have all been," Shelly said. "Let's go find a vase and start supper."

"Where's Grandfather?" Amy asked as they entered the apartment.

"He said he'd be back later," Shelly answered.

"They put the car back up on the trail for us," Jake reported.

"Well that was sure nice of them," Shelly said with a smile. Then she looked at the female and thought the words, "I think I might have said something wrong to the general."

She heard a chuckle from the kitchen, where Jake and Funny—as Shelly had named this glowing male—were opening cabinet doors, and looking for a pan to cook the fish in. She went to the kitchen, shooed the boys out, and then did a little happy dance when she discovered how well it was stocked. She found butter and dill for the fish, brown rice, salad greens, fresh fruits, vegetables, and the bread left from lunch. In no time she had everything cooking, and she turned to survey her new domain. Amy and Patience, the glowing female, were arranging the flowers in the lemonade pitcher. "Patience—the name fits," Shelly thought. Jake was sitting on the floor, explaining a chess game that he had set up on the coffee table to Funny, who was sitting across from him on the sofa. A knock at the door sent Amy scampering to wave it open. She came back carrying a tube and handed it to Shelly. "You didn't say thank you," she chided her daughter.

"Yes I did, Mommy," Amy said with a confused look.

Shelly searched Amy' face. "She did," Funny thought to her.

"Good for you, baby girl," Shelly said brightly. "Come on; let's see what this is."

Shelly removed a lid from the tube, pulled out a long, rolled-up paper, and spread it open on the dining room table. It was a map of the cave system. "Neat," Jake said, studying the map from the other side of the table.

"Yes," Shelly agreed.

"This place is as big as a small city," she thought. Shelly rolled up the map and placed it back in the tube. "We'll look at this later," she said. "Right now let's set the table and eat Jake's fish."

During the meal, Amy gave Shelly a tutorial on why the glow beings didn't eat what humans ate and why it wasn't rude or ungrateful when they didn't eat together. "Our food would make their tummies hurt," Amy said. "And it might make them sick. They don't need to eat as often as we do, and they brought their own"—Amy paused for a moment, trying to think of the word—"… nourishment with them."

When the kitchen was clean, the children had been bathed, and the good night kisses had been planted, Shelly tucked each child into bed. "Mommy, did you see my rock collection?" asked Amy sleepily.

Shelly stopped and looked at the eight rocks arranged on top of the dresser. She examined a few, commenting on each rock's color or sparkle. Then she picked up a yellow rock that seemed a little heavy for its size. "This yellow one is pretty," Shelly said.

"Mmm, my favorite," mumbled Amy.

Sitting at the table with Patience and Funny, the map spread out before them, Shelly leaned back in her chair and looked at Patience. "Okay, now tell me what I said wrong to the general," she demanded in her thoughts.

"It is not that you said anything wrong," Patience replied. "It is that you are a different species. You must understand that, compared to yours, our species has a long life span. Our reproduction is much different. Our babies, and the very young, are rare, cherished. Most of us go our entire lifetime and never communicate with an elder until we become one. You have been given a great honor, and a privilege. Elders are power; one simply doesn't say no, question, or make demands to an elder."

Shelly waited for Patience to say more. When she didn't, Shelly shook her head. "No, it was something about the window," she insisted.

Funny chuckled, and Shelly turned on him. "You seem to find this so amusing; you explain it!" she snapped, not amused.

"It is easy," Funny said. "When this mission came up, Elder jumped on board. Elders seldom go on missions. Because of his birth name, different species have always fascinated him—your species extensively, but most information we have is secondhand. When we were given the design for the cave system, it was right. It was complete. Then here you come and ask to have the design changed. You want a window not just for your apartment, but for all the apartments. That meant that the design had a flaw. You must understand Elder simply does not create a flawed design. You get the window, and the first thing you want to do is cover it up. If you did not want to see the window, then the design was not flawed. But then you had to ask if it opened, so the design is again flawed."

"I didn't really expect the windows," Shelly groaned. "I was being flippant." She looked at Patience. "It really is a matter of being different species, isn't it? I'll have to watch more closely what I say and think. I will apologize to the elder when he gets here," Shelly promised.

"No need," Funny said. "Elder knows."

"What do you mean he knows?" Shelly asked.

"He is Elder," Funny replied. "Elder hears everyone."

"What!" Shelly exploded.

Patience and Funny both leaned back in their chairs, their eyes blinking. "Please try to control your emotions before you injure the young ones," General's voice echoed in her mind.

"They are asleep," Shelly replied.

"Not yours," snapped the general. "Ours."

Shelly looked at Patience and asked, "How old are you?"

"We would be the equivalent of fifteen years old in the time of your species," Patience answered, lightly rubbing her temple.

"Enough," thought Shelly to herself, she didn't want to know more. "Let's get started on this map," Shelly said, standing to get a better overview.

CHAPTER 5

Shelly admired the layout before her. The shopping district was larger than she had thought. There were also parks, a hospital, and churches, all conveniently placed. There was a knock at the door, and Shelly thought, "Come in."

"So you are learning the map," Grandfather said as he walked up to the table to join the three of them.

"How many apartments are there in this place?" Shelly asked.

"Twenty thousand," Grandfather answered.

"Where is number one eight four eight two?" Shelly asked.

"Here," he answered, promptly laying his finger on the map.

Shelly grabbed her pillow and tried to think of a way to change the map without making it flawed. "You have a suggestion?" Grandfather asked.

"If I left here right now with this map, I doubt I would be able to find that apartment. However, if we call this street Main Street," Shelly said, indicating a street that ran down the middle of the city, "and we prefix the streets west of Main Street with 'West' and east of Main Street with 'East,' and if we number each street one, two, three, and up, then people can find their way from west to east. The streets that cross north to south should be named Avenues and numbered in the same manner. Then we can find our way in here."

Grandfather studied the map. "But should not there be a Main Avenue that splits north and south?" he asked.

"It's too confusing to have two Mains, especially to the younger ones, but we could call it Patience Avenue," Shelly said with a smile. "And this street where the entrance to the cave is would be close enough to the middle to make it easy," she added, running her finger along the street on the map.

"Noted," said the general.

"May I see the assignment sheets?" Shelly asked, still studying the map.

"Of course," General answered.

"General," Shelly said aloud, pointing to an unnamed location on the map. It was a large prime spot, located not far from the shopping district, next to the hospital, and across from the school. "What's this?" she thought, not taking her eyes off the map.

"The nursery. It is for your babies, nurses, and caregivers," answered Grandfather, speaking softly.

A knock on the door signaled the arrival of the assignment sheets. Shelly scanned them quickly—and then more closely, with surprise. "How does he do that?" she thought. The list was complete, with new addresses included. As she studied the occupations and addresses, she wasn't sure she liked what she saw. "You have a suggestion?" Grandfather asked.

"All the laborers, tradesmen, and service workers live on the north side of the shopping district. Teachers, doctors, and shop owners live on the south side," she said.

"This is efficient," Grandfather stated.

"Yes, it is," she said, "But by dividing like this, it could also lead to class warfare in time. Some workers might feel that, because of a certain address, they are better than other workers."

"The apartments are basically all the same," Grandfather said. "Wouldn't the people be happy to be alive and to have others to live and work with?"

Clearly the elder did not understand her concept of class division. Shelly looked at him and said, "One thing about humans is that they aren't satisfied with being happy. There are always some who will stir up trouble, find something to gripe about, and thrive on making the rest of us miserable."

"You are positive this war would happen?" General thought.

Shelly realized he truly did not grasp the concept of class warfare. So she shared with him the memory of her devastation when, as a first grader, her best friend of a whole week, whom she adored, came to her and told her they could no longer be friends because she lived on the wrong side of town.

"Noted," General thought. And then he added "Your species has a long way to go."

"We'll probably need a jail too," thought Shelly, and she was startled when she heard "Noted" come from the general yet again.

Shelly nodded and started to look at the names on each sheet—a task that she had purposely avoided. She stopped, and wondered if she could contain her joy, when she found her two friends Grace and Christy, from North Carolina. She had met them when Doug had taken her and the children on vacation. Jake had been a toddler and Amy a baby. Grace, a childless widow, had run a bed-and-breakfast on a mountain in North Carolina. Christy, a long time friend of Grace, moved permanently in with Grace when her daughter married, to help with the workload and do the cooking. Since both her and Doug's parents had passed away, Grace and Christy had volunteered to become Jake and Amy's foster grandmothers. Shelly stared at their names on the list. "I thought all the people on the East Coast were dead," she thought.

"They locked themselves in their home with Christy's two granddaughters," Patience said quietly. "They were among the first from your memories to be rescued."

"Shelly looked at Grandfather. "You really are angels, aren't you?" she said.

"No, we are keepers," he replied. "It is our species assignment to make sure sentient beings on other worlds do not become extinct."

A knock at the door brought the delivery of a revised map. When it had been spread out on the table, Shelly noted the names of the streets had been added along with a jail, gym, dance studio, and theater. "How many people were rescued?" Shelly asked. "12,862 total—2,776 males, 3,824 females, and 6,262 children under the age of eighteen," Grandfather answered.

Shelly sat down. "So few," she thought. There were almost as many children as adults, though teens could work. Shelly scrubbed at her eyes and pushed back her hair. "You tire, and you need sleep," Grandfather said aloud. "There is much to do tomorrow, and you need to be rested. You will make one final inspection before the first drop."

"First drop? What does that mean?" Shelly asked.

"It means we will start delivering your people to the dormitory," he answered.

"How many will be in the first drop?" Shelly asked.

"Two hundred," Grandfather answered. "Many of them will recognize you, and we are trusting your presence will help make the transition easier."

Shelly awoke the next morning with Amy and Jake bouncing on her bed. She couldn't even remember going to bed. "We're hungry," bubbled Amy. "Can we have cheese omelets and toast?"

"Of course you can," Shelly replied, hugging them both. "Scoot, now, while I get showered and dressed," she laughed.

"I'll start your coffee and breakfast, Mom," Jake said as they ran out of the room.

In no time, Shelly was in the kitchen, sliding the last omelet onto a plate. There was a knock at the door. "Come in," Shelly thought.

Amy had dashed to wave it open. "Grandfather," Amy squealed.

Shelly turned just in time to see Amy throw herself at the grandfather, and a split second before the little girl touched him, the glow disappeared. The grandfather took Amy's hand and led her to the table. When he had sat down, Amy climbed into his lap, hugged his neck, and kissed his cheek.

"I'm so happy to see you," Amy said to the elder. "I missed you last night at supper. See my flowers? I wanted to give you a kiss good night. Why, Grandfather, you're not glowing. Are you sick?" Amy said with heartfelt concern.

The grandfather hugged her and then directed her to a place at the table where a plate holding an omelet sat. Then his glow came back on. "We missed you too, little one," Grandfather said. "We are not sick. For our species, yours is a hostile world. Our glow is sort of a personal force field to keep anything bad from happening to us. You must not ever touch the glow. It could injure you."

"Okay," Amy said. "Want to see my rock collection?"

"After you eat," Shelly said quickly.

"Can we go outside again after we eat?" Jake asked.

"The others are arriving shortly," Grandfather commented. "They will be happy to escort the children and pets outside."

"I think that is a good idea," Shelly said.

Amy and Jake finished their meal, rinsed their plates, and stacked them in the dishwasher. Amy ran to retrieve her rock collection, and Jake went to put on his sneakers. Shelly cleaned the kitchen while Amy showed her rocks to Grandfather. "And this is my favorite," Amy said, handing the yellow rock to him.

"It is beautiful. You have good taste," Grandfather said, handing the rock back to her after examining it.

By the time Patience, Funny, and the two other males arrived, both children were ready to go.

Shelly and the grandfather watched the little troop until they turned the corner. A bullet car pulled up almost immediately afterward, and they set off to continue the tour of the city. "Suggestions?" General thought at her.

"Maybe a kiosk with a map outside the restaurant for people to refer to," Shelly thought.

"Noted" was the reply.

They checked most of the public places on the map. Shelly was astounded when she saw the nursery. It was the only place she had visited that had color on the walls and ceiling. Their surfaces were bright and vibrant, with colorful scenes of people, birds, flowers, and animals. In the play areas, there were wooden boxes, shelves, and bins of toys and books. Soft muted colors adorned the areas for resting and sleeping. There were dressers, closets, and shelves full of clothes, diapers, and everything else a baby needed. There was a kitchen, and a dining area where small tables, chairs, and high chairs lined the wall. "You have done well here," Shelly said as they left. "I can think of nothing to add."

They inspected the fish farm, and she was impressed with the long rows of tanks, pumps, and equipment that she didn't understand. Last, they went back to the dormitory, where Shelly again walked through the office of the head of personnel. "Will everyone wake at once.?" she thought.

"They can," General answered. "Or it can be spaced out."

"They will be hungry," she thought. "It might be good if they woke up smelling something good to eat."

"Noted," General sent back.

"Are there any policemen in the first drop?" she thought.

"They can be added," he replied. "Do you expect trouble?"

"They are humans," she said aloud. "I expect anything and everything."

CHAPTER 6

Shelly noticed a printer sitting next to the computer. She opened one of the file cabinets and saw it was full of files with names on them. She shuffled through the papers on the desk. Next to them was a file with Robert's name on it. She opened the file, scanned the detailed job description, and then picked up a paper with "LAWS" written across the top. She felt a chill go through her as she read the last one, and she slowly sank into the desk chair. She looked at the general and thought, "These are the Ten Commandments—well, almost."

"They are the laws that every sentient being in the universe must learn to obey to live in peace," he stated.

Shelly had so many questions bouncing around in her mind. She couldn't decide which to ask first. General held up his hand and thought to her sternly, "Not all of your questions will be answered."

"It figures," thought Shelly. "What is your name?" she asked him.

"We are keepers," he answered.

"No, what is the name you were born with?" she thought.

He stared at her a moment, and sat down in one of the chairs in front of the desk. "We do not have names as you do," General explained. "It is more of a signature aura. When a child is conceived, it emits an aura—a feeling. The elders are immediately touched by the new aura and pass it to the collective; it is like a birth announcement.

You did surprisingly well in your naming of Patience and Funny. Those names fit their auras."

"So what name or word would fit your birth aura?" she thought to him.

"'Curiosity' would be close," he thought.

"Are there others that could be called Patience?" she asked.

"Of course" was his answer.

"Well, how do you tell them apart?" she thought.

"If you had an identical twin of Amy, and you named that twin Amy also, would they be the same? Would you be able to tell them apart?"

Shelly looked at him for a bit and then nodded affirmatively. "No one is exactly the same."

She didn't quite understand it all but thought she was close enough for now. "Who gives the keepers their assignments?" she asked.

"The instructors," he replied candidly.

"Who gives the instructors their assignments?" she asked

"You would have to ask the instructors to get that answer," he replied.

Shelly felt that if she tried to get more information, she would end up in a loop, and so she decided it wasn't worth the time. "So what's next?" she thought.

"We must talk about your children," Grandfather said aloud, kindly. Shelly sat up and felt fear, and then anger, start to grow. "They will not be harmed, but we need to block the memory of us in their minds," he said.

Shelly started to ask him why but stopped. She knew why. There was no way Amy, or even Jake, would be able to keep from talking about the glowing alien beings. Slowly, she nodded. She could feel the tears wanting to fall. They had been so happy the last couple of days. She wished they could keep some small part of it. "Amy may keep her rock collection," Grandfather said. "She will not remember where she got it, but her feelings for it will be the same."

"You said 'block'; can you also remove the memories?" she asked. Grandfather slowly nodded affirmatively. "Will there be a danger of them breaking down or getting past the block?" she asked.

"If they grow strong enough in willpower and self-control, they can get past the block," he said. "But if they grow that strong, they will also have the wisdom not to discuss how they arrived here."

"Why don't you just remove the memories?" she asked.

He looked at her a long moment before answering. "We have grown very fond of your little ones," he said. "It would please us to know that, at some point in their lives, they will remember us."

"When will you do this?" she asked.

"When they return," he answered.

Shelly felt as if she were too heavy to stand up. She had grown to care for this glowing being. She knew she would miss him when they left.

"Thank you," Grandfather said softly.

She pushed herself up and started for the door. "We might as well wait in the apartment," she sighed.

"You must learn to use the contact chair," General thought.

Shelly wondered if she would miss the general.

As they walked through the dormitory to the narrow-hall door, Shelly thought about the contact chair. She tried to imagine what might be in store for her. She wondered if there would be some kind of upside-down bowl with wires attached that would fit over her head. She tried to remember if she had seen anything like that above the chair. She wondered if she would have to pass some kind of test. "I'm not so good with tests," she thought as they approached the conference room doors. By the time they entered the conference room, her palms were sweating and she had managed to work herself into a nice state of nervousness. General had Shelly open the control room door to make sure she knew where the lock was and to assure her that she could do it.

"Please take a seat in the chair," he thought at her.

The chair was taller than a normal chair. Shelly had to half-hop to get up into it. The general walked over to a panel near the chair and waved his hand in front of it. What looked like an old X-ray plate slid out. "We will communicate with the machine from here," he said. "When we lay our left hand on this plate, it tells the machine that a keeper is instructing it."

He placed his left hand on the plate. "When a small green dot appears on the screen in front of you in the upper left-hand corner, it means the machine acknowledges us as a keeper.

"I see the dot," Shelly said.

"Notice the silver plates on the arms of the chair. When you place your left hand on the left plate, the machine will scan you," General said.

Shelly hesitantly placed her left hand on the plate and saw a green dot appear in the lower left-hand corner of the screen.

"When I place my right hand on this plate, it tells the machine an elder keeper has granted access to you," General said.

A green dot appeared in the upper right-hand corner of the screen. "When you place your right hand on the plate on the right arm of the chair, it tells the machine you have been granted permission to use the chair."

Shelly placed her right hand on the plate and saw the green dot on the lower right-hand corner appear. She felt a slight hum go through both her hands as the chair activated. General raised his hands off the plate and waved one hand over the panel, and the plate slid back. Both dots in the upper and lower corners disappeared. "We have, as you might say, calibrated this chair to you. From it you will be able to reach us after we have gone," General stated.

"That's it? That is all there is to it?" Shelly asked with relief as she jumped down out of the chair.

"Yes, and the children are returning," General sent, walking out the door.

Shelly double-stepped after him, and the door automatically slid closed behind her. She stopped and looked back at it. "That's probably a good thing," she thought.

The others were already in the apartment when Shelly and the grandfather entered. "I didn't catch any fish, Mom," Jake said.

"I didn't find a pretty rock to add to my collection," Amy said.

Jake sat at the dining table with his chin in his hand. Amy sat on the floor and pulled Misty into her lap. "You know, you guys look worn out. Why not go lie down and rest for a bit," Shelly suggested. "We will eat when you get up."

"Okay, Mommy," Amy said, setting Misty in front of her.

Jake stood up, and Shelly was surprised to see all five glows drop their shields. The three young males shook Jake's hand and hugged Amy. Patience hugged them both. Then the grandfather gave both children a hug and kissed Amy on the cheek. "Have a good rest, little ones," the grandfather kindly said.

Both children turned and walked down the hall to their bedrooms. Amy stopped and returned to the grandfather. She took his hand and looked up at him trustingly, saying, "You'll be here for me when I wake up, won't you, Grandfather?"

The grandfather nodded and said, "I will always be here for you, Amy."

When the children had closed their doors, Shelly sank into a dining room chair and laid her head on the table, struggling to swallow the lump in her throat. Patience, as if receiving some silent instruction, handed Misty to the elder and quietly left the apartment on some unknown errand. "It is done," the grandfather said a few moments later.

CHAPTER 7

Shelly looked up and let the tears fall. It hurt her to think her children were losing precious happy memories. After a moment, she went into the kitchen, ran some cold water on a towel, held it to her eyes, and took several deep breaths. Just when she felt herself regaining control, there was a knock at the door. "Come," she automatically thought. When she turned around, Patience was standing there. She had returned with a bundle of folded clothes in her arms.

"You need to change into these," Patience thought to her. "We will have to remove your things from the apartment."

Shelly nodded and, without a word or a thought, walked into her bedroom to change. Patience had brought her a cream-colored tunic top with two pockets in the front, and a pair of roomy pants. It looked like one of the outfits the keepers wore, only these were made of cotton. She was given underwear that was serviceable, and comfortable soft-soled shoes that were just a step above slippers. "Well," Shelly thought, "at least we will see our friends soon." She returned to the living room. Funny was carrying Jake, and Misty's male was carrying Amy. Golly's male carried a sleeping Golly and Jessie, while Grandfather held a sleeping Misty. The children were dressed in tunic outfits similar to Shelly's, and Shelly could see the lumps of Amy's rock collection in a pocket. "I didn't think about the animals sleeping too," Shelly said.

"We try to minimize the stress. A kennel has been installed, and all the animals are to be taken there," Grandfather said.

"You picked up people's pets too?" Shelly asked.

"Your species seems to have an unusual attachment to them—especially your young ones," the grandfather said.

As they left the apartment with the children and pets, the keepers with the pets turned right toward the door that led to the street, and the rest went left to the narrow hallway that led to the dormitory. After the children had been tucked into beds close to the personal office, the male keepers left. Patience sat on a bed and asked Shelly to join her. "Elder has requested I speak with you about the babies," she said softly.

"Grandfather told me about the forty-two babies picked up at the hospital," Shelly said, suddenly distracted by Jake's left arm dropping off his bed, hanging suspended in midair.

"Not those babies—the babies you and the rest of the surviving females over the age of twenty-three and under the age of sixty-five will deliver in nine months," she said.

Shelly jerked around and glared at Patience. "Tell me I just heard you wrong," Shelly slowly said. "I cannot be pregnant; it is impossible. I just misunderstood what you said."

"You were implanted last night while you slept," she responded cheerfully. "You are with child and will deliver a boy baby in nine months."

"How dare you do this!" Shelly exploded off the bed, screaming. "What gives you the right?"

"Control your emotions," ordered General.

"You shut up!" she shouted, her anger mounting.

Shelly felt a vise clamp onto her brain; she couldn't speak or move. She could barely think. She struggled with the sensation, but it tightened even more. "Not a vise," she thought. "It's more like my mind is wrapped in a tightly woven net."

"If you cannot control your emotions, it will be done for you," General stated.

He had marched into the dormitory and was standing in front of her. "You have injured three of us, and it is only a wonder that Patience's injury is not permanent," he scolded.

Shelly cut her eyes to Patience to see her curled on the bed, holding her head with both her hands. Shelly felt her anger deflate. It was replaced with compassion and guilt. Shelly would have gone to Patience if she could only have moved. Then the net loosened slightly. "How did I hurt her?" she thought.

"We have tried repeatedly to convince you how strong you are—not only you but your children as well. We have known since you first backed over the side of the mountain. Your family nearly crippled half of our crew with your fear. If Elder had not been on this mission, things would be much different for you and your family," he stated.

"You helped us down the mountain," Shelly thought skeptically.

"We helped you," General sent to her mind. "It took nearly all of us to control your fall down that mountainside. Do you honestly believe you could have fallen to the bottom of that drop safely without help?"

A female keeper entered the room and went straight to Patience. She laid one hand on the injured alien's forehead and the other hand on the back of Patience's head. "Will she be all right?" Shelly asked with concern. "How long will she hurt?"

"She will be healed in a moment and be fine," General thought. "Her injury would not have been serious if she had not been opened to you so completely. She was expecting happiness and joy, not anger. She has learned a valuable lesson."

The mind net had been loosened enough to allow Shelly to start pacing. "If you had just told me about the babies," she thought.

She still felt the net controlling her feelings of anger and betrayal. "Patience did tell you how we feel about babies," he said.

"Telling me you like babies is not the same as telling me I would be impregnated against my will," Shelly thought angrily, gritting her teeth as she felt the net on her mind tighten.

"The mission was explained to you," he thought.

Shelly stopped pacing, faced him, and felt the net tighten again until she could no longer move. She thought at him in a whisper, "You told me you were here to keep us from dying."

"No, you were told our mission here is to keep your species from becoming extinct," he sent. "And the best way to do that is to make sure we get the widest variety of DNA we can accumulate into your gene pool."

Shelly glared at him. She was angrier than she had ever been in her entire life. She felt betrayed. She had trusted these beings. She started going over everything she could remember any of them saying to her. They had always been kind and gentle, generous and honest, with her family. She felt the net loosen enough to allow her to move. She walked over to the office and stood with her back to them, looking in but not really seeing anything. She was trying to see it from their perspective. This pregnancy wasn't personal. It wasn't about her as an individual. It was about the human species as a whole.

Suddenly Shelly saw it all with crystal clarity. The biggest difference between the two species was that the keepers were not individuals. They were all part of each other, part of a whole. The mind net loosened almost to the point of being gone, but she knew it was still there. Patience truly had no idea she would be upset or angry about being pregnant. She was still angry, though not so much at the pregnancy as at the fact they had impregnated her without her knowledge or permission. Somehow she knew it was something they would never understand. They might know it, but they would never be able to understand it. On the other hand, there was certainly plenty about them she knew and didn't understand.

Shelly turned and saw the healer stroking Patience's temples. As she walked toward them, she felt the mind net rustle in her head. "In control," she thought.

"We are just reminding," came the reply.

"Are you the one that impregnated me with my children's half-brother?" she thought at the healer.

"We did the procedure, but your child is a full brother," the healer snarled.

Shelly blinked at the grouchy answer. "That is impossible," Shelly stated.

"No it is not. We extracted enough of your husband's viable DNA from his jacket," the healer snapped.

"You cloned Doug?" Shelly thought, fighting for control as the net tightened.

"We do not clone. Enough DNA was recovered to …" She stopped. "You are not permitted the information on how the procedure was done. Be assured the child you carry is not a clone. He is a full brother to your other two."

With that the healer turned and left the dormitory. "Doug's baby." Shelly closed her eyes and thought for a long moment.

CHAPTER 8

Opening her eyes, Shelly asked Patience aloud, "May we talk?"
"Of course," Patience said.

"Will you please drop your shield?" Shelly said. "I would like to hold your hands."

Patience's glow disappeared. "I am so sorry I hurt you," Shelly said earnestly, pressing Patience's hands into hers.

"We have been healed," Patience said softly. "The fault was ours." Patience squeezed Shelly's hands gently. "We were warned against opening to you, but so few of us are granted children—such joy and happiness. We just wanted a chance to have the feeling."

Shelly looked into Patience's eyes. "Doug's baby—I am having Doug's baby!" she thought, letting her feelings flow. Shelly's feelings were bright and sunny with happiness. She closed her eyes, continuing to think of the baby, as she allowed the feelings to grow and build until her entire being was bursting with unbridled joy. Shelly wasn't sure how long they sat there, but when she finally opened her eyes, she could see the happiness in the beautiful alien being she was holding hands with. She knew the shield was down, but she could have sworn Patience was glowing.

"Thank you," Patience said reverently.

Shelly patted her hands, stood, and turned to face the general. "It is a good thing you have just done for us," Grandfather said humbly.

"She deserved it," Shelly said.

Shelly started to pace the room. "Okay, I have always considered myself easygoing. Let me tell you right now this is not going to be pretty. We are going to have to figure out how to tell the rest of these women about this breeding program of yours."

"We will trust our communications expert to handle it," General replied curtly.

"You have a communications expert? Who is it?" she asked with a feeling of dread.

"You are the communications expert," he sent.

"I knew it! I just knew it. You are dumping all this right in my lap!" Shelly yelled. As she continued to pace, she felt the net tighten. "You keep me from moving right now, and I will blow up into little bitty pieces all over you!" she screamed. "Do you have any idea how angry some of those women are going to be—especially the ones that don't even like children? And you expect *me* to tell them! I won't do it. I am not going to do it!"

Stepping in front of the general, she poked him in the chest for emphasis. Her finger poked into his glowing shield instead. "Ouch!" she yelped. "Ouch, Ouch, Ouch," she repeated, hopping around in a circle, and shaking her hand in the air. "Oh, ouch!"

She bent over and held her finger between her knees. "We thought you understood not to—" General started.

"Not to touch your blasted personal force field!" Shelly said, finishing the sentence. She then stuck her finger in her mouth, pulled it out, and shook her hand a few more times. "To heck with it; it's just too much," Shelly said loudly. "I'll worry about it later," she thought, sticking her finger back into her mouth. The healer arrived with Funny and the other two glowing keepers that had become her pets' pals. The healer dropped her shield and touched Shelly's hand, and the pain stopped immediately. Before she got her finger out of her mouth, the healer was walking away. "Well, thank you, Dr. Grouch," Shelly thought at the healer's back.

Funny snickered, and Shelly glared at him. "Don't touch the force fields," the healer thought back at her.

Shelly had a sudden thought and aimed it at General. "Does my baby have an aura?" she asked.

"Yes, but it is not like those of our species. Yours is more of a soft, shimmering shadow," he said.

"Can you touch him?" she thought.

"No, not at all," he replied.

For some reason she felt a wave of relief. She looked at Golly's friend and asked aloud, "Why have you never spoken to me?"

"Etiquette dictates we must wait for you to speak to us first," he answered.

She thought at him, "Can you hear my thoughts?"

"Most definitely," he thought to her.

He was strength; she would always think of him as Strong.

"And you?" she said to Misty's friend.

"Same," he replied.

"You can hear my thoughts also."

"Yes," he thought to her.

"Why did Misty choose you?" she thought to him.

"We are compatible," he thought back.

This alien was somehow familiar. She had it! Curiosity—he was another grandfather, but different. She could feel the difference. To her he would be Curious. Shelly knew she had just gained a small bit of understanding of the keepers.

The four young keepers all approached her, dropping their shields. Funny, Strong, and Curious shook her hand in turn. Patience hugged her. "We will remember you always," she whispered into Shelly's mind.

Shelly watched as they left through the narrow hall at the back of the dormitory. "The drop is ready to begin," General sent.

Shelly thought, "About the order of awakening."

"You have a suggestion." His thought was a statement.

"I would like to have Jake and Amy awake about thirty minutes before others begin to wake. This will give me time to explain things to them. They can be a help, calming the other children. Then wake the cooks and policemen. I will get the cooks started in the kitchen, and they should have enough time to get something that smells good cooking. Then wake the head of personnel and allow her time to get organized. After that, I guess it doesn't matter."

"Noted," General sent.

"One last question. I didn't talk to Funny first, but he spoke to me," she thought.

"Would we expect less from Funny?" General sent with a touch of resignation. "If you have questions or problems, contact us," General thought, and then he turned and walked toward the narrow hallway.

"Good-bye, General," Shelly thought as he walked away.

"Good-bye Shelly," Grandfather thought back at her.

Shelly shook her head and laughed. "He just had to throw me one more curve," she thought.

CHAPTER 9

Shelly sat on a bed watching, expecting something—such as the air above the beds to shimmer and a couple hundred people to suddenly appear sleeping in the rows of beds. She laughed at her fanciful ideas when large double doors at the back of the dormitory opened, and keepers began filing into the dormitory three at a time. One line was carrying sleeping pets, and the other two were on each side of what looked like a floating inflatable raft with a sleeping person on it. They worked quickly and silently. The two along the sides of the raft stopped at an empty bed. One pulled down the sheets. Then both gently laid the raft's occupant on the bed and covered the form. The raft seemed to automatically flip sideways, and the two left. She was surprised at the number of pets that were carried through the doors. Most were dogs and cats, but some were birds in birdcages, and there was even a lop-eared rabbit. Shelly didn't know how, but she spotted Funny. His tunic pocket was bulging, and he was carefully carrying a large octagon-shaped fishbowl with a small goldfish swimming in it. "Hey, Funny, you even picked up fish," she thought to him. "It doesn't look to be asleep. And what's in your pocket, a guinea pig?"

"Fish belongs to a little one; it was deemed unwise to put him to sleep. I have a parrot in my pocket. Elder drew the line at rodents and reptiles." He smiled as he responded in her mind.

Shelly laughed, and then he was gone through the door. The whole process seemed to take no time at all, and the doors closed behind the last one out. Shelly walked back to look at where the doors were, and like the secret door in the conference room, they were completely hidden. As she turned, thinking to look for her friends, she saw Jake sit up and look around. "Mom," he called.

"I'm here, Jake," she answered, hurrying over to reassure him.

"Mommy," Amy belted out just as Shelly reached Jake's bed.

"Here, baby girl. Come sit with us on this bed," Shelly said calmly.

Amy bolted to them, firing off questions nonstop. "Are we at the cabin, Momma?" she asked. "How did we get here? Are we dead? Where are Misty and Jessie? Who are all these people, Momma?"

"Shh," Shelly said, gently wrapping Amy in her arms. "We're not at the cabin, not dead. We must be quiet so we don't wake anyone up," she said.

"There's an office over there, Mom, Maybe someone can tell us something" Jake reasoned.

"Good idea, Jake," Shelly said as she took each child's hand and went to the office with them.

Jake went to study a map hanging over the sofa; Shelly had not noticed it before. Shelly picked up Roberta's folder and read the children an introductory letter. "To the residents of the cave community: You are the last of those living without protection in this country. You have been transported to this safe haven to preserve life. We extend our apologies for any inconvenience now and in the future. Your stay here may be as long as two years, so we urge you to be frugal with your supplies. It is now up to you to build a strong and peaceful society. Any questions or concerns should be directed to your head of personnel."

Both children were quiet, so Shelly picked up the assignment sheets. "Oh, look guys," she said. "We have an apartment. Here is the address."

Shelly showed the assignment sheet to them. Jake looked at the map. "Here we are, Mom," he said, excitedly pointing to a spot on the map.

"Can we go see it now?" Amy asked, bouncing up and down.

"You lead the way, Jake," Shelly said brightly.

Jake took one last long look at the map, and Shelly knew he was committing it to memory. "This way," Jake said confidently as they headed out.

He quickly led them through the restaurant, across the shopping plaza, past the fountain, and down the street to the short hallway door. Shelly noticed pet doors had been added to the apartment doors, and she wondered when the keepers had done it. Jake reached out and waved the door open. "How did you know to do that?" Amy asked her brother.

Jake stopped and shrugged. "Works in *Star Trek*," he said, and he continued on to the apartment door.

"Let me try," Amy said as she scooted in front of Jake and waved the door open.

They entered the apartment. The children stood looking around while Shelly watched them. "I like it," Jake stated. "It feels happy, like home."

"Oh, Mommy, it feels like love in here, and look at the pretty flowers," Amy said, running over to the bouquet in the lemonade pitcher.

Shelly swallowed the small lump in her throat as she realized that Patience had left the flowers for Amy. "They are pretty, and they can be all yours, baby girl," she said to Amy.

"It's perfect," cooed Amy, "except we should have curtains on the window."

Shelly agreed with a smile and felt a small twinge of guilt.

"Let's go check out our rooms," Jake said as he sprinted toward the bedrooms, Amy running after him.

Shelly followed and watched as they both went to the rooms they had slept in the night before. "Mommy, can I decorate my room with my rock collection?" called Amy as Shelly and Jake arrived at her door.

"Where did you get a rock collection?" Jake asked.

Amy looked confused for a moment and then answered, as she finished arranging the rocks in a circle with the large yellow one in the middle, "I don't remember. But isn't it beautiful? I just love it."

Jake picked up a smooth oval-shaped black rock and looked at it closely. "Neat," he commented, putting the rock back in its place. "You know, Mom, I have my own bathroom," Jake said. "And, it has everything I need: a toothbrush, a comb—all that stuff."

"I think we should go back to the others now," Shelly said, and she started for the door with the children following.

When they entered the dormitory, they saw a large bald man sit up and look around. "Stay here, guys," Shelly ordered, going over to him.

"Where am I? The bald man asked. "How did I get here?"

"Jake, bring me the assignment sheets and that letter," Shelly said. "I'm not sure where we are or how we got here," she told the man as Jake handed her the papers. "What's your name?"

He stood, and she handed him the letter. "Zeke—Zeke Robard," he answered, reading the letter.

"You're head chef," she told him.

"That's right," he said, still staring at the letter.

"No, you're head chef of the restaurant through that door," she told him, pointing.

"There's a restaurant?" he said, his head jerking up. "Can I look at it?" He handed the letter back to her.

"Sure," Shelly replied as she turned and led him into the restaurant. He passed her as they got close to the kitchen. Shelly watched as he went through every cabinet, drawer, cooler, and refrigerator and ran his hand lovingly over one of the stoves. He turned and looked at her. "This is the kitchen of my dreams," he announced happily.

They both looked at the dormitory to see Jake pointing a small group of four men and a woman their way. The woman was in the lead. She was tall and had straight black hair that hung to her shoulders. Shelly noticed her long legs because her pants stopped just short of her ankles. "That little girl in there said we are in heaven," she said shakily.

Shelly groaned. "No, *Haven*," Shelly said, handing her the letter.

The men grouped around, trying to read over her shoulder. "Could you give me your names?" Shelly asked them.

Shelly showed them their occupations and addresses on the assignment sheet as they called off their names.

They were three line cooks and two prep cooks. "Zeke is the head chef, and it looks like you five are his crew," she said.

Shelly looked at Zeke and said, "I'm betting there are close to two hundred people in there that are going to be hungry. It might be nice if they smelled something good when they awoke."

Zeke nodded to her and smiled. Rubbing his hands together, he boomed out, "Let's get it together, team. We have a service to prepare."

Shelly returned to the dormitory. Jake and Amy were talking to four men that were sitting on their beds while looking around the large room. As Shelly approached, the men stood. They were huge; three of them were easily over six foot two, and one stood a head taller than the others. She noticed that their tunics, pants, and shoes were dark blue. "We're in heaven," she heard Amy pipe.

"*Haven*," Shelly quickly corrected.

"Is my family here?" one of the men asked, looking around.

"If you will give me your names, we can check to see," she said.

"Jim Anders" said the man.

"Scott Cutter." The second man made a slight bow.

"Mike Strand," the third man said.

"Sergeant Thomas Williams, US Marine Corps," the fourth and largest man stated firmly. "You can call me Sergeant."

Shelly handed them the letter, which each man read and passed to the next man. Shelly quickly found the first three names on the assignment sheet. She showed them their occupations, addresses, and family members listed. She found the sergeant's name last, and noted he had no family listed. She showed him he was head of security, wondering at the word "radio" in parentheses next to his occupation. She looked up at him. He was staring at her. She recognized the look in his eyes as he studied her. "A ladies' man," she thought, noting that it didn't seem to bother him that he had no family listed.

"Can we find our families now?" Scott asked.

Shelly hesitated. She wasn't really sure it would be a good idea.

"Can I show them the jail?" Jake asked.

Shelly sent him a grateful look. "That would probably be best," she said. "I assure you that if you have family members on this list, then they are here."

Sergeant gave her a measured look before saying "She's right. Might be a good idea to see what we will be guarding before the rest of these good citizens wake. Lead the way, soldier." He ruffled Jake's hair as they walked to the door.

"Sergeant, you might want to look around for some kind of radio when you get there," Shelly called after them.

Sergeant gave her a wave of acknowledgment.

Shelly smelled coffee and went in search of a cup. She was soon settled on her bed, preparing to enjoy her coffee. "This is going pretty good," she thought, pleased with herself. At that moment, she saw Roberta Black sit up. Shelly set her coffee cup on the floor and gathered up the papers; she and Amy got to Roberta's side at the same time. "Where am I?" Roberta said, looking around confusedly.

"In Heaven," Amy sang.

"What!" Roberta said, grabbing her chest with both hands, building up to panic.

"*Haven*," corrected Shelly, looking sternly at Amy while she handed the letter to Roberta. "You are to stop saying that to people, Amy," Shelly scolded. "You're scaring them."

"It's *like* heaven," Amy replied saucily.

Roberta finished the letter and glared at Amy.

"You're Roberta Black, aren't you?" Shelly asked pleasantly.

"Do I know you?" Roberta asked stiffly.

"Um, I'm Shelly Bradford; we met at a party once. You are head of personnel. These are yours," Shelly answered, handing her the assignment sheets.

"I remember you—the friend of Jane Fillmore," she said as she looked closely at the paperwork. "You're the waitress. If these are mine, what are you doing with them?" she demanded.

"My children and I woke up and looked around. We found those on the desk in your office," Shelly answered gesturing toward the office.

"My office, you say," Roberta said, standing immediately. "You went into my office, went through my desk, and removed my papers?" She spit the words at Shelly as she entered the office.

Roberta immediately spied the nameplate and picked it up, moving to the map. "What exactly were you doing with my papers?" Roberta snapped, looking closely at the map while stroking the nameplate.

"Well, the kitchen and security staff woke up, so I showed them the letter and their occupations. Security is checking out the jail. And a suggestion was made to Zeke, the head chef, to start food preparations," Shelly answered, thinking to herself, "This woman isn't just uppity and pushy; she's formidable and intimidating."

Roberta turned away from the map, walked around the desk, and sat in her chair. She looked up at Shelly and spoke, her words dripping venom. "Just who gave you the authority to do *my* job?"

Shelly was more than taken aback. What was wrong with this woman? She squared her shoulders and said crisply, "Well, you're awake, so you can handle it. If you will excuse me, I will go and check on my children now." She turned to leave the office.

Shelly was almost out the door when Roberta barked, "Bring me coffee—black. You might as well start doing your own job for a change."

Shelly bit back the retort that was on the tip of her tongue and mentally erased the bad word she was thinking, replacing it with female dog. She retrieved her coffee cup, went through to the restaurant, and was immediately hit with the glorious aroma of fresh-baked cinnamon rolls. She set her cup on a table, walked to the serving line, and helped herself to a new cup of coffee. Daniel Porter hurried over with a tray of big cinnamon rolls covered in thick white icing. "How about a nice warm roll, Shelly?" he asked, scooping one onto a plate with a spatula and handing it to her.

"Thank you, Daniel," she said. "I'll take this one to our head of personnel and be back for mine."

"Call me Dan" he said.

Amy skipped up. Her eyes widened, and she asked politely, "May I have one of those? The mean lady said I had to leave."

"Mean lady?" Dan said as he plated Amy a roll, which she snatched, leaving him holding the empty plate.

"Our head of personnel is having a slight adjustment problem," Shelly said graciously. "Did you tell someone else they were in heaven?" she asked Amy sternly.

Amy nodded, swallowing a bite of her roll. "I didn't scare her, though," Amy said with a mischievous twinkle. "She said it was wonderful."

Shelly was heading back toward the office when the Security team and Jake entered the restaurant. All looked to be following their noses. Shelly nodded to Jake's questioning glance, and he didn't stop. She went into the office and saw Carol White sitting opposite Roberta. Carol had worked for the children's pediatrician; she was his office manager, and one of the sweetest, warmest people Shelly knew. Shelly smiled at Carol and set the coffee and roll on Roberta's desk. "I didn't order that; get it out of here," Roberta growled, pointing at the roll without looking up.

Shelly picked up the roll and saw Carol look at it longingly, so Shelly offered her the roll and asked if she would like a cup of coffee. Roberta slammed her hand on the desk and said coldly, "Unlike you, we are working here. Now, will you get out of my office—and take that messy kid with you. I have already told her to stay out of here. She almost made poor Carol pass out, telling her she was dead."

"Oh, she didn't; I knew we weren't in heaven, and I thought it was cute," Carol clarified, smiling at Amy.

Shelly felt her anger rising. "Control your emotions," she thought. Shelly nodded at Carol, took Amy's sticky hand and the roll, and left without speaking. When they were back in the restaurant, Shelly looked at Amy's face and laughed. "You are a mess," Shelly said. "Let's go to the restroom and wash up. Did you manage to get any of that icing into your tummy?"

"It was really good, but I'm still hungry. And Momma, I didn't tell nobody they was dead, honest." Amy said.

"I know you didn't, baby girl," Shelly assured her. "Now let's wash up and eat."

Shelly leaned back in her chair. She was stuffed. The serving line food bins were filled with scrambled eggs, bacon, sausage, toast, biscuits, gravy, hot cakes, french toast, and warm syrup, all under lights to keep them warm. There were shallow bins of a variety of fruits and juices sitting on ice to keep them cool. Jake and Amy had eaten and then gone off to explore. Shelly had told them not to go into the kennel until an attendant arrived. Now she was sipping coffee and, like many others, anxiously watching the dormitory door, waiting for her friends. Sergeant Williams pulled out a chair and sat down at her table. "You have a fine boy; good head on his shoulders," he commented.

Shelly felt a tickle of irritation, wishing Doug were still alive and here with her. Other men had tried to come on to her using similar tactics, trying to get close to her through her children. "I know," she replied a bit sharply. "He favors his father a lot."

"Jake told me about him. He must have been a pretty great guy," the sergeant said as if not hearing the unfriendly tone.

Shelly looked at his face and saw the sincerity in his eyes. "Green eyes," she thought. "No, brown. Hazel—that's it."

CHAPTER 10

Shelly jumped up as people started filing into the restaurant with different expressions. They were scared, sad, shell-shocked, happy, and crying, with many sniffing the air and looking hungry. Shelly stood next to the dormitory door and welcomed them warmly, gesturing to the food line, encouraging them to get something to eat and drink. She wasn't surprised when she saw a few familiar faces, but she was startled at the number of people that seemed to know her. Then there was Grace, her best friend, holding an eleven-month-old baby while a small, solemn seven-year-old girl held on to her tunic. "Oh Grace, I'm so happy you're here," Shelly cried.

"Shelly, you're here too," Grace cried, and they did their best to hug one another around the squirming, fussing baby. "Where are my grandbabies?" Grace asked.

"They are off exploring," Shelly told her. "Where's Christy?"

"Some dragon lady read us a letter and then told the people whose last names began with *A* to stay in there for processing. Then the old heifer told us to come through this door," Grace said. "What's with that woman anyway?"

"Don't ask," Shelly said as she knelt down to the little girl. "You must be Karla, I met you when you were a little baby. You know, I knew your mother." The little girl's sad blue eyes looked at her with interest. "Yes, I loved your mother," Shelly said. "She was so pretty, bright, and funny, and she sang so beautifully. She loved you very much, didn't she?" Karla nodded with a little more animation. "Would it be all right to get a hug? Because when I do, I'm going to feel all the love your momma gave you. I miss her so much. Okay?" Karla nodded again and threw herself into Shelly's arms. Shelly hugged her, kissed her cheek, and pushed her wavy dark brown hair away from her face. "Now, do you know what I'm going to do?" she asked. Karla shook her head. "I'm going to take that fussy baby Kerry from Miss Grace. And I'm going to go find a high chair for her while you and Miss Grace go over there and get a big plate of pancakes with lots of syrup. Okay?"

"Okay," Karla said shyly.

Shelly stood, took the baby, and pointed to the table they would meet at. The sergeant was gone, she noticed. She had just gotten the baby settled and strapped in when Jake and Amy sat down. "We found the park and the kennel," Jake said.

"We didn't go in, though," said Amy. "Whose baby?" She glanced up. "Granny Grace!" she squealed as Grace set her tray on the table.

"Come give your granny a big hug, you two," she said, holding out her arms toward them.

Hugs were given all around. Amy prattled nonstop about all the wonders of the cave, while Grace, Karla, and baby Kerry ate. Grace had just returned from washing syrup off Karla and Kerry when they all saw Christy trotting into the restaurant. The children met her halfway to the table, and she nearly tripped over their enthusiastic hugs. She continued toward Shelly and Grace, laughing and dragging the children still wrapped around her legs and waist, waving a paper at the two women. "I got a card shop," she called as she got closer.

They could see Christy beaming. When she got to the table, Christy stopped long enough to pull the children off her and hug Shelly. She then sat at the table. "Look; I have my very own card shop. I've always wanted a card shop," she said, wiggling on the chair.

"The card shop is right across the street," Jake said.

Christy jumped back up. "Oh, we have to go see it now."

"Don't you want to eat something first? How about your sugar?" Grace cautioned, knowing Christy had suffered from diabetes over the past several years.

"I feel fine," Christy said. "In fact, I haven't felt this good for a long time."

"Come to think of it," Grace said, "I feel great too. My back doesn't hurt at all." Grace had been forced to retire from her position as manager of a textile plant. She had fallen off a ladder and broken her back while inspecting the work of a machine repairman. She had suffered chronic back pain for years.

The group walked across the plaza. Christy was bubbling about her shop. "I wonder what occupation you will get, Grace?"

"I can't even imagine," Grace replied. "There isn't much I can do."

Shelly smiled. she knew Grace was going to have her dream fulfilled too. Christy stopped in front of the shop, looking at the window. "Do you think it will be all right if I change the name of it to Christy's Card Shop?" she asked. "Oh, and in fancy lettering," she added.

"I'm sure it will be fine," Shelly said, grinning.

Once inside, Christy spun in a circle trying to see everything at once. She went behind the counter and started opening drawers and cabinets, running her hand slowly down the stack of multicolored paper in much the same way Zeke had done to his stoves. She turned to face them with tears in her eyes. "This is really all mine?"

Grace and Shelly nodded.

"Mom, may we show Karla the park and stuff? Jake asked.

"It's all right with me if it's all right with her granny," Shelly answered.

"Is it safe?" Christy asked. Shelly gave a nod of assurance. "Then of course, dear; have fun," Christy said.

The three children were gone at a run. Christy went to a shelf and pulled down a book. "This is all about advanced techniques," Christy said, turning the pages.

"I think I had better go and see if the *B*s have been called," Shelly said.

"This little one needs a new diaper," Grace said, jiggling the whining baby.

"There are clean diapers in the ladies' room at the restaurant," Shelly said.

When they reentered the restaurant, Grace headed for the restroom with Kerry, and Shelly took her place in the short line that had formed at the door of the dormitory. Shelly noted a paper had been taped next to the door with a large *B* printed on it, and she wondered why they couldn't wait inside the dormitory. She had worked her way up to be the next one called when she heard Amy's frantic call. "Over here, baby girl," Shelly called back, kneeling as Amy flung herself into her mother's arms.

Through Amy's sobbing, all Shelly understood was that something was gone. "They're gone, Mommy. All gone."

Shelly rocked her gently, trying to settle her down. "Hush, baby. Slow down and tell Momma what's gone," Shelly soothed.

"My rock collection—all my rock collection—and my beautiful flowers too," Amy said, hiccuping and sobbing.

Shelly looked up at Jake as he came to stand next to them. "They're gone, Mom," Jake affirmed. "Amy wanted to show Karla her rocks, but they were gone. The flowers too. Who would take rocks and flowers, Mom?"

"Please stop crying, Amy; Momma will fix it," Shelly said, still rocking Amy gently. "We'll find your rock collection."

"You promise, Momma?" Amy asked, wiping at her eyes with the backs of her hands.

Shelly nodded and stood as Carol called her name. "Ms. Black will see you now, Shelly." Carol said tiredly.

Shelly searched Carol's face; it looked worn and tired. "Have you had a chance to eat?" Shelly asked.

"I'm fine," Carol said. "I'll have something later."

Shelly, Amy, and Jake went into Roberta's office. "My flowers," Amy said, reaching for them.

"Don't touch those; they are mine," Roberta said sternly, looking at Amy with distaste.

Shelly put Amy behind her and faced Roberta. "Those flowers were in our apartment," she said, gritting her teeth, and thinking to herself the mantra "Control your emotions; control your emotions."

"No, they were in *my* apartment. Here is your occupation and address. Now you may leave." Roberta spoke dismissively, handing Shelly a sheet of paper.

Shelly read the paper and felt her anger mounting. "Occupation: waitress. Address: 931 W 22nd Street," she read on the page. "This is not the information that is on the assignment sheet," Shelly said evenly, handing the paper to Jake.

"Well, let me just double-check *my* assignment sheet," Roberta said, pretending to hunt for Shelly's name. Shelly noticed the wastebasket was full of papers. "Yes, here it is; see for yourself," Roberta said, holding up the sheets.

Shelly felt her control slip as she grabbed the sheets away from Roberta. She looked at them and felt it slip even more when she saw that Roberta had separated the people in much the same way as the keepers had. "You give those back. Those are none of your business," Roberta shouted.

"These are not the original assignment sheets. You have changed them," Shelly said, wadding up the sheets of paper in her hands.

Roberta stood, leaning forward with both hands on her desk. "You get this straight right now, Shelly Bradford. I am in charge here. I am the one who decides who will do what and live where. And there is not a single thing you can do about it."

"Oh, really?" Shelly said, so angry she was shaking. "Have you forgotten we have a security team here?"

"Go ahead; tell them. See where it gets you. You'll find out soon enough that I can't be touched," she said smugly as she sat back down, turned to the computer, and proceeded to print out new copies of her assignment sheets.

"Where are my sister's rocks?" Jake demanded.

"Try looking in your own apartment," Roberta said, not bothering to look around.

Shelly ushered her children back to the restaurant. "You know where that apartment is, Jake?" she asked.

"All the way down by Farming," Jake answered readily.

"How about you guys go check to see if the rock collection is there," she told them.

"What about my flowers, Momma?" Amy said, sniffing.

"I will fix it, baby girl. I promise," Shelly said with confidence.

After Jake and Amy left, Shelly located Sergeant Williams sitting at a table, watching the crowd. She went to the sergeant's table and sat down. "What's up?" he asked, seeing the anger on her face.

"You have to do something about Roberta," Shelly said. "She has changed the assignment sheets, and she isn't supposed to do that."

"She is head of personnel. It sounds like she's doing her job," he said slowly, knowing that was not what Shelly wanted to hear.

"But she has changed them," Shelly stressed to him.

"Shelly, please understand," he said. "I don't have the authority to stop her; she would simply change my occupation if I tried, and that goes for everyone on my team."

Shelly sat back, stunned, clutching the balled-up papers in her hand. She ran her fingers through her hair, trying to think. This had to be stopped, but how if not by security? Then the contact chair came to her mind. She was going to have to contact General. He was going to have to fix this. It was his fault anyway. His stupid mind probe was supposed to reject anyone that was that was a danger to their new society, and that petty tyrant of a woman was definitely a danger. "Don't worry about it," Shelly said calmly, rising from the table. "I'll figure something else out."

CHAPTER 11

Shelly went to the conference room and laid her hand on the dark spot on the wall, and the door to the hidden control room opened. It closed automatically behind her when she entered. She hopped up into the chair and gingerly placed her hands on the contact plates. She saw the two green dots appear on the bottom of the screen, closed her eyes, and mentally called, "General."

"Get out of that chair!" General bellowed.

His thoughts blasted in her head so intensely that Shelly fell trying to get out of the chair, hitting her head on the way down. "Must you insist on crippling us? Why are you using that chair?"

"You told me to use the chair to contact you," she said, sitting on the floor while rubbing her head.

"You were instructed to use the chair when we were gone," he stated forcefully.

"But you *are* gone," Shelly stated flatly.

"We are not gone," he barked. "We are still here."

"Where?" Shelly asked, looking around the room.

"Still in your atmosphere. That chair is an amplifier. You do not use it until we have left your solar system."

"Well, that is not what you told me," she said, standing up. There was a long pause. "This is another one of those 'different species' things isn't it?" she said.

"Evidently," he agreed. Then he asked, "Is there a problem?"

"There is a big problem with the head of personnel," she said, smoothing out Roberta's crumpled assignment sheets. She quickly proceeded to fill him in on Roberta's changes, giving him only the information that pertained to assignments.

"You have a head of security," General said.

Shelly repeated what Sergeant Williams had explained. After another long pause, General said, "It will be handled. Return to the restaurant. Wait for one of the security team to come for you. *And stay out of that chair.*"

Shelly returned to the restaurant. She checked for Jake and Amy but saw they weren't there. Then she helped herself to a glass of juice and a biscuit, and she found an empty table to sit at. She watched as the sergeant stood, holding a radio to his ear. She saw a look of surprise come over his face. She watched as he quietly contacted the rest of his team, pulling them away from their families and taking them to a deserted corner of the restaurant to speak to them. She saw the sergeant, Jim Anders, and Mike Strand walk toward the head of personnel's office, and Scott Cutter headed her way. "Shelly, I have been ordered to escort you to the conference room," he said, looking uncomfortable.

Shelly raised her eyes and said calmly, "What if I don't want to be escorted to the conference room?" He looked pained but determined. Shelly rose and smiled sweetly. "Just asking," she said, patting him on the arm. "Oh yeah, those other three are definitely going to bring Roberta," she thought as she led Scott to the conference room.

Shelly entered the conference room and took a seat at the far end of the table. Scott stood next to the door. She noticed three things. The first, sitting at the other end of the table, casually reading some papers, was General. He wore dark wraparound sunglasses and was dressed in a military uniform. His hair was pulled back. Strong, wearing the same sort of sunglasses and also in military dress, stood at attention behind the general. The second thing she noticed was that a desk had been added to the far left-hand corner of the room. On the desk was the shortwave radio that had been in her car. It had belonged to Doug; it had been one of his hobbies. He had shown Jake and her how to use it. The third thing she noticed was that the keepers were not glowing; they had their shields down. "Your little one, Amy, is crying," General thought to her.

"Is she hurt?" Shelly thought as she started to rise.

"Sit. She is not injured. She says she cannot find her yellow rock," he thought back.

Shelly settled back in her chair with a sigh, laying clasped hands on the table, and quickly thought to him what had transpired concerning the rocks and flowers. "The little one found all her rocks except the yellow one … interesting," he sent back.

The doors opened, and Roberta entered, head held high and arms crossed in front of her. Carol followed with an air of quiet dignity, and Sergeant Williams came after her. Roberta and Carol sat together at the middle of the table, with Carol placing several files next to her on the table. The sergeant stood at the door opposite Scott. Shelly noticed that the sergeant had a large red handprint on the left side of his face. Still looking at the papers, the general said mildly, "I am General Elder. It has been brought to my attention that there is a problem with the assignment sheets."

His statement was like a green light to Roberta. "There is absolutely no problem with my assignment sheets," Roberta stated firmly. "This sneak is a troublemaker. She and her brats have caused me nothing but headaches from the time I awoke. First, that … that woman rifles through my desk, wandering around poking her nose into what is none of her business and doing my job before I woke up. That ill-mannered little girl of hers told me I was dead as soon as I awoke. Now, tell me exactly what right you have to come in here and question me? I am the head of personnel, and now that I think about it, I don't recall your name being on my list."

Shelly stared at her hands, wondering to herself how deep a hole Roberta was going to dig for herself. "Explain what made the original assignment sheets undesirable," the general said, sounding almost bored.

"Well, an *intelligent* person knows you simply do not house common laborers among the genteel, sophisticated, and educated," she said, waving her right hand dismissively.

The general, still not looking up, and still speaking in a bored voice, said, "There also seems to be an issue with flowers."

Roberta sat straight up and said, "Those are *my* flowers, in *my* apartment, and she had no business in an apartment that had not been assigned to her. I am the head of personnel, and I intend to have that apartment, and *this* room will be my office."

Shelly wondered if Roberta was really this clueless, and whether she had any inkling of the danger she was in. She peeked around at the others in the room. Carol sat staring at her hands resting in her lap, her back not quite touching the back of her chair. Sergeant and Scott had not moved and were staring straight ahead. She thought, "I'd bet money they know the danger and see it."

"They know," Funny thought at her as he entered, dressed in the same military uniform and sunglasses.

Funny handed General a single sheet of paper. "May we have those files now, Miss White," General said.

Carol rose and walked around the table, handing the files to the general. She then returned to her chair. "That one is strong; she has excellent control of her emotions," Funny sent.

"Really?" Shelly thought. "You're right; she doesn't look a bit scared."

She heard a chuckle as Funny thought, "On the contrary, she is trying not to laugh out loud, but there is something wrong with her."

"She is probably hungry and thirsty. I don't think Roberta has let Carol have anything to eat or drink since she woke up," Shelly thought.

General raised his head for the first time, turned toward Carol, and spoke crisply. "Miss White, do you know what is missing from these files?"

"Yes, sir," she answered. "The laws."

When Roberta heard "laws," she rolled her chair back from the table, fixed General with a glare, and crossed her legs, swinging the top one back and forth in a defiant motion. The general ignored her and continued to question Carol. "Miss White, may I ask who removed the laws from the file."

"I removed them, sir."

"Miss White, did you remove the laws from these files on your own or at the direction of Miss Black?"

"I removed them at the direction of Miss Black."

"Miss White, did you agree with that directive? Did you try in any way to dissuade that action?"

"I did not agree. I tried to dissuade the action to the point of threat of replacement if I did not comply."

"Miss White, you are dismissed to the restaurant. You are to wait there for our summons. It may be a while, so if there is anything you would like to do while you wait, please feel free to do it."

When Carol stood to leave, Roberta exploded. "You sit right back down. You are my assistant, and you do not have my permission to leave this room."

With cool composure, not even looking at Roberta, Carol left the room. Roberta turned her venom back to General. "You have no right to give my assistant orders."

"Your *assistant*, Miss Black—not your puppet or personal robot," General said.

His voice returned to its bored tone as he continued to look at his papers. "Let us get back to these laws, Miss Black," the general said. What exactly are your objections to them?"

"You of all people should know the U.S. Constitution says there is to be separation of church and state," Roberta said sanctimoniously.

"The Ten Commandments have no place whatsoever in any US literature, and I refuse to be a part of breaking the law."

"Let us go through these laws and see if they are exactly the Ten Commandments, shall we, Miss Black? One: 'You will have but one God.' Is this exactly like the first commandment?" the general said, sounding bored.

No, that is not exactly like it. The wording is different," Roberta huffed.

"Two: 'You will not use the name of God to coerce others to break a law, for you will be the greater law breaker.' Exactly, Miss Black?"

"No, not exactly, General, and I know what you are doing; you are changing words to circumvent the separation of church and state," Roberta said.

"Three: 'Six days you will work, and on the seventh you will rest or do God's work.' How about that one? Four: 'Honor your mother and father.' Five: 'You will not murder.' Six: 'You will not engage in adultery.' Seven: 'You will not steal.' Eight: 'You will not bear false witness against your neighbor.' Nine: 'You will not covet your neighbor's home, belongings, or spouse.' Ten: 'You will allow none to go hungry in time of plenty.' Are any of these exactly the Ten Commandments you speak of, Miss Black? Or are these laws that, if observed by every member of a civilized society, ensure an everlasting peace for that society?" the general asked.

"Those are the Ten Commandments no matter how you tweak them, and according to our constitution, they do not belong in our government," Roberta insisted vehemently.

General shuffled through the papers in front of him "Maybe you should read the Constitution you keep referring to, Miss Black. Nowhere in that document does it say anything about the separation of church and state. In fact, you should read the First Amendment to that document; that will give you a better understand of how your forefathers felt about religion. Mister Cutter, will you escort Amy

Bradford to the conference room please," General said, still bored and reading his papers.

While they waited, no one spoke a word. "Are many of your species like this one?" General thought to Shelly.

"One is too many, but sadly, yes, there are many," she sent back.

"Your species has a long way to go. It is ones like this one who hold you back," General sent.

CHAPTER 12

Scott returned with Amy, and she approached Shelly. "Hello, Amy, my name is General Elder, and we would like to ask you some questions if that is all right," Grandfather said.

Shelly sent him a quick thought of thanks. Amy nodded.

"Would you mind coming around here so we can make sure we hear your answers?" Grandfather asked, turning his chair around so Amy could stand directly in front of him.

Amy made a wide berth around Roberta and went to stand in front of him. "Now, Amy, tell me all about when you woke up this morning," Grandfather said, gently holding her hands.

Amy thought for a moment and then said, "Well, I woke up, and Momma and Jake were there. We went into the office, and Jake looked at a map. Momma read us a letter that said we are in heaven. Then she looked on a paper and saw where our new home was, and we went there."

"Did you like your new home, Amy?" Grandfather asked.

"Oh yes," Amy replied. "It felt full up with love. There was even a whole bunch of flowers, and Momma said they were all mine. It was perfect, except we needed curtains. Then I decorated my room with my rock collection. I put them all in a circle except my favorite one—the big yellow one. I put that one in the middle of the circle."

Grandfather nodded. "Now, Amy, when did you find out your rocks were missing?"

"Me and Jake took my new friend Karla to our new home so I could show her my rock collection, and it was gone. And my flowers were gone too." Amy said with a slight tremor to her voice.

"Can you tell me about how you found your rocks?" Grandfather asked.

"We went back to the office where the mean lady was, and she had my flowers. She said that I wasn't allowed to touch them and that they were hers, but Momma said they were mine. Then the mean lady took away our new home and gave us another one. And the mean lady said my rock collection was in the other place."

"Where did you find your rocks, Amy?" Grandfather prompted.

"On the floor inside the other place. They were everywhere, but I can't find the yellow one. Jake helped me, and we looked hard, but we can't find it. I love my other rocks, but they aren't my favorite like the yellow one is." Amy's lip trembled, and her eyes filled with tears. She looked at him and said, "Are you going to help me find my yellow rock, Grandfather?"

"We will help you, little one," he said, touching he cheek tenderly.

Roberta rolled her eyes and emitted a loud, exaggerated sigh.

"Mister Cutter, will you return Amy to her friends," General ordered.

Amy waved to her mother just before going out the door. "Did she remember you?" Shelly thought to the general.

"No, she was responding to her feelings," he answered in thought.

General turned his chair back to the table and went back to reading his papers. "Where is the child's yellow rock, Miss Black?" General asked firmly.

"How should I know where some stupid rock is? The brat said she couldn't find it. She probably lost it herself," Roberta said, tucking a loose strand of hair behind her ear and smoothing the front of her tunic.

Shelly felt her face flush with anger. She was gripping the edge of the table and imagining ripping out Roberta's hair. "Control your emotions," General sent.

"I'm doing the best I can," Shelly sent back. "Why don't you just mind-probe her to find Amy's rock?"

"The rock is in the right front pocket of her tunic. We have known that since she entered this room," he sent.

Shelly let out a snort of laughter, and everyone in the room looked at her. "You find this amusing," Roberta said snidely.

"No, I just imagined you bald," Shelly said, and Funny coughed into his hand.

"Sergeant Williams and Mr. Cutter," General said, "we would like you to search the apartment—"

Before he could finish the sentence, Roberta shouted, "Go ahead! Search my apartment! You won't find any rocks!"

"As we were saying," continued General, "Sergeant Williams and Mr. Cutter, we would like you to search the apartment where Amy found her other rocks—after you search Miss Black."

"You cannot search me. I have rights. Anybody lays one finger on me and I'll sue you for everything you've got!" Roberta screeched.

Deadly calm, General said, "Miss Black, you will reveal the whereabouts of that child's rock or these men will perform a complete search of first your clothing and then your person, and there is nothing you can do about it."

Shelly thought, "I do so love when someone has to eat her own words." Roberta was breathing hard. Her body was rigid. General raised his head and, with the slightest movement, nodded to the security men. Both, moving in unison, stepped forward to stand behind her chair. Roberta jerked the rock from her tunic pocket and slammed it onto the table. "I didn't mean to keep it," she said defiantly. "I was in a hurry, and I just overlooked it when I put the other ones in their apartment. I was going to give it back later, when I had time."

General raised his index finger slightly. Funny went around, picked up the rock, and carried it to the general. The general examined the rock and said, "Mr. Cutter, you have had a bit of education in metallurgy, correct? Tell us, what is your opinion of this rock?"

Roberta started to squirm, looking around at the doors. Scott stepped to the general and took the rock. Shelly saw the surprise on his face as he turned it all around and then moved his hand up and down as if weighing it. "In my opinion, this rock is a solid gold nugget with a weight of over five ounces," he stated, handing the rock back to General.

"I didn't know it was gold," Roberta whined. "How was I supposed to know it was gold? The kid said it was a rock. Everybody said it was a rock."

"You knew it all the time, didn't you?" Shelly thought to General.

"Of course," he replied before continuing aloud with Roberta. "Miss Black, what was your father's profession?"

"I ... I don't remember," Roberta stammered, her voice going up an octave.

"Miss Black, what was your first job?" General fired at her.

"I don't remember. It was a long time ago. I really didn't know it was gold," she said, her response directed at Shelly.

"Let us refresh your memory, Miss Black. Your father was a jeweler, and you went to work for him at age sixteen."

"So what? That doesn't prove anything," Roberta said. "You have no right to question and accuse me. I'm not taking any more of this." Roberta stood and walked stiffly to the doors, but the security men each took one side step toward the other, effectively blocking her exit.

"Restrain her if necessary," General ordered.

"You have no right," said Roberta going back to her chair.

Shelly wondered if she should get a bucket because Roberta looked as if she were going to be sick. Then General stood, and Shelly felt the power of the elder rise with him. The very air in the room felt charged with it. For the first time since they had entered the conference room,

General focused his entire attention on Roberta, and she seemed to shrink in her chair as he spoke. "Your behavior, Miss Black, has been reprehensible. You were assigned a profession, with detailed descriptions of your duties, and procedures that were to be strictly followed. You held a position of trust, and you were to help and reassure your fellow man. Instead you corrupted that position to gain power, distribute abuse, and wreak havoc on what should have been a smooth transition. You, who profess to be so well versed on the Ten Commandments, broke two of those very commandments within an hour of waking, and a third right here in this room. You have talked about your rights without regard for the rights of others. You have declared the rights of your position, giving not the slightest thought to who gave you that position. You have referred repeatedly to your government, with no understanding that your government—and your country, for that matter—no longer exists. You, who is without the smallest bit of honesty or integrity, stole the cherished possession of an innocent child—a possession that was not only cherished but also extremely valuable. Miss Black, for your irresponsible behavior and for having committed a crime, your assignment is suspended as of this moment. You will—"

Roberta stood with a haughty expression on her face and interrupted. "Just who gives you the authority to suspend anything? Your opinion of my behavior means nothing," she objected. "You can't just waltz in here and suddenly judge me like that." She snapped her fingers loudly for effect.

General sat back down and went back to his papers and bored voice. "You are absolutely correct, Miss Black. Our authority here is limited, which is why we merely suspended your assignment instead of revoking it. As far as your crime, we have no intention of judging you. That will be left to your peers. Now Sergeant Williams and Mr. Cutter will escort you to their facilities, where you shall be held until such time as your peers decide to judge you. Sergeant Williams, Mr. Cutter, see to Miss Black's detention immediately."

"You will come with us now, Miss Black," Sergeant said as he and Scott stepped to either side of Roberta.

"I'm not going anywhere with you!" Roberta yelled, and the sergeant took hold of her left arm just above the elbow.

"Don't you dare touch me," Roberta said as she swung her right hand toward his face.

Sergeant Williams caught her wrist, saying, "You only get that shot one time, Miss Black, and you have already had your shot."

Sergeant quickly forced both her hands behind her back, and cuffed them with a pair of nylon handcuffs. As the two men started toward the doors with her, the general said, "Sergeant, when you have finished with this little errand, please stop by the restaurant and ask the new head of personnel, Miss White, to join us in the conference room."

"Yes, sir," Sergeant replied while dodging a vicious kick.

Shelly knew she was going to have to wash her ears twice to get out the filthy language that spewed from Roberta as they half dragged her from the room. "For a high level of intelligence, that woman sure has a low level of vocabulary," Shelly thought.

CHAPTER 13

Shelly leaned back in her chair and looked at the general. "You have questions?" he thought.

"Yes. You said your mind probe would reject any of our species that would be a danger to our society. So how did she get through?" Shelly thought.

"Those who would cause physical harm were rejected. Her problems are emotional. They escalated when she was given a position she perceived as giving her unlimited power," he answered.

"Are you telling me that you knew she had emotional problems and you still put her in such an important position?" Shelly thought. "That was a mistake."

Funny put his hand to his mouth and coughed.

After a long pause, the general thought, "A miscalculation."

"Have you ever made a mistake?" Shelly sent.

"Yes, when we acted on some of your suggestions," he replied quickly.

Funny chuckled aloud, and then suddenly became quiet, standing up straight, and squaring his shoulders. "Slapped you down, didn't he?" Shelly sent at Funny, getting no answer. "I'm just wondering what kind of mother she is going to make," she thought to General.

"Possibly a good one," he sent. "Her emotional problems stem mainly from being unhappy. We know that much of her unhappiness was caused by her inability to have a child."

"Well I hope having a baby makes her a better person" Shelly thought.

"She is not having *a* baby," General said, noting Shelly's skepticism. "She is having twins."

Shelly threw back her head and laughed until tears rolled down her cheeks.

"Control your emotions," General sent.

"Oh, General, I may have a chance to get control over anger, fear, jealousy, and a few other emotions I can't think of right now, but some emotions cannot be controlled—humor being one of them. Ask Funny." She knew she could never have said that aloud.

There was a knock on the door. A refreshed-looking Carol White entered in front of Sergeant Williams, and both resumed their previous places. Carol noticed Shelly's tear-streaked face. "Are you all right?" Carol asked with concern.

"Yes, Carol, I'm fine," Shelly answered. "I've just had the best laugh I've had in over two years."

Pushing the papers aside, General gave Carol his full attention. "Miss White, you are now assigned as the head of personnel. You have an understanding of the duties and strictures of this position?"

"Yes, sir, I believe I understand," Carol stated with confidence.

"Your first duty will be to correct all deviations from the original assignment sheets; then you may proceed normally. You start immediately," the general instructed her.

Carol nodded her head and rose to leave, but the general stopped her. "One more thing, Miss White; your basic duty is to mitigate the stress and confusion of the populace. As long as there is no interference with your stated assignment, you are free to accomplish this in any way you deem necessary."

"Thank you, General," Carol said with a smile.

Shelly wasn't sure, but she could have sworn she saw Carol skip as she went through the doors. The general dismissed Sergeant Williams. "You were right to contact us," General thought at Shelly. "This episode has given us a better understanding of your species."

"Carol will do a good job," Shelly sent.

"Yes. It disturbs us that we did not hear sooner that she needed to eat," he thought back.

"She was probably trying hard not to think about it," Shelly replied, tilting her head at him.

"You have a question?" General sent.

"Carol was able to keep you from hearing her hunger, and Jake is also able to cover his thoughts from you. I understand how and why Carol could do it, but it wasn't intentional. Jake does it on purpose. Why?"

"Jake believes you can read his mind," General answered.

"No, what makes you think that, if you can't hear what he is thinking?" Shelly asked, confused.

"We are elder," General stated, as if that explained everything.

"Well, for heaven's sake. Why should Jake think I can read his mind."

After a short pause, Grandfather answered aloud. "This is something you should discuss with Jake."

Shelly thought about it to herself a moment, nodded, and asked, "So what's next?"

"Because of our increased understanding, the next drop of survivors will be smaller than we had planned. After that, we will proceed per the original plan," General answered. He then continued as they all four walked to the doors. "Contact me if you have a problem. And stay out of that chair."

"Well how am I supposed to contact you if I'm not to use the chair?" Shelly demanded.

"You simple call us mentally" was his reply.

"I'm sorry if I hurt you guys," Shelly said to Funny and Strong.

"Most were not hurt; we were covered against the elder," Funny replied with a hint of humor.

"I thought you couldn't keep him from hearing you," Shelly sent mentally.

"We cannot, but we try," he sent back.

"So what happens if one of you is successful? Will you be reprimanded?" she said, kidding him.

"Why, no, then we would become the elder," Funny answered respectfully.

Shelly turned toward the Twentieth Street door, but she stopped and looked back to watch as General, Strong, and Funny walked to the end of the short hall. General laid his hand on the wall across from the door to the narrow hall. A hidden door opened, and they were gone. Shelly walked through the plaza, observing people grouped around three sides of the kiosk. The kiosk was four-sided; the map was on the two sides opposite each other; the other two sides had been empty. She was curious about what was on the third side. As she slowed, she heard an older woman say, "I swear they are new teeth. See for yourself. Go ahead; try to pull them out."

"Oh, Momma, those are your dentures," a younger woman replied, shaking her head. "No way am I going to pull on them. Ick!"

"Well, I know they're new." the older woman grumbled. "And I don't care if you believe me or not."

Shelly smiled and edged around to see what had been added. She saw that it was a list of professions. "Well I see it doesn't include the oldest profession," a sultry female voice said.

Shelly turned to see who had said it, and she couldn't stop the gasp that escaped her lips. The woman was extremely striking. She was a little taller than Shelly, with dark brown eyes, an olive complexion, and a full, thick mane of wavy waist-length jet-black hair. It was what she had done to her clothes, though, that had elicited the gasp. She had found a pair of scissors and cut the tunic into a short V-neck halter top, and her pants were rolled down past her navel to the top of her hips, leaving her entire midriff completely bare. She looked like an exotic belly dancer—a very curvaceous one. Shelly turned and continued toward the restaurant with a smile, thinking, "Now that girl is going to keep things lively."

She met Sergeant coming out of the restaurant as she was going in, and she asked him if he had seen Jake and Amy. "I'll tell you where they are if you will tell me what that little smile is about," he said with a grin.

Shelly's smile widened as she glanced back over her shoulder with a slight nod of her head. The sergeant looked, stared for a moment, and then sighed. "That one is going to cause trouble." He looked back at Shelly and said, "Jake and Amy are eating in the restaurant."

"Thanks," Shelly said.

"Catch you later," he replied, walking down the plaza.

Shelly watched him walk away, noticing that he never even peeked at the belly dancer as he passed the kiosk.

Shelly walked into the restaurant and spotted Jake and Amy. She waved to them on her way to the serving line. There was a different crew working, but Zeke was still there. She helped herself to a bowl of stew, salad, and yeast rolls. As she was adding extra vegetables and fruit to her salad, Zeke walked over and said with a smile, "Hey, Shelly, if you want something different, I'll be happy to make it for you. Alice came back after checking out her digs. She said her apartment's kitchen pantries are full. I wasn't sure how many might be back to eat, so I thought it best to make stew."

"This looks and smells great," Shelly said. "I can't think of anything else I might want. Thanks for the offer though."

CHAPTER 14

"Momma, the kennel attendant is there, but Jake wouldn't let me get Misty and Jessie," Amy said when Shelly was close to the table. "He says we have to wait for you."

"Jake is right, baby girl," Shelly told her. "Let me eat this really quick, and we will go get them."

Shelly had just stacked her empty dishes on a tray when she heard Grace shout her name from across the restaurant. She stood and watched Grace run toward them, dodging tables, chairs, and people. Grace grabbed both of Shelly's upper arms and shook her, laughing and talking at the same time. "Do you know what they gave me?" Grace asked. "You'll never guess. Hot dang, I can't believe they gave this to me. Shelly, you are looking at the new equine administrator."

Shelly laughed as she watched Grace do a circular happy dance. "Come with me, guys," Grace pleaded with a smile. "Shelly, please, you and the kids have to go with me to see the horses and their barns."

Shelly looked at Jake and Amy and asked, "Do you guys mind if we pick up the dogs and cat on the way back?"

"I know the way," Jake said.

"I want to go too," Amy said.

It was a long walk to the double doors that led to Farming. They went through the doors. The barns looked small; they were almost indistinguishable in the distance. "Hey, those are neat, Mom," Jake said, pointing. "Do you think we can use one?"

Shelly and Grace looked to where Jake was pointing and then walked over to a row of at least twenty golf carts with keys in them. They looked at each other. Shelly giggled, bowed, and gestured to the first cart, saying, "Your chariot awaits, O new equine administrator." Everyone piled into the cart laughing.

When they arrived at the barns, Shelly realized how little she had seen when she had been there with General. There were at least ten barns, grain silos, sheds, pens, and corrals. The horse barn was the first one. It had three offices, one each for the administrator, the head trainer, and the head groom. Each office had a desk, a chair, a computer, and two extra chairs. Amazingly, each also included a compact kitchen, a small table with two chairs, a twin bed, and a full bathroom. There were twenty-five box stalls, a bathing station for horses, a feed room, a tack room, and a loft full of hay. The stalls were equipped with automatic drinking fountains, hay racks, and feed boxes. Grace looked at it all, touching everything she passed and smiling as she felt the textures on her fingertips. Lost in the wonder of disbelief, she was opening and closing a stall gate when her face lit up with what Shelly had come to think of as a "dream come true" look. "Can we go check out the loft?" Jake asked.

"Go for it, kiddos," Grace said. "That is, if your Mom don't mind."

"It's fine; just be careful." Shelly said.

Grace leaned back against the stall. "You know, Shelly, I did some rodeo shows back when I was young—trick riding, barrel racing … was pretty good with a bull whip. Always dreamed of having a place just like this. Not sure how I got off track. Guess I listened when folks told me I needed to grow up and get a real job. I think I didn't really give up the dream, though, until I broke my back. I may not be able to ride anymore, but dang it, Shelly, I'll run this outfit from a wheelchair if I have to.

"Your back been bothering you?" Shelly asked.

"Yep, it's been getting to where I have fewer good days." Grace shrugged. "No use complaining. Ya gotta play the hand life deals ya. But you know what, my back hasn't hurt at all since I woke up here. Guess I'm getting a couple of good days for a change." Grace shook her head. "I have got to tell Christy about my new profession. She is never going to believe this."

After parking the golf cart back where they got it, they made their way back to the plaza. Shelly visualized how hard it would be for a pregnant woman to make this walk in eight or nine months. "Noted," General's voice suddenly echoed in her mind.

Shelly jumped and looked around. She shook her head and wondered if General was always listening to her thoughts. They stopped to pick up the pets and then continued on to Christy's apartment. She and Grace also lived on East Twentieth Street, not far from Shelly. Their apartments were across the hall from each other. Christy invited everyone in. After she and Grace finished their hugs, squeals, and happy dancing over Grace's new position, Christy showed off her new home. She was especially excited about the brand-new computer. The apartment was almost the same as Shelly's; the only difference was the style of furniture. "I wonder if there is paint for the walls?" Christy mused. It struck Shelly that she hadn't even considered painting her own light-gray rock walls.

They declined refreshments and left with promises of meeting up the next day. The dogs and cat raced ahead of them, zipping through the pet doors, and were already in the apartment by the time Shelly and the children arrived. "How did they know where to go?" Amy asked.

"Probably followed our scent," Jake reasoned.

Shelly remained quiet as she watched Golly go from room to room whining. She knew he was looking for Strong. After examining the apartment, all three animals jumped back through the pet doors.

"Hey," Jake yelled, running after them with Amy and Shelly on his heels.

They chased the pets down Twentieth Street, turning left on Patience Avenue. Shelly turned the corner, trailing Jake and Amy, and was just in time to see the animals slip through a pet door at the cave's entrance. For the first time, Shelly saw a set of huge wooden double doors. A solid metal bar was slid into a metal bracket on each door to lock them in place, effectively closing the cave opening. A regular-size entrance door with a pet door in the bottom was to the left of the double doors. Shelly marveled at the workmanship of the keepers.

It was dark when they went outside, and although they couldn't see the pets in the tall grasses, they could hear Golly's intermittent barks. "Now, I wonder why they came out here and how they knew they could get out," Jake said, scratching his head.

"They had to tinkle and followed the scent," Amy said reasonably.

Jake looked at her for a moment and said, "You're probably right."

Shelly knew the keepers had somehow "cavebroken" their pets—and more than likely all the other pets too. Jessie was the first one back, wagging her tail and wiggling around Amy's feet. Golly returned to Jake with his tongue hanging out. Misty returned at a lope and didn't stop but leaped back through the pet door.

When they all got home, they headed to their bathrooms for showers. They found long nightshirts hanging from pegs on the backs of their bathroom doors. Shelly realized that all the doors on the inside of the apartment were regular doors with doorknobs. Then it hit her that the doors to the shops were regular doors also. She quickly dismissed the idea of wondering why.

After Shelly tucked in the children, she wandered back to the living room and heard soft beeping coming from the computer. She sat down and wiggled the mouse until the screen lit up. "You have a caller" was displayed on the screen. She clicked on the Answer icon, and Grace appeared. Grace looked at Shelly and started smiling and talking. "Aren't these great? Grace said. "We don't have telephones, but these are almost as good. You just can't put them in your pocket."

"Well, maybe people not having loud conversations in public is a good thing," Shelly mused. "I just wish I had learned more about computers."

CHAPTER 15

They were finishing the cleanup after breakfast the next morning when the computer began beeping. It was Karla calling for Amy. Shelly left them giggling, walking to her bedroom to dress for the day. When Shelly came back to the living room, Amy was jumping up and down with excitement. "There are new people at the restaurant, Momma," Amy said. "Can we go meet them, please? *Please?*"

"There might me more kids there," Jake said.

Jake and Amy really had been a big help the day before, and Shelly was curious to see what General had up his sleeve, so she agreed to take them to the restaurant. In the plaza, there were several new arrivals looking at the map on the kiosk. Shelly stopped, introduced herself, and welcomed them to the cave. Then she continued to the restaurant. There were more people than she expected in the restaurant. It seemed many individuals from the previous day's drop had come to meet the new arrivals. Shelly gave the children permission to go find Karla. She noticed a medium-size man with a shock of thick snow-white hair rubbing his eyes, holding his paperwork close, and then holding it far away. It looked to her as if he were having a problem reading it. Shelly introduced herself, and offered to read his papers for him. "Hello, thank you for the kind offer, but I can read this just fine," he said, looking at her in surprise. "I'm just trying to figure out how it's possible without my glasses. Oh, I'm Clarence Barker."

Shelly encouraged him to eat, told him to let her know if he needed anything, and went to pour herself some coffee. She found an empty table, and spied Sergeant and Jim Anders on the other side of the restaurant, eating. It wasn't long before Grace, Christy, Karla, Jake, and Amy had joined her. The children each had a glass of milk and cinnamon rolls. Grace and Christy had settled for just coffee. Shelly was thinking she should be doing something useful when the belly dancer arrived. The striking woman had done more work on her outfit. The neckline of the tunic, now a crop top, was lowered even more, and the pant legs had been taken in to make them skintight. She paused in the doorway, tossed her hair over her shoulder, and slowly swayed toward the serving line. The restaurant grew quiet as she walked, and Shelly glanced around to see almost everyone gazing at the belly dancer. Grace, Christy, and the children were eying the woman as she moved down the serving line considering the offerings. "So where's the baby?" Shelly asked Christy.

"I dropped her off at the nursery. You should see that place; it is great," Christy said.

All of them continued watching the belly dancer as she sat at a table in the middle of the restaurant with only a small bowl and spoon and began eating what looked like yogurt. "She must not be very hungry if that little bowl is all she got," Amy said.

"She must be starving," Karla said. "Look at the way she is licking every little bit of it off the spoon."

Jake just watched. It didn't take long before first one man, and then a second, sat down at the belly dancer's table. Shelly watched as Sergeant scooted his chair around to keep an eye on the table. The belly dancer threw her head back and laughed. Then one man grabbed the front of the other man's tunic. "Knew that was coming," Grace mumbled.

Sergeant and Jim were on the move. A punch was thrown, and both men were soon rolling on the floor, knocking over chairs as people scattered to get out of the way. Sergeant grabbed one man, and Jim held the other one. Shelly leaned back, feeling a small quiver of thrill go through her as she watched Sergeant easily handle one of the angry men. She was just thinking how interesting Sergeant was as he ducked a punch. "Where is Sergeant Williams?" General thought at her.

"In the restaurant," she thought back distractedly.

"What is he doing? He is not answering his radio," General snapped.

"He's breaking up a fight," she answered in thought, wishing General would quit bothering her right now.

"Who is fighting, and why?" he asked.

"Two men are fighting over a woman," she answered as Sergeant hauled the now compliant man off the floor and stood him up.

"Why would males fight over a female?" General asked after a pause. "There are more females than males in your group."

"Because of her assets," Shelly replied lazily.

"That cannot be correct," General firmly replied. "No one was dropped at the cave with assets."

"Not material assets," Shelly sent with a touch of humor. "This woman has female assets."

After a long pause, General asked, "Can you find Judge Barker and escort him to the conference room?"

"We have a judge?" she asked, watching Sergeant turn the man and cuff him.

"Yes, Judge Clarence Barker," General informed her.

Shelly remembered the white-haired man. "Can do," she said as Sergeant, with the man in tow, passed close enough for Shelly to see beads of sweat trickling down the side of his neck.

"Control your emotions," General barked.

"General, this is another one of those emotions that can't be controlled," Shelly thought to him, smiling in her mind.

She pushed her chair back and informed the group at the table she had an errand to run.

"But I wanted you and the kids to go with me to find my horses," Grace said.

"I shouldn't be long. Why don't you finish your coffee, and I'll meet all of you outside," Shelly replied.

Shelly went to Judge Barker's table and told him General Elder wanted to speak with him. He took one last sip of coffee and then rose and walked with her from the restaurant. As they were walking through the plaza, he asked, "So who is this General Elder?"

"I believe he has something to do with our being brought here," Shelly answered.

"This should be interesting," he said.

When Shelly opened the short-hall door, Golly, Jessie, and Misty piled out of the pet door, and began a welcome-home dance around her feet. When she started to put them back into the apartment, she heard Grace and the children's voices on the street behind her. "Go find Jake," Shelly said to Golly.

The dog dived out of the hallway pet door with the other two animals following. Judge Barker chuckled, saying, "Quite a crew you have there."

Shelly agreed and led him across the hallway to the conference room. General was sitting in the same chair at the end of the conference table. Strong was standing behind him. Both were in uniform and were wearing dark wraparound glasses; their glows were down. Shelly introduced Judge Barker and General Elder to each other. Acknowledgments were made, and the general motioned Judge Barker to take a seat to the right of him, dismissing Shelly by saying, "Corporal Strong has something to go over with you."

"Hi, Strong; Golly misses you," Shelly sent as they left the conference room.

The only reply Strong gave was a slight nod of his head, until they were out of the conference room. "Elder has requested we instruct you on your computer to access the computer in the office of the head of personnel," Strong sent.

Shelly nodded, and they went into her apartment. Strong sat at the computer, pressed a few keys, and brought up a screen asking for a file name. He typed in a series of numbers, and another screen came up asking for a password. Again he typed in a series of numbers. "Now you do it," Strong sent.

"You have got to be kidding," she thought at him. "I'll never remember all those numbers. Can we change the file name and password to something I can remember?"

"If you wish," he replied, striking keys. "What would you like to name this file?" he asked mentally.

"I don't know; something I can remember. How about 'toenail fungus'?" she sent.

Strong typed "toenailfungus" into the Name of File text box. "And the password?" he asked.

"'Eat it all,'" Shelly said immediately.

Strong hesitated and then typed "eatitall" twice. Shelly heard a chuckle in her mind and thought, smiling, "Funny, do you find my choices amusing?"

"Not your choices," Funny sent. "Strong's confusion."

Shelly nodded and then thought to Strong, explaining, "If people go poking around in my computer files, they are not likely to be interested in looking at one titled toenailfungus. If they do, it is even less likely they will come up with 'eatitall' as the password."

Strong sat back shaking his head and sent, "We like your species, but we do not think we will ever understand it."

"I understand perfectly how you feel," she sent him. "Let me ask you, does it bother you when Funny laughs at you?"

"No, we are not bothered," he sent back.

"Well what's it like when you get two Funnys together?" she asked mentally.

"Disturbing," he answered aloud as he stood, and they left the apartment.

CHAPTER 16

Shelly was outside, holding her hand above her eyes to shield them from the glare of the sun, trying to find Grace and the children. She spotted them in the far distance. It looked as if they were herding the horses toward her. She walked to meet them. Rounding a slight bend at the base of the mountain, she was greeted with the sight of a long barn and large corral. It looked to be about the same distance that the other barns inside the cave were from the cave entrance. Shelly arrived at the corral before the others. She opened the swinging gate and then stood away from it. The horses took their time getting to the corral, stopping to tear mouthfuls of long grass as they went. Shelly watched as every once in a while a horse would veer off and then suddenly stop, turn, shake its head, kick up its hind feet, and go back to the herd.

Though Shelly couldn't see him, she could hear Golly barking. She was not surprised to find Golly knew how to herd. The horses filed into the corral, some snorting and nipping at the horses next to them. Shelly was closing the gate as Amy, Jake, and Grace walked up. They were discussing the merits of the individual animals. Amy and Jake climbed up to sit on the top board of the corral fence while Shelly and Grace leaned their arms on the top board to look closely at the beautiful animals.

"Where's Karla?" Shelly asked.

"Christy thought she was too young to be messing around with horses," Grace answered.

"Granny Grace said we could learn to ride," Jake said excitedly.

"Can we ride right now, please?" Amy begged.

Grace laughed, patting Amy on the back, saying, "We have to get each and every horse checked out first to make sure they are sound and to find out what kind of temperaments they have, but we should have lessons set up soon. Now I'm going to get them into stalls. Then the both of you may give them a little grain. It will make it easier to bring them in next time if they know food is here," she said as she climbed over the fence, hopped into the corral, and headed toward the barn.

Grace went into the barn and came out a moment later with a lead rope. She went among the mingling horses, caught a large bay mare, and led her into the barn. The other horses followed quietly behind her. "I'll be darned, Shelly said. "How does she do that?"

"She caught the lead mare, and the others follow her," Jake replied, proud of his new knowledge.

After the last horse went into the barn, it wasn't long before Grace waved them inside. This barn had two long rows of tie stalls with a wide aisle between. In each stall was only room enough for a horse to stand, a feed box with a hay rack over it at the front end, and a gate at the back. To exit a stall the horse had to back out. There was a narrow aisle in front of the row of stalls for workers to use to distribute feed. A set of doors opened at the far end of the barn. Grace called from the far end of the barn. Shelly, Amy, and Jake went to find her. She was in a feed room, shoveling oats into a wheelbarrow. Inside the feed room were two closet-size rooms lined with what looked like aluminum. A grain chute was sticking out of the far wall. The doors to the feed closets were blocked by two-foot-high solid metal gates. When Grace had the wheelbarrow full, she handed Amy a gallon scoop and told Shelly to push the wheelbarrow down the feeding aisle while Amy gave each horse a scoop of feed. She and Jake would do the same on the other side. "Start at the far end," Grace instructed.

"One scoop doesn't look like much for such a big animal, Shelly commented.

"They aren't working and don't really need the grain, but this will make them want to come to the barn," Grace said.

When the first scoop of feed hit a box, the horses started nickering, whinnying, and stomping. Amy loved it. Shelly was surprised at how quickly the feeding went. By the time Shelly and Amy had fed the last horse, Grace and Jake were turning the first ones fed back into the corral. Some were trying to come back into the barn, but Golly was there to keep them out. Jake opened the pasture gate, and Golly made it his job to see that every horse left the corral. When all the horses had been turned out, and the corral gate closed, Amy looked around and said, "Where's Misty?"

"Golly, go find Misty," Jake said.

"If this is done every morning at the same time, we will never have to go out after these horses again," Grace said. "They'll be here waiting for us."

"We saw llamas, Momma," Amy said.

Shelly looked at Grace, who nodded in agreement. They heard Misty yowl. Golly came out of the tall grass carrying her by the nape of the neck. "Golly, drop Misty now," Jake laughed.

When Golly turned her loose, Misty turned, arched her back, hissed at him, and ran to Amy. "Come on, guys; I have a surprise to show you," Grace said as she closed the barn door with them inside.

They followed Grace the length of the barn and then through an access door next to a set of double doors at the far end. "Wow, neat," Jake said.

They were in a large equipment room and a fully equipped blacksmith shop. Two large horse-drawn wagons sat to one side. There were three golf carts, each with a name on it: "Equine Administrator," "Trainer," "Head Groom." Each cart had two bench seats and a small pickup truck–style bed on the back. Shelly grinned as she took a seat in Grace's golf cart, saying, "At least we get to ride back."

"It gets better," Grace said as the children and pets climbed into her cart.

Grace opened a door, and they could see they were just outside the horse barn in the cave. "I don't know who thought of all this, but it looks like they have thought of everything," Grace said with a smile.

As they rode through Farming, Shelly looked at Grace and said, "So how many horses do you estimate there are, and what did you think of them?"

"There are seventy-eight head," Grace answered. "All look to be well-bred. Most are quarter horses, I think, but there are eight Belgian draft horses. There is one exceptional yearling stud colt. The rest are geldings and mares. It looks like most, if not all, of the mares are in foal—and not far from dropping. I'll know more when we see how they work."

Shelly smiled at Grace's enthusiasm.

They parked the cart at the beginning of the farming area and walked to the plaza. They were heading to the restaurant and passing the belly dancer when Grace said, "I wonder where we can get another set of clothes?"

"Oh, you can come see me," the belly dancer said.

Shelly and Grace looked at her in surprise.

"I'm Rosa Garcia. I'm a clothing designer. Well, really I worked for a clothing designer as a seamstress, but I was working my way up to designer. I have the clothing shop. It came with shelves full of clothes like those we woke up wearing. I've been experimenting with ways of changing them though."

She was so engaging and sincere that Shelly and Grace warmed to her immediately. "Boy, that sure is some experiment you are wearing," Grace said with a smile.

Rosa laughed. "I know what you mean. The security man had a talk with me. He told me he didn't have a jail big enough for this kind of outfit. I was going now to do a little redesigning. My shop is down at the corner of the plaza. Stop in and I'll fix you right up with a couple of changes of what you are wearing."

Shelly and Grace both promised to see her later and then headed toward home. At the kiosk, they saw Carol closing one of its doors. They stopped, and Shelly said, "Hi, Carol, posting something new?

Carol smiled. "Just adding the new occupations that came in this morning."

Shelly and Grace read down the list. Most were educators. Grace pointed to one and looked at Shelly, and they said in unison, "Head of transportation!"

"I thought I had the market cornered on transportation," Grace said.

Maybe he's going to be in charge of the golf carts," Jake said.

"You may be right," Shelly agreed.

Shelly and the children went back to their apartment, showered, put on their nightshirts, and put their clothes in the washer. They were eating a late lunch when the computer beeped. Jake got to the chair first and brought up a screen that read, "You Have a Message." he quickly opened the message, and they all read it:

Shelly, please contact all citizens and have them report to the restaurant at 3:00 p.m. for a mandatory meeting. Only those adults in child care may be exempt, and it is urged that children under six not attend.

Thank you,

Judge Clarence Barker.

"How am I supposed to contact everybody?" Shelly said, running her fingers through her hair.

Jake looked up at her, smiled, and said, "With the computer, Mom, like this."

Jake hit some keys and in moments had the entire list of residents, shops, and every establishment where a citizen might be.

"Jake, you are a genius," Shelly said. "Now, let me sit down there, and you show me how to do this."

Jake walked Shelly through sending an alert to every computer that would be in use in the cave. "Now show me how to talk with Rosa at the clothing shop."

In moments Shelly was explaining to Rosa how their clothes were in the washer and wouldn't be dry in time for the meeting.

"No problem," Rosa said. "Give me your address, and I'll be right there."

A few minutes later, Amy waved the door open. "Oh, Miss Rosa, that is awesome!" Amy said.

"Awesome is right," Shelly agreed.

"You like?" Rosa said as she twirled slowly.

Rosa had taken the plain tunic and somehow applied the vibrant and colorful image of the head, neck, and body of a peacock to the front, and a fully spread peacock tail on the back. The pants had a green leafy vine running the length of the outside seams. "It is beautiful; surely you didn't do all that since we last saw you," Shelly said.

"No, I had the painting done," Rosa said. "All I did was take it in here and there."

Shelly observed Rosa had indeed taken it in and added darts here and there. The outfit was a perfect fit to her body, but it was tasteful. "This is what I have really been working on," Rosa said as she unfolded Amy's tunic.

The tunic had small daisies painted around the neck, and on each pocket was a large daisy with leaves. "Oh, Miss Rosa, thank you so much," Amy cooed. "I just love it. Look, Momma; Miss Rosa made it just for me."

"Thank you, Rosa, that was so thoughtful," Shelly said.

Rosa stroked a pocket daisy, saying, "It's what I always wanted to do—design clothes that make people happy."

"Well, you have certainly made this little girl happy," Shelly said, laying her hand on Amy's head. "And I have no doubt you are going to be kept very busy."

"I hope you're right. Since you are my first customer, I'm going to design you something very special. I have to run now though; a few women stopped me in the plaza, and I told them to meet me in the shop," Rosa said as she sailed out the door.

As they left for the meeting, Jake ordered Golly to stay, hoping the other two animals would stay with him.

CHAPTER 17

Shelly and her children met Grace, Christy, and Karla in the plaza. Amy proudly showed off her new tunic, assuring Karla that Rosa would make her one too. They all made their way into the restaurant a little early for the meeting. Amy and Karla managed to claim a table close to the stage. "How's the baby doing?" Shelly asked Christy.

"She is fussy no matter what I do for her" Christy said. "The nurse at the nursery said she is teething, but I'm sure she misses her mommy. I'm doing my best for the girls, but I am just too old to be a full-time mother."

"Oh, come on now, Christy; you're not that old," Shelly said. "And you are looking good. How are you feeling?"

"You know, I feel good," Christy said. "I'm worried about my insulin, but the nurse couldn't find any. A doctor arrived in the last drop, but I didn't want to bother him on his first day here. I think I've lost weight, but how do I tell if I don't have a scale and I'm not wearing my own clothes? I mean, if I had my own jeans I could tell because they would be loose, right?"

"Right," Shelly answered as she looked around the restaurant and then the stage.

In the center of the stage was a podium. To its right was a desk with a solid wood front. A chair facing the audience sat to the left of the desk. At precisely three o'clock, Judge Barker entered the stage carrying a folder. He stood behind the podium, opened the folder, and began to speak. "My name is Judge Clarence Barker," he began. "I awoke here this morning. After a brief respite, I received a request from General Elder to meet with him in the conference room. We are assembled here so that I may relate to you what we discussed in that meeting.

"General Elder is a member of a centuries-old secret elite paramilitary group of scientists, engineers, inventors, chemists, and other learned people. No world government has ever known of their existence. Over hundreds of years, they periodically revealed various inventions and products that would be of benefit to mankind. Their technology far surpasses what the rest of us know. The main purpose of this organization is to guarantee the continued existence of the human species. We here are not the only survivors of the virus in the United States. There is a group that took refuge in a bunker beneath the White House in Washington, DC. A large group in Colorado sheltered at NORAD, and many smaller family and militia groups prepared private shelters. Australia, because it is surrounded by ocean and was able to keep out the virus longer, gave the elder group time to save a great number of its population. In the United States the elder group picked up only those twelve thousand eight hundred sixty-two people that were alive and without protection. What we are being given here is the chance to begin a society—a new civilization—one that may finally live in peace.

"The elder group gave us a beginning with the Ten Laws, but it will be up to us to build the kind of government we will have to live with. Those that received notice this morning will please meet me in the conference room to form a foundational government, to be voted on by our entire adult population in the near future. From the elder group, we also received the gift of renewed health. All who suffered from illness, maladies, or deformities have been cured. Eyes have been corrected, new teeth implanted, hearts repaired, and excess weight removed. The elder group saved our lives, healed our bodies, and provided us with a safe haven to guarantee the healthy continuance of mankind. To further ensure this agenda, every female over the age of twenty-three and under the age of sixty-five has been impregnated and is now carrying a child. For those females with husbands, the children born to them will be biologically from their spouses' DNA. Those females without husbands can rest assured the children born of them are not related to anyone in this community."

Shelly took Christy's hand as Christy stared in disbelief at the judge. Shelly looked around the room and saw the same looks on the faces of not only the women but the men too. She watched as, in many cases, that disbelief turned to anger. A man stood and addressed Judge Barker. "I am Doctor Murphy. Some of what you are claiming is not medically possible. Many of these women are past the age of childbearing. How are we to believe that this General Elder knows what he is talking about, or that you didn't somehow misinterpret what he told you?"

The judge calmly, but sternly, answered Dr. Murphy. "I am not here to debate the how or why of the elder group. I can only pass on what was revealed to me in my meeting with him. You do the exams, doctor. You can come up with your own conclusions. However, let me tell you this: people in bunkers or shelters are mostly older or with related family members. Where will they be in the next couple of generations? Those of you women that are with child are carrying the building blocks of mankind for this continent. Those of you that are adamantly opposed to raising a child may place the child in the nursery to be raised there or to be adopted into a loving home. No one will think less of you if this is the decision you wish to make."

Several people stood, and hands shot into the air. The judge quickly said, "I am not here to answer questions. Any questions you have may be directed to the head of personnel. Now we have one more order of business here. Is there a court reporter among us?"

No one answered, but then a woman stood and said, "I'm not a court reporter, but I know shorthand."

"You will do," the judge said. "Your name, please."

"My name is Velda Biggs," the woman answered.

The judge instructed Sergeant to get her a notepad, pencils, and a small table and chair, which were set in front of, but to the right of, the desk. The podium was removed. Judge Barker sat at the desk and waited until Miss Biggs was settled. He covered his microphone while he gave her instructions, and then he read from his folder. "Yesterday Roberta Black, the former head of personnel, knowingly broke three of our laws. She coveted the home that belonged to another, she bore false witness, and she stole. The facts and guilt are not at issue here; what we are here to decide is the punishment for Roberta Black."

Judge Barker nodded to Sergeant, who in turn nodded to someone standing offstage. Mike Strand went to a storeroom off the kitchen, collected a petulant Roberta, and escorted her to the chair next to the desk. Roberta sat, head held high, and glared at the crowd. Judge Barker read the charges to Roberta and then asked, "Roberta Black, do you have anything to say before I pass sentence?"

"You have no right to judge me," Roberta said arrogantly. "I was put in charge here. None of this is legal, and I demand this whole farce end now."

Judge Barker looked at the crowd of people and asked, "Is there any here who will speak for the defendant, Roberta Black?" There was not a sound in the restaurant. Judge Barker looked at Roberta and stated, "Roberta Black, for your flagrant disregard for the laws, and the unrepentant behavior exhibited in these proceedings, you shall be permanently removed from this community."

Roberta folded in on herself, holding her face in her hands and sobbing, her arrogance gone. Judge Barker said, "Sergeant Williams, you will escort Miss Black out of this community."

Amy's voice rang out as she ran on to the stage. "No, no. We can't do that."

"You wish to speak for this defendant?" the judge asked her.

Amy nodded.

"Sergeant, find a microphone for this child," he ordered.

Sergeant quickly complied. Amy spoke. "This is a mean lady. She stole my favorite rock from my collection, but she gave it back. Miss Carol has her job now, so she can't take anybody else's home, and we shouldn't make someone go away because of a rock. Mr. Judge, you said all the grown-up ladies are going to have a baby, so that means the mean lady is going to have a baby too. Please, Mr. Judge, we just can't make her go away."

Judge Barker studied Amy for a moment and then turned to Roberta and asked, "Roberta Black, will you promise to obey the laws of this community and to accept the occupation assigned to you by Miss White?"

Roberta stared at the judge for a moment and then asked cautiously, "What did this child mean about women having babies?"

The judge quickly explained the pregnancies to her. Everyone there witnessed the change that came over Roberta. Her entire demeanor transformed, and it showed plainly on her face. Placing both hands on her stomach, she said, "I had a bad infection when I was nineteen. A total hysterectomy was preformed. How is it possible I can have a baby?"

"The elder group fixed you," Amy said.

"Is this possible?" she quietly asked the judge.

"That is the information given to me," the judge answered.

Roberta sat, her hands still resting on her stomach, and her head bowed. Suddenly she stood and, with no sign of pretense or arrogance, humbly said, "I, Roberta Black, promise to obey all the laws of this community and to accept the occupation that will be assigned to me by Carol White, head of personnel."

She sat back down, bowing her head and looking at the floor. Judge Barker wrote something in the folder and then announced, "Roberta Black, you are hereby released from custody with the expectation that you will honor your promises. Miss Biggs, you will type up a transcript of these proceedings. A copy will be retained in Miss Black's permanent file."

Judge Barker banged a gavel on his desk and announced the meeting adjourned. Amy went to Roberta and said, "Please don't be sad, Miss Black."

Roberta looked up at Amy with tears in her eyes and replied, "I'm not sad, Amy. I am so very happy to be having a baby."

CHAPTER 18

Shelly filed out of the restaurant with the others. Around her she saw and heard the anger and unrest of the people. Christy was angry, speaking as she followed Shelly. "I don't want to have a baby. How am I going to handle Karla, Kerry, and a new baby, *and* run the card shop?"

Grace was one of the few that were beaming with the baby news, and she told her, "Oh, Christy, don't worry about it so much. Shelly and I will be here to help you, and there is always the nursery. It's all going to work out."

"What we all need is rest," Shelly said. "We need a break. All of this is so overwhelming. It's too much too fast."

They agreed and decided to go home to rest and think. Shelly was hoping that, given the time to think it through, Christy would be more accepting of the baby. Shelly's tension melted away when she and the children returned home to a welcome dance from the dogs, and Misty winding herself between their ankles. The children took the pets outdoors while she checked for questions on her computer, answering them with what she thought were the right responses.

The next day, Amy, Jake, and the pets disappeared to find Karla. Shelly headed to Rosa's clothes shop. All three of them needed at least one more complete set of clothes. She jumped when she heard a beep behind her. It was Grace on a motorized tricycle. She laughed as she pulled to a stop beside Shelly. "I just had to check out that transportation guy, and look what I got," Grace said.

Shelly looked it over. It had a wide, comfy seat, a big basket in back, and a small motor under the seat. "Talk about riding in style," Shelly laughed. "You headed to feed the horses?"

"Shoot, I done fed them and turned them back out early this morning," Grace said. "I had to show Christy and you my new wheels. Now I'm headed to the restaurant to see if I get a trainer or groom today."

"I have to see Rosa," Shelly said. "Then I'll meet you for coffee."

Grace nodded, and Shelly watched as she motored off down the street.

"Oh Shelly, I'm so glad you're here," Rosa said. "I want you to try something on so I can see how I need to alter it. You wait right here. Don't go away; I'll be right back." Rosa rushed to the back room.

"Not going anywhere," Shelly called as she looked around the shop. Rosa had several tunics she had applied her artwork to on display. Rosa returned and spread out an outfit that had no resemblance to the tunic and pants. The sleeves and pockets were gone from the tunic. The front neckline was cut in a V, and the back was a low V. The pants had been made into a flowing floor-length skirt with a slit up the left side. The whole thing was dyed a soft yellow. "Do you like it?" Rosa asked. "Take it over there to the dressing room and try it on. I want to see how it fits."

"Rosa, this is so beautiful," Shelly said as she carefully carried the outfit to the dressing room, wondering where she would ever wear something like this in the cave.

She came out to stand in front of the mirror and gasped. Rosa had a way of bringing out the very best in a woman's body. Rosa walked all around her and said, "Come into the back. I need to pin you in a few places."

"Rosa," Shelly said gently, "I love it, but I'm pregnant, and this isn't going to fit me for very long."

"Not to worry," Rosa said with a wave of her hand. "I thought of that, and trust me, you will be able to wear this until you are at least six months along, unless you get huge quick."

"How do you feel about being pregnant?" Shelly asked tentatively.

"I missed the baby thing by ten months; I'm only twenty-two," she answered.

The front door opened, and Sergeant stepped in. He stopped and stared at Shelly. Both women waited to see his reaction. Sergeant slowly raised his right hand and rotated his index finger in the air, his eyes never leaving Shelly. Shelly twirled with a nervous giggle. Rosa looked from Shelly to Sergeant, and a knowing smile flitted at the corners of her mouth. Sergeant moved slowly toward Shelly and said, "Rosa, you keep this up and I am going to have to build a bigger jail."

"She is beautiful, isn't she?" Rosa said proudly.

"And then some," Sergeant agreed still staring.

"Did you come in for something specific or just to ogle at my customer?" Rosa said, laughing.

"Um, yes, of course," Sergeant said. "I need a couple of changes of clothes, and I was told you have them."

Rosa went to the back room, leaving them alone. "You got a date for that?" Sergeant asked.

"No, Rosa wanted to make something special for me," Shelly answered.

Sergeant walked around her, "She sure has a way with a needle, doesn't she?" he commented.

"She really is talented," Shelly agreed.

Rosa returned and handed Sergeant a bundle wrapped in scrap cloth and tied with a strip of material. "Anything else?" she asked as Sergeant continued to eye Shelly.

"Oh, no, this is all. Thank you, Rosa," Sergeant said, backing to the door. "Later, Shelly." He threw the parcel over his shoulder as he left.

"That man has a thing for you," Rosa laughed.

"No, he's just your typical ladies' man," Shelly replied.

"That man is not a ladies' man. Believe me; I can spot them. He has a thing for you, and you have a thing for him," Rosa said, smiling.

Shelly felt her cheeks burn. "I still love my husband. There is no way I could have a man like him in my life," she stated adamantly.

"Virus get your man?" Rosa asked softly.

"No, a drunk driver, two years ago," Shelly answered sadly.

"You haven't had a man hold you and tell you how beautiful you in two years?" Rosa asked as if stunned. "Of course you love your husband. And there will never be another to take his place. But that doesn't mean you can't love someone different. You're going to have a baby, and you have two great kids that deserve to have a father figure."

"I don't know," Shelly said, walking to the back room. "It would be so complicated here."

"Spare me. Things got complicated when those crazies started mixing up that virus juice. I'm telling you now, Shelly; that is one fine man, and if you don't snatch him up, some other girl will get that pleasure," Rosa said firmly.

"If he is so fine, why don't you snatch him up?" Shelly asked.

"Because he's not for me. He's too old. He's looking for a family. Yours would be perfect. The good Lord didn't mean for us women to raise children alone; that's what men were made for."

Shelly shook her head with a laugh, saying, "You sure are wise for only being twenty-two."

Rosa smiled sadly. "Not me. I just repeated what my momma taught me."

Rosa finished pinning, and Shelly went into the dressing room to change back into her tunic and pants. Rosa had a bundle ready, and she exchanged it for the dress Shelly handed her. Shelly nodded and smiled at two women that were walking in as she was leaving. She promised Rosa that she would return in a day or two for another fitting.

Shelly stood outside the clothes shop trying to decide if she would rather visit Christy at the card shop, catch up with Grace at the restaurant, or go see about getting herself a tricycle. Suddenly Sergeant was beside her, taking her bundle and saying, "May I carry your package, pretty lady?"

"Why, thank you, kind sir. I'm trying to decide where I want to go," she replied, smiling up at him.

"Just what I like—a female who thinks about her options," he joked. "How about a cup of coffee and a bite of something sweet," he suggested.

"Just what I like—a man that knows my weak spot," Shelly quipped, turning toward the restaurant.

"I do like him," she thought as they strolled down the street together. "He makes me feel girly and young again."

"So you got that hot new dress in here?" he asked, shaking the bundle.

"Changes of clothes for me and the kids," she answered. "I didn't want to hurt Rosa's feelings, but darn if I know where I'll ever wear that 'hot new dress.'"

"I was wondering if you would mind if I took Jake to the sporting goods shop for some fishing tackle," Sergeant asked, changing the subject.

"He would enjoy that. Sure—as long as he's home for lunch. And you're invited if you don't mind potluck," Shelly replied, pushing away the thought that this man might be using her son.

Shelly and Sergeant entered the restaurant. They saw Grace sitting at a table with two men; she waved them over. They each picked up some coffee, and then headed to the table. "I have my trainer and groom," Grace said as they sat down. "This is Martin Harman, my head trainer, and Dale Pickett, the new head groom."

Shelly and Sergeant shook hands with the men and completed the introductions by giving their names. "What kind of horses have you trained, Martin?" Sergeant asked.

"Call me Marty. Mostly working quarter horses, but I dabbled in a little racing here and there."

Grace here tells us we got a nice bunch," Dale said. "But she won't let us go look at them until we eat."

"She's right," Shelly said. "Besides, they are all out in the pasture now."

"Not exactly," Grace said. "I brought a dozen in to the main barn to start working with them."

CHAPTER 19

The five of them sat watching as more new arrivals entered the restaurant and walked to the serving line. Shelly pushed her chair back, saying, "Well, I want to go see about a tricycle and maybe visit Christy. It was nice meeting you both."

Sergeant stood, offering to show her to the transportation garage. "Oh, you don't have to do that, Sergeant," Grace said. "We are going that way right now. Marty and Dale need to get their trikes too."

Disappointment flashed across Sergeant's face, and his eyes lingered on Shelly for a moment longer. "Right," he said. "Well, see you later."

"Later," Shelly agreed as she watched him leave, and then she turned back to Grace, smiling.

Grace looked first at Shelly and then at Sergeant, and said, "Why the heck didn't you kick me or something?"

"What?" Shelly said, knowing her cheeks were turning pink.

"I got your 'what,'" Grace said with a wink.

The transportation garage was just inside the Farming doors. Shelly stopped and looked in wonderment. Where the golf carts had been parked now stood a large garage. Grace laughed. "I was going to tell you about it, but I wanted to see the look on your face."

Shelly shook her head, telling herself that new things appearing should stop being a surprise. The head of transportation, Gus

Striker—a stocky, red-haired, freckle-faced man—tended the counter. A taller, younger version of Gus, that had to be his brother, brought around the tricycles. Grace shifted from one foot to the other impatiently while they waited in a short line. Marty took his place at the counter. Gus asked for his name and had Marty give a thumbprint impression. "Larry will bring your bike around." Gus said. "Give him this nameplate to put on the trike, and he will show you how to operate it."

Marty stepped aside, and Dale took his place as Larry brought up a tricycle. Grace left with Marty and Dale when they had their trikes, and Shelly took her place at the counter. She was the last in line, and Gus relaxed as they went through the procedure.

"Does everyone get a tricycle?" she asked.

"Only the adults," Gus answered.

"Is Larry your brother?"

"Baby brother. Our parents died when he was twelve. I was eighteen and finished raising him. He's a good man, but he doesn't really like working in a garage."

Shelly was caught completely off guard by Gus's statement. This was the first person she knew of that wasn't working at something he or she loved. "So you're going to take care of maintenance on the trikes and golf carts?" she asked.

"That and run cab and bus services," he answered.

"Well, you will be busy in a few months," Shelly laughed.

"That's what I hear," Gus replied, smiling.

"So is this work anything like what you used to do?"

"No, I used to run a junkyard," Gus said. "I didn't know anything about electric motors. Still don't, really, but there are detailed instruction manuals that were here for the trikes and carts. Funny thing is, I can't get to the battery. It's completely encased, with just a cable running from it. The manual says not to try to open the case. Of course I couldn't help myself. I had to see what kind of battery it was, so I took a chisel and hammer to it and got enough of the corner loose to peel back the cover and look inside. I lifted what looked like the battery out of the case, and I'll be darned if the thing didn't disintegrate right in my hands."

"You mean it blew up?" Shelly asked, looking closely for burns or injuries to Gus's hands.

"No," he said. "It just turned to a gray powdery dust." Gus scratched his head and said, "If the manual says 'don't touch,' you can believe me—I won't touch it no more. Hate ruining something that was working perfectly."

"I know what you mean." Shelly nodded and moved to receive her trike from Larry. As she handed her plate to Larry, she introduced herself and said to him, "I hear you don't really like working in the garage."

Larry shrugged and said a bit shyly, "It's all right."

"What would you rather be doing, Larry?" she asked.

"I don't know," he answered. "I like being outside in the woods, but that isn't really a job."

Larry pointed to a round disk in the middle of the handlebars, and told her it was the on/off button; that was where she was to place her thumb to start the trike's motor. "The motor turns off automatically when you get off the trike," he explained. "When the motor is running, it automatically engages the drivetrain. If you would rather pedal or push it like a regular trike, just don't push the start button."

Shelly nodded in understanding, though all she really understood was how to push the Start button. Shelly placed her bundle of clothes in the trike's basket. She thanked Gus and Larry, and headed for Christy's card shop.

Shelly turned into the shopping district and saw Amy and Karla leaving Rosa's clothes shop. She pulled to a stop next to them. "Look, Miss Shelly; look! I'm just like Amy, only I got violets. Isn't it beautiful?" Karla said, dancing in a circle.

Shelly smiled, running her finger over the tiny deep-purple violets at the neckline and the big violets on the pockets. "It is beautiful," she agreed. "And you look so pretty in it. Do you girls know where Jake is?"

"He went fishing with Sergeant," Amy answered.

"Really," Shelly said thoughtfully.

Sergeant had said he wanted to take Jake to the sporting goods shop for fishing tackle, but he hadn't mentioned they would try it out. Shelly smiled to herself, knowing that Jake would be enjoying himself and that maybe Sergeant was good for him. "Well, Karla, are you going to the card shop to show your granny your pretty new tunic?" she asked.

Karla's face lost some of its animation as she replied, "No, Granny went home to take a nap. She said Kerry kept her up all night."

"Then how about a snack at the restaurant with me?" Shelly suggested.

"We can't, Momma," Amy stated. "We got jobs at the toy shop. The man and lady there said we could dress the baby dolls and put the furniture in the dollhouses."

"That sounds like a pretty important job. May I walk with you and meet the people who run the toy shop?" Shelly asked them, getting vigorous nods and smiles. Shelly got off her trike and walked with the girls, pushing the vehicle as she went.

Isaac and Elizabeth Taggart were a delightful couple in their late sixties. Elizabeth was petite in size, with round sky-blue eyes and a crown of thick, curly silver hair. Even with wrinkles on her face, she made Shelly think of a china doll. Isaac wasn't much taller than his wife. He had a ruddy complexion that made his cheeks rosy. His appearance brought to Shelly's mind an elf. They were both toy makers. She specialized in porcelain. He specialized in wood. They proudly showed Shelly around the shop. Their back room was totally equipped as a workspace for both. On one side of the room sat a bench with tools precisely lined up and hanging on a pegboard behind it. Around the room were saws, a drill press, a small lathe, and everything one would need to work with wood. On the other side sat a table, a sewing machine, paints, brushes, a kiln, molds, bags of porcelain mix, and drawers filled with doll parts. Elizabeth stroked the kiln, saying. "I'll be able to design my own dolls now instead of just painting unfinished ones. Amy and Karla will have the first Taggart dolls."

Shelly did a quick double check with the couple to ensure the girls were indeed a welcome help before getting back on her trike and leaving their shop.

As she motored toward the restaurant, she thought about joining Jake and Sergeant, but she wasn't sure she wanted to hike up and down the creek trying to find them. She stopped at the kiosk. The fourth side held a notice that read, "Personal supplies may be obtained free at individual shops. Personnel will answer all questions on where you may obtain an item. Please do not come to the quartermaster for personal needs. Thank you, Roberta Black."

"Well I'll be darned," Shelly thought. She pushed her trike to the restaurant and parked it. Inside, she poured herself a cup of coffee, waved to Zeke, and went in search of a table. She spied Judge Barker and Carol sitting at a table with their heads together, reading over some papers. "Am I intruding?" Shelly asked them.

"Of course not; sit," the judge replied.

"So how is the government building going?" she asked.

"Fine; all agree to the original US Constitution," the judge answered. "Now we are working on community laws, and what to do with our workforce. Of course, not many people have been dropped yet. So far, most of the people are over the age of forty or under the age of eighteen. Most adults have occupations. However, we have a small number of adults in the labor pool."

Shelly nodded in understanding, saying, "Looks like the teenagers may have to pick up some of the slack."

"You're probably right, but it doesn't seem right to work children," Carol said.

Shelly laughed, saying, "Are you kidding? Most teens want to work rather than go to school all day. Also it will give them a better idea of what occupation they want to pursue."

Judge Barker looked at her and said, "You may have something there. Four solid hours of basic academics would be as much as or more than students received in school anyway. Class sizes could be smaller if some teens worked mornings and others worked after lunch. I have a meeting to go to right now and will bring this up with the members of the board while I'm there." He pushed back from the table, stood up, and walked toward the conference room.

Shelly called after Judge Barker, "You might also think about what to do with workers that have been assigned to occupations they don't like."

Judge Barker turned. "Do you know of someone that is working at something but would rather do something else?"

Shelly nodded affirmatively.

"We'll work on that." The judge nodded and continued to his meeting.

Shelly looked at Carol and said, "So tell me, how did Roberta end up with the quartermaster?"

"He picked her out of the labor pool. She is not going to have it easy with that one either. He is all business, and he expects his orders to be obeyed immediately. His name is James Fielding, and he's a retired army master sergeant. So who doesn't like their job?" Carol asked.

"Larry Striker, in Transportation," Shelly answered. "But he said the only other thing he really likes is to be outside in the woods."

"That's interesting," Carol said. "We had a man come in this morning whose occupation is master huntsman. His name is Jim Lightfoot. He wasn't here thirty minutes before he picked up some extra food from Zeke and left."

"So how are you doing?" Shelly asked. "You look tired."

"Gets a little hectic at times," she admitted. "Most of the women don't believe me when I tell them they are expecting a baby. I'm not here to convince them, though; I just pass along the information. I've been on the lookout for some help, but so far there haven't been any likely candidates."

Then Carol lowered her voice and whispered secretively, "I'm tired because I stayed in the office last night to see how the new people are dropped off. But I couldn't stay awake. I woke up this morning with my head on the desk. I'm going to try it again tonight."

"Good luck," Shelly laughed as she stood up. "I'm going to try to round up my crew for lunch. Catch you later."

CHAPTER 20

Shelly parked her trike at the toy shop and gathered Amy and Karla. As they departed, the Taggarts urged the girls to return whenever they liked. Shelly walked home with both girls, pushing her tricycle beside her. When they arrived at the apartment, Amy waved the door open. Shelly parked her trike in the short hall and followed the girls into the apartment. Jake and Sergeant were there; they had potato wedges and fish baking, and they were putting together a salad.

Sergeant grinned at her as Jake told her proudly, "We almost have lunch ready for everybody."

The girls sat on the sofa while Shelly picked up a knife to help cut vegetables for the salad. The guys were joking about who had caught the biggest fish, and the girls were discussing their work at the toy shop. Amy was dragging a string back and forth, playing with Misty. Jessie was curled up in Karla's lap. Golly wasn't in the apartment. "This is nice and homey," Shelly thought, feeling relaxed as she worked.

"There is a male using a shortwave radio to call for others that may be alive," General thought to her.

Shelly paused and thought back, "I can't answer right now. There is a government meeting in the conference room."

"No need to hurry," he sent back. "I just wanted you to be aware of it. You may want to move the radio into your apartment."

"One thing, General," Shelly sent. "Could you drop some help for Carol in Personnel? You are tiring her out."

"Noted. She would not be tired if she slept in her bed."

"Agreed," she sent with a smile.

Shelly looked up and became flustered when she saw Sergeant staring at her curiously. Realizing she had been standing there with the knife halfway through a tomato, she said, "I was just wondering how many of these to cut."

"At least more than just that one," he replied, and he then went back to talking bait with Jake.

Lunch was pleasant, with conversations about the toy shop, the sporting goods shop, fishing, tricycles, and the gym, which had a swimming pool as its most interesting feature. Jake, Amy, and Karla cleared the table while Shelly and Sergeant cleaned the kitchen. The children left to check out the swimming pool, and Shelly was fixing coffee for Sergeant and herself when there was a knock at the door. "Come," thought Shelly automatically as she took cups out of the cupboard. Another knock brought her up with a start, and she hurried to answer the door. Sergeant leaned back in his chair, just watching.

Shelly welcomed Judge Barker into the apartment. As he entered, he said, "We are taking a lunch break and thought you might want to know there's a red light blinking on the radio in there." He nodded to Sergeant and left.

Shelly sat and stared at the radio she and Sergeant had removed from the conference room and set up next to the computer in her apartment.

"General," Shelly thought.

"You have a question?" General sent.

"I don't know what is with this blinking red light. Did you do something to this thing?" she sent.

"We made some minor improvements. Simply turn it on; the radio will automatically go to the frequency that is calling," General answered.

"Stay close," Shelly thought. "I'm not good at first contacts."

"A word of caution: those that are calling have many weapons in their shelter," General advised.

Shelly nodded and flipped the switch, and the red light turned green. Shelly depressed a button on the microphone and answered the call. "This is Shelly Bradford. Who am I receiving?"

"This is the government of the United States. What is your location?" came the demand out of the radio.

"We don't know our location. Where are you?" Shelly answered.

"How many people are in your party?"

"What is your location? And how many in *your* party?" Shelly asked firmly.

"You are speaking to a representative of the US government, and you will answer all questions," the voice ordered.

Shelly looked at the radio for a moment and then flipped the switch off. She knew it wasn't necessary, since nothing would be broadcast unless she had the mike button depressed, but she decided in this case to use the utmost caution. She turned to Sergeant and said, "I think we'd better get Judge Barker in here."

"Shelly, can you give me your reasoning as to why you don't want to answer his questions?" Sergeant asked.

"Number one, do you know where we are; and number two, how do we know who they really are?" Shelly answered. "We are here with more women and children than men. We have no weapons to defend ourselves. I don't think it would be wise to confide too much to a single voice on a radio without the consensus of a few more people here."

Sergeant nodded. "You are good at this. You handled it the way I would have, but there is more to you, Shelly. You're keeping secrets."

Shelly blinked in surprise and said, "What secrets could I possibly be keeping?"

"I don't know, but I'm working on finding out," Sergeant said as he left to find the judge.

Shelly sat unmoving, staring at the red blinking light, trying to figure out what she had done or said to lead Sergeant to suspect her of having secrets.

Sergeant returned with Judge Barker and two other men. Judge Barker introduced the men as Calvin Johnson, professor of history, and Harold Vickers, professor of political science. Shelly relayed what had transpired on the radio and gave her reasoning for not answering the questions. Harold Vickers rubbed his hands together, saying, "Of course we must tell them everything. They are our government; it is our duty."

Calvin Johnson shook his head and said, "It is my opinion that we should go very slowly here. There isn't much of a country left. Are we really sure this will be government as we knew it before the virus?"

"Maybe we should hear a little more and try to get a feel of what is going on," the judge said.

Shelly flipped the switch on and reinstated contact. "You say you are a representative of the government. Do you have a name?"

"My name is John Drummond. By order of the president, as commander-in-chief of the military, martial law has been declared. You are required to give your exact location, a complete census of your party, and a detailed list of your assets. You will comply with this order or face a charge of treason."

Shelly flipped off the switch and turned to the four men listening. Judge Barker said, "I don't like the sound of this. Why would martial law be declared? There certainly are no riots or invasions."

"We could just put them off," Calvin said thoughtfully. "It's going to be a minimum of one year before anyone will dare venture out of shelters and chance infection from the virus."

Judge Barker nodded in agreement, saying, "We will go slowly, Shelly. Put them off."

Shelly flipped the switch and spoke into the mike. "Mr. Drummond, we respectfully decline to answer your questions at this time. There are things you have said we don't understand—for instance, the reason for enacting martial law."

John Drummond replied, "Martial law was enacted to stop the rioting and looting. When those are under control, the president will lift restrictions."

"Are you saying there is rioting and looting still going on?" Shelly asked.

"Of course the unrest is still going on, but our military is handling it, just as they will handle any that do not cooperate at this time. You, Shelly Bradford, will answer all questions put to you or face a charge of treason. And may I remind you the penalty for treason can be death."

Shelly flipped the switch and looked around at the men. "He just flat-out lied."

Harold Vickers shook his head in bewilderment and said, "That doesn't sound like our government."

"It's not. History shows that often in times of crisis or upheaval, a group of the military or opposing factions will take over an existing government. I'm afraid that is what has happened here. It would be interesting to know if the president himself is involved," Calvin said.

"Or if he is even alive," Judge Barker added.

Shelly nodded and flipped the switch. "Mr. Drummond, I would like to speak to the president before we go further."

"You do not make demands of us, but we will grant this one request," he replied.

"Why did you ask to speak to the president?" Harold asked.

"To determine if he is alive and has any involvement in all of this," Shelly answered.

"We have the president here; you may speak with him," Mr. Drummond said.

Shelly pressed the mike button. "Sorry to bother you, Mr. President, but we need to know if you gave the order for martial law."

"Yes, I issued the order," the unique voice of the president said, sounding weak and resigned.

"One more question, Mr. President. Did your entire family get to shelter, including your new kitten, Misty?" Shelly asked.

Without hesitation, and sounding a little stronger, the president answered. "The first lady and my children are here. Sadly, we couldn't find the kitten."

"Thank you, Mr. President. Please inform Mr. Drummond that we are in an underground shelter in Kansas. Our number is eleven: four men, four women, and three children. Our only assets are a limited amount of food and this radio."

"He will be informed," the president replied.

Shelly flipped the switch and said, "Well, that tells us all we wanted to know."

Harold Vickers looked confused. "Why did you lie to the president about how many of us there are?"

Shelly looked at him and answered slowly. "I didn't lie to the president; I lied to Mr. Drummond. The only cat I know of named Misty is mine. If the president had gotten a kitten, it would have been all over the news."

"Then why did you tell him where we are?"

"Mr. Vickers, it is obvious you haven't been outside yet. We are surrounded by mountains. There are no mountains in Kansas that I know of."

"It sounds as if they are using the president as a puppet; there isn't much we can do about it though," Calvin said.

"General," Shelly sent.

"You have a question?"

"Can you pick up the president and his family and bring them here?"

"No. It is forbidden to pick up those that are in shelters."

"Can you hear what their plans are?" she thought.

"No, we cannot hear them," General answered.

"But I thought you could hear everybody," Shelly thought.

"We can hear our own species, but not all of yours. You and your children are stronger than most. To hear your species, we must either be close or use a mind probe," General explained.

"Are you telling me that my children and I are the only ones of my species you can hear?" she sent.

"There is one in a Colorado shelter and another in a family shelter in a place you call Georgia on your continent," General answered.

"I wonder if the elder group can pick up the president?" Judge Barker asked.

"No, they won't pick up anyone that is in a shelter," Shelly answered.

Shelly looked up to find Sergeant studying her closely. She ran her fingers through her hair and said, "There isn't much we can do for the president until it is safe for us to leave the valley."

"Well, I for one am not willing to live under a military or any other kind of dictatorship. And make no mistake; that is what it will be," Calvin said.

"General," Shelly thought.

"You have a question?"

"Can you tell us what our best course of action is?"

There was a pause, and then General sent, "Sadly, we cannot interfere. This is for your species to work through. It is part of your growth."

The judge, looking thoughtful, said, "We are not in a good position. We have the opportunity to start a new peaceful world here, but it is a fragile start."

"We are going to have to fight them. We need weapons and trained solders," Harold said.

"Can you give me one instance in history when war has brought lasting peace?" Calvin asked.

"Well, we aren't going to settle anything here. Our main concern now is the peaceful running of this community for the next year or so," Judge Barker said, ending the debate before it got started.

"The red light is blinking again," Sergeant said.

CHAPTER 21

Shelly turned to the radio. "It's a different frequency." she flipped the switch and depressed the mike button. "This is Shelly Bradford; who are we receiving?"

"You've got NORAD here—Cheyenne Mountain, Colorado," said a male voice on the radio. "We monitored the conversation you had with our president."

Shelly started to shake and turned off the mike. This was becoming too much for her. She looked around at the men in the room. "What in heaven's name do I say to these people?"

Sergeant brought chairs from the table so they could all sit around the radio. "You might want to see if they still have tracking ability and if they have pinpointed our location," Sergeant suggested.

"Good hearing from you, NORAD; have you pinpointed our location?" Shelly said into the mike.

"Affirmative, Shelly. Nice little high spot you found in that wheat field in Kansas. It's a shame about the president's kitten. We all hope she can make it alone. She will be a real asset in keeping the rat population in the White House under control."

"Cats are pretty good at surviving. I'm sure she can make it for at least a year—more if she has to."

"Our doctors and scientists are advising the president it will be at least eighteen months before he can leave the shelter," NORAD answered.

"Thank you, NORAD. Please keep us abreast of any news we should be aware of," she said.

"Will do, Shelly. And our commanding general is interested in speaking with you personally about some of the features your contractor has built into your little underground shelter. NORAD signing off."

Shelly flipped the switch and excitedly turned to the men. "They know. They understand the president is in trouble. They are going to help him when the time is right."

"General," Shelly thought.

"You have a question?" he asked.

"Does NORAD know about you?"

"Our ships have been monitored, but there has been no contact," he answered.

With the exception of Sergeant, the men stood. Judge Barker patted Shelly on the back, telling her he now understood why she was the communications expert. The three men left to resume their meeting in the conference room. Sergeant kept his seat. "Whom were you talking to, Shelly?" Sergeant asked.

Shelly feigned confusion, saying, "I'm talking to you now."

"You know exactly what I mean. If you are going to be my wife, there shouldn't be secrets like this between us."

"Where did you get the crazy idea that I am going to be your wife, Sergeant Thomas Williams?" Shelly demanded, wondering why she was feeling so panicky.

Sergeant leaned closer and said softly, "Shelly, you can put it off for a while, but from the time Amy said we were in heaven, I knew you were my angel."

Shelly looked at him and began to giggle. She put her hand to her mouth, trying to stop it, but the giggle turned into laughter. The more she tried to stop, the harder she laughed. She moved her hand from her mouth to her stomach, doubling over in the chair and clutching her stomach with both hands. Sergeant sat with his arms crossed, his head tilted, and one eyebrow cocked, waiting for her laughing fit to end. Shelly began taking big gulps of air, trying to catch her breath. After a couple of failed starts, she was finally able to stammer, "Sorry, but what you said was so out of a bad romance novel."

When she saw the disgruntled look on his face, the laughter took hold of her for yet another uncontrollable round. Suddenly the laughter turned into sobs and she couldn't stop. Sergeant gently lifted her out of the chair, set her on his lap and held her close, not speaking.

"Are you injured?" General thought to her.

"No. I can't take it anymore. It's too much. And now he knows. I don't know what to do," she thought.

"Believe in the laws. They will guide you." Grandfather sent softly.

Shelly pushed away from Sergeant and went into the bathroom to wash her face. She needed some time alone to be sure she understood what Grandfather meant. With a cold washcloth held tightly to her eyes, Shelly decided. She would tell Sergeant that he was right about her ability to talk to General, but she wasn't sure how much more she should tell him.

When she returned to the living room, the chairs had been put back in place and Sergeant was gone. Shelly sank down on the sofa, her elbows on her knees and her head in her hands. She thought of what Sergeant had said to her. Why did he think she was going to be his wife? How could she be when she still loved and missed Doug so much? She realized that when she thought of Doug, the pain wasn't as sharp and crippling as before. She had put her grief aside by concentrating her focus on others with losses as great as, and more recent than, her own. It was time to stop grieving. She saw what it had done to her children. But that didn't mean she had to be another man's wife. She was just going to have to calmly explain that to him.

"I am attracted to him though," she thought. She remembered how pleased she had been when he hadn't drooled over Rosa the way other men had done.

The knock at the door brought a sigh of irritation as she went to wave the visitor in. The door slid open, and Sergeant entered carrying a tray with two covered plates on it. "I thought you might need a few moments to compose yourself, so I brought you comfort food," he said as he set the tray on the table and lifted the dome covering one plate.

Shelly whimpered with pleasure as she beheld a huge slice of chocolate cake smothered with chocolate whipped-cream icing. "You brought us cake!" she said, scampering to the kitchen for forks.

"I brought *you* cake. I brought me *man* comfort food," he said, revealing a mound of chili-cheese fries as she returned with the forks.

Shelly laughed, shaking her head, and they both closed their eyes and reveled in the first bites. They had eaten about half of their treats when Sergeant began pushing a fry around on his plate and said, "Can you tell me about it?"

Shelly ran her fork through the icing and asked, "Can you tell me what you think you know first?"

Sergeant continued worrying the fry, but his voice took on the tone of one giving a report. "You and your children were the first to wake. You were the only ones here with personal items: Amy's rock collection and the flowers. After your confrontation with Roberta in her office, and my refusal to stop her, you stomped down the street toward the conference room looking like you wanted to rip someone's head off. You came back calm. You looked almost smug when I received a call on my radio from a man claiming to be a general, who I doubt has ever been in the military. Shelly, you may not know it, but when you are mind-talking your eyes get a glazed kind of look. I know you are mind-talking. And I know you are mind-talking with more than one person. What I don't know is this: are you using extrasensory perception, or have they implanted some sort of sending/receiving device in your head?"

"It's ESP," Shelly said.

"Are you sure?" he asked.

"General," she called mentally.

"You have a question?" General sent. "Did you plant something in my head so I can hear you?"

"No, that would be forbidden," General answered. "Shelly, your species have had abilities for thousands of years. Unfortunately, during wartime, your species has a habit of killing those that are educated, priests or holy men, and teachers of the defeated. Books and reference materials are destroyed. Over hundreds of years, those that showed themselves to have abilities were murdered. Because of this, your species has buried and denied your abilities. But just because such abilities are buried does not mean they are not still there. You are not unique in your ability; there were many others with your strength before the virus, and there are still a few left."

"It's ESP. They didn't put anything in my head," she assured Sergeant.

"Can you trust them to tell the truth?" he asked.

"Yes," she answered. "That I am sure about. The laws they gave us are what they live by."

"There is more to them, isn't there?" Sergeant said softly.

Just as softly, Shelly said, "Yes, but please don't ask for more. I won't lie to you, but you will be asking me to break a confidence, and that is something I don't think I could forgive you for. You must understand that the elder group has no interest in any of us personally. Their main objective is for the human race to survive and learn to live peacefully."

"So they are here to advise and help us," he said.

"No, they refuse to give us advice, and help will only come if there is a danger to this community as a whole. Even then it will be minimal."

Sergeant nodded as Shelly pushed back her chair. Laying his hand on her arm, he said, "There is one more thing we must discuss."

She sighed and said, "I'm sorry I laughed at you, but you blindsided me with the wife stuff."

He looked at her earnestly and said, "I realize that. I know now I should have waited for a time when you were under less stress. Shelly, I know you still love your husband and that you always will. I care a great deal for you and your children, but that isn't the only reason we should be together. In case you haven't noticed, most of the women coming in are over forty or under eighteen. I'm thirty-four. Remember the fight in the restaurant over Rosa? There will be more fights as long as there are unattached young women living here. And, quite frankly, I am already tired of dodging nubile teenage girls."

Shelly laughed, saying, "Well, as campy as your first declaration was, I think it might be preferred to this one." Then, on a more serious note, she said, "I understand perfectly what you are saying. I can't continue to think of only what I want, but what is best for my children, the community, and the human species as a whole." She looked him in the eye and said, "When our entire population has been dropped in the cave, if you or I don't find someone else we would rather be with, and if both my children are receptive to the idea, I will be your wife. But Sergeant, I can't promise to love you like I love my husband."

When Sergeant started to say something, the door slid open. Jake, Amy, and the three pets noisily poured into the room.

CHAPTER 22

"**S**ergeant!" Amy squealed, throwing herself into his arms.

She laughed as he lifted her up with a hug, saying, "Here's my pretty little daisy girl." He ruffled Jake's hair, saying, "How's it going, soldier?"

The children both tried to be the first to tell him of the new children that had arrived, and their escapades inside and outside the cave. Sergeant listened attentively to each story, making comments and asking questions. "He really does like them," Shelly thought as she watched. "And they like him." She thought about Sergeant being there all the time and found the idea comforting.

The drops continued. Every morning there was a new group of four to five hundred new residents found sleeping in the dormitory. Carol was rewarded with not one but two assistants. The task of telling the women to expect childbirth in nine months fell to Carol. She handled it with sympathy, empathy, or firmness, as called for by each situation. More children arrived, and the schools were opened.

Jake and Amy developed a circle of friends. Their days and evenings were full of school, dance lessons, swimming, horseback riding, and exploring inside and outside the cave. Golly had taken to disappearing during the day; he was gone when they woke up in the morning and returned just before Jake came home from school. Shelly would often see Sergeant talking to different women, but he would shake his head ever so slightly whenever he caught her eye. She always returned the gesture. Shops were open, services were running, and a feeling of normalcy was taking hold. Nevertheless, over it all there was a pall of sadness. Everyone had lost family and friends, homes, and treasured keepsakes.

Shelly was on her way to the gym, concerned about the solemn faces that passed her, when she saw the theater. She parked her bike, went in, and looked around. She was astounded to see how large it was. There was seating in rows sloping down to a very large stage. On the stage sat a dozen people who were talking, reading, or simply lounging. Shelly walked up to the stage and asked who was in charge. "It seems I have been honored with the title of head thespian," the baritone voice of a tall, well-built man said.

"Now ain't he pretty, and he knows it," Shelly thought as the man made a sweeping bow. Shelly introduced herself and asked to speak to him privately.

"Of course, if you will follow me," he said.

They passed what he was quick to explain were dressing rooms. When they were settled comfortably in his office, he said, "Marcus Murphy, at your service, pretty lady. Do you want to do a little acting perhaps?"

"No, not me, Shelly said, "I was wondering when your first show is going to open."

Marcus looked at her as though she were speaking in a foreign language and said, "We are just actors here. We act out scripts. We don't produce or direct plays."

Shelly leaned forward. "Marcus, have you ever been in a play and thought you could do a better job of directing it than the director was doing?"

"Of course," he said with a wave of his hand. "Who doesn't think he can do a better job than the boss every now and then?"

"Well this is your chance," she said. "What are you waiting for?"

"You just don't seem to understand," he replied as if talking to a child. "We don't have set designers, costume designers, scriptwriters, songwriters, or choreographers, and that is just a short list of what it takes to create a play."

"Mr. Murphy, we are not talking about putting on a Broadway play here. We are talking about some much-needed entertainment for an audience of sad, hurting people that have lost almost everything they hold dear. Many of these people are working at jobs they never held before, but they are working. They are not sitting around waiting for someone to hand them a script. Go to the head of personnel. She will find the people that will help you with whatever details need to be worked out. Everyone has a job to do here. It's time for you to take advantage of the opportunity you have been given."

Shelly stood, turned to leave, and then said over her shoulder, "Let me know when opening night is; I have a fabulous dress to wear."

Shelly headed toward Carol's office. She wanted to give Carol a little time to get a list together for Marcus. She was secretly pleased that she could alter her course away from the gym. She turned onto an avenue, heading for Twentieth Street. She wanted to avoid riding through the shopping district. What had been a peaceful plaza to be strolled along was now often busy with shoppers, children, and other trikes. It was getting so crowded that many times it was necessary for her to walk her trike. She had gotten in the habit of parking her trike beside the cake shop, and walking across the plaza to the restaurant.

Shelly was a few doors from Twentieth Street when she noticed a beautiful rose painted at eye level in the middle of a door. She stopped and got off the trike to take a closer look. It was about three times the size of a real flower and was very well done. Each petal was shaded and slightly curled. There was even a glistening dewdrop just ready to fall, and the stem and leaves ran almost to the bottom of the door. "Impressive," she thought as she remounted the trike. She smiled when she saw a shoe turned upside down on an anvil with another shoe beside it, on the door across the street from the rose. "There will be more," she thought, and she wondered if it was a human trait, this need to assert one's individuality. She knew the keepers would never understand. She turned onto Twentieth Street and saw an older woman with something in her hand standing outside the short-hall door. As she got closer, she smiled, seeing the board with splotches of variously-colored paints on it. The woman was in the process of painting a huge daisy on the door. She looked to be in her fifties; a long, steel-gray braid hung down the middle of her back. Shelly saw that a strand of hair had escaped the braid and was streaked with yellow paint. As Shelly stood admiring the flower, the woman said, without looking away from her work, "If you want something painted on your door, you will have to catch me at my shop and be added to the list."

"Have you done many of these?" Shelly asked her.

"Yes, and I'm sorry, but I can't discuss details of what you want now. I'll never remember them unless I write them down," the woman said briskly, not stopping the flow of her brush.

"Amy," Shelly thought. She and the children were going to have to talk about getting permission before ordering things from the shops. Shelly said, "It's just that I'm Shelly Bradford and this is my door. Did Amy ask you for this?"

The woman paused and turned to her. There was a streak of yellow paint above one eye where she had brushed the strand of hair out of her face. "My name is Mary Sanders," the artist said. "I don't know an Amy. The head of security asked me to paint a daisy on this door, and on the first door to the left just inside here."

"Really," Shelly said.

"Look, if you don't want this, I can take it off or add something more," she said. "It would be a shame to remove the flowers though."

"No, no, it's perfect," Shelly told her. "Just a bit ago I was admiring the rose on a door around the corner and wondering what we might choose for our door. I would have never thought of a daisy, but it's absolutely right."

"The rose was the first door I painted. Now everyone wants something on their door. Most want something that pertains to the work they do. I could add something about your work. What do you do?"

"I'm the communications expert," Shelly said.

The woman stared at her for a moment and then turned back to the door, saying, "Yes, well, the daisy did come out nice, didn't it?"

Shelly laughed and agreed the daisy had most definitely come out very nice. She thanked Mary and headed down the street to talk with Carol. Mary went back to her painting.

CHAPTER 23

Shelly parked her bike next to the cake shop, walked across the plaza, and entered the restaurant. Sergeant was at the far end of the serving line, talking to Zeke. He held up his coffee cup to Shelly, and she held up her index finger to signal she would be back in a minute. When she got to Carol's office, Marcus was already there. They had their heads together, going over lists. They didn't even notice as Shelly quietly backed out of the office and returned to the restaurant. She went to the serving line and poured herself coffee, eyed the ever present cinnamon rolls, and thought about her missed workout at the gym. With a heavy sigh, she went and sat at a table with Sergeant. "Thank you so much for sending Mary to paint the daisies. Amy is going to love them."

"How about you?" he asked.

"Of course. They are a perfect choice. I have been wondering what we should have."

"I've missed you," he said. "You've been avoiding me."

"Yes, I have." she admitted. "I wanted us to focus on the new arrivals."

"I've tried, Shelly," he said. "But after a few words with other women, I find myself looking for you."

Shelly nodded. "Same with me."

"There are over twelve thousand people here now. The drops are almost done. Have you talked to Amy and Jake yet?" he asked.

"Not yet," she said. "I know you've been spending time with them. They talk about you all the time, but I need to have a serious discussion with them. We need to know soon how they would feel about you living with us."

Sergeant had just reached across the table to take her hand when Marcus pulled out a chair and sat, saying, "Well, pretty lady, it won't be long before I'll be entertaining you."

Shelly felt Sergeant tense as he let go of her hand and leaned back in his chair, eying Marcus. She quickly introduced the two men and asked Marcus if Carol had been able to help. "That is one efficient lady," he said. "She not only helped but also had some excellent ideas to get the people involved. I'm looking forward to working closely with her. She said I was to ask you whether we should put a notice in the kiosk or use it as an alert on the computer."

"An alert about a play coming soon to a theater near you?" Shelly asked, smiling.

"No, we're going to hold open auditions," Marcus answered.

"That is definitely something for the kiosk," Shelly said. "All it's going to take is for one person to read it, and the news will spread like wildfire. First it will be 'Did you hear about the auditions at the theater,' and then it will go around again: 'Did you hear who made the cut?' Yes, this is going to be very good for the people."

Marcus had just pushed back his chair to leave when a child's scream reverberated through the restaurant. Sergeant was on the move before the screams of a mother started. By the time Shelly and Marcus ran out of the restaurant, Sergeant was already cradling a small boy while the boy's mother stroked the whimpering child's forehead. A woman standing next to her trike, wringing her hands, kept repeating, "He ran right out in front of me; I couldn't stop."

"You were going too fast!" screamed the boy's mother.

Sergeant looked up at Shelly and told her to contact the doctor. "Tell him I'm bringing in a boy with a broken arm."

Shelly went through the restaurant to Carol's office and used her computer to alert the doctor to be ready for the boy.

Shelly settled back for a nice chat with Carol. "So the drops are almost complete."

"Yes, and I never did figure out how they get here," Carol said with a laugh.

"Did you spot any individuals that may be future problems?" Shelly asked.

"A few may be the chronic complainer types. But it looks as though we have a very good mix of stable citizens." Carol said.

"At least you will get a little more sleep now that you won't have as much to do," Shelly predicted.

"Are you kidding? I'm going to be very busy helping Marcus, and there are always people with questions," Carol said.

"Marcus, huh? It sounds like this is a project you are going to enjoy," Shelly said, smiling.

Carol blushed bright red and said, "Well, he is very good looking. One of my assistants checked him in, so I just met him. I know he didn't come in with family, but he may already be attached to someone."

"He certainly didn't sound like someone attached when he spoke about you to Sergeant and me," Shelly said lightly.

Carol leaned forward. "What did he say? Do you think he likes me?"

"Oh, just that you were efficient and he was looking forward to working with you," Shelly said, enjoying the pleased look on Carol's face. "I think it would be better if the audition announcements were in the kiosk. It's going to be fun watching people get excited about something besides work."

"Oh, good. I guess I'll just have to go speak with Marcus about how he wants this announcement worded," Carol said with a wink as she got a legal pad and pencil out of her desk drawer.

Shelly giggled, wishing her good luck, and said, "I'll ride with you. I started for the gym earlier and never made it."

Carol collected her trike from outside the restaurant. Shelly explained that her trike was next to the cake shop, as she didn't like riding in the plaza because of the traffic. Carol agreed as she watched a woman with a full basket weave between pedestrians. "I know it is none of my business, but it might be a good idea if everyone parked on the side streets and the plaza was only for foot traffic," Carol said.

Shelly stopped and looked at her seriously. "Oh, Carol, anything that concerns the community is everyone's business. Too many of us lost sight of that before. We let, even demanded that, someone else take care of or fix problems that should be handled within the community. Human beings around the world sat back and let a few run their lives; while the men in power gave lip service to wanting to help the masses, they helped themselves. Slowly, those power brokers stripped the populace of their freedom, their dreams, and their very individuality. We, as a populace, must never let that happen again. We need to tell our leaders what we expect from them. If they stray from those expectations, then they should be replaced. We should never again allow the few to bring down the many."

"Maybe you two should be sitting in on the government conferences," a voice said from behind them.

They both jumped and turned to find Judge Barker smiling at them.

"No, you have so many educated people in on that already," Shelly said.

"Maybe some people with good old common sense are needed too," the judge said.

"I don't think I would be much help with the legal parts of it," Shelly said. "But you know I will be more than happy to look it over and tell you where I think old-fashioned common sense may work."

"You scholars put it together; there are plenty of people that will help with the common sense end of it," Carol added.

Judge Barker nodded and, as he walked away, said, "I'm going to hold you to it."

Shelly continued on to the gym as Carol entered the theater. The gym was full of assorted pieces of equipment to keep a body strong and fit, but there was also a climbing wall and an Olympic-size swimming pool. Shelly had intended to make use of some of the equipment, but instead she opted to join the group swimming laps in the pool. Swimsuits were stocked in the locker room. They were one piece and were made of the same material as the tunics and pants, only thicker.

Shelly had completed several laps and was treading water when Sergeant entered and waved her over. He squatted down next to the pool as Shelly swam up to the edge. "Jim Lightfoot came in. Can you come and talk with us?" he asked.

"Sure; shall I meet you in the restaurant?" she asked.

"No, Jim and I will wait for you outside the gym; I think we should talk in your apartment," he answered, and he walked away before Shelly could ask what it was about.

They were sitting at her dining room table, and Sergeant asked Jim to tell Shelly what he had found. Jim was twenty-eight and was wide shouldered but slightly built. His face looked as if it had been chiseled by weather. He had dark, intelligent eyes that missed nothing in his surroundings, and the long black hair tied back at the base of his neck with a leather thong spoke of his Native American heritage. "I have explored our surroundings outside the cave. The valley runs north to south. I believe it's about twenty miles long, not including the forested areas to the north and south, and at least five miles wide. There is a stream that runs the length of the valley about three miles east from the cave. From the way it looks, we have mountains all around us. I wasn't able to find a trail or road out of here, because the whole valley and forest areas are enclosed by a barrier. I don't know what it's made of, but it's clear, it won't cut or break, and liquid passes right through it."

"I don't understand why you are bringing this to me," Shelly said carefully.

Sergeant studied her for a moment and then handed Jim his radio. "Will you please keep this on you so we can contact you? And I don't see any reason to discuss the barrier with anyone else right now."

Jim nodded and left without a word.

"What do you know about the barrier?" Sergeant asked.

"Why would you think I know more than you do, and why does the barrier bother you so much?" she asked.

"I think you know because you were the first awake, because you are in contact with the elder group, because the barrier bothers Jim as well as me, and because neither of us likes feeling trapped," he stated firmly.

"That's the second time you have said something about me being awake first. Why do you keep bringing that up?" she asked, starting to lose her patience.

"I keep bringing it up because it doesn't make sense. The first one awake should have been Roberta. That would make sense, but it was you, coordinating everything as if you knew exactly how everything should be. I could accept this without question before, but now Jim has found we are trapped in here, and I do not liked being trapped," he said, frustration making his voice louder than normal.

Shelly ran her fingers through her hair. "Why don't I just ask the elder group what the barrier is about?"

"How can you be so darn sure they are being completely honest with us?" he demanded.

"Because if not for them, none of us would be alive," she answered, deceptively calm.

Shelly watched him visibly deflate, and he said with resignation, "Ask them."

"General," Shelly thought.

"You have a question?" General sent.

"They have found the barrier. What do I tell them? They don't understand how it was made. They feel trapped."

"The virus is airborne; the barrier will drop when it is safe for you to leave the shelter," General answered. "The technology for the manufacture of the barrier is forbidden to you."

Shelly relayed the information to Sergeant.

"So we have to wait a year, or more, to see if they are telling the truth," he replied.

She glared at him, saying coldly, "Do you want out now, Sergeant?"

"I don't have that choice, now do I?" he said mockingly.

"Yes, Sergeant, you have a choice," she said. "If you want out, you will be let out, but you will not be able to return."

"You can remove the barrier?" he asked.

"No, I cannot remove it. And tread carefully with your questions. Either you trust me or you don't. One thing is certain: I will not tie myself to a man that will not trust me," she said, standing and heading toward the door. "Now, we can go get you through the barrier, or we can go to the restaurant and eat chocolate cake. It's your call, soldier."

She stood by the door, both hands on her hips, her chin stuck out slightly, waiting for his answer. He looked at her. She didn't have that stop-your-heart gorgeous beauty that Rosa had, but she was pretty. Her true beauty lay in her strength of character and her loyalty. The more he knew her, the more beautiful she became to him. "Can I have chili-cheese fries instead of cake?" he said with a crooked grin.

Taking her in his arms, he hugged her, kissed her temple, and inhaled the scent of her hair. Shelly was surprised at the strength of the feelings that ran through her body at his nearness. She looked up, raised onto her tiptoes, and softly touched her lips to his. Then she gently pushed him away, thinking, "I have got to talk to Jake and Amy very soon."

CHAPTER 24

At the restaurant, Shelly decided on a salad loaded with fruits and vegetables, while the sergeant stuck with the chili-cheese fries. They were enjoying the food, and each other's company, when Judge Barker set a toasted cheese sandwich and glass of lemonade on the table, pulled out a chair, and sat, saying, "Hope you don't mind if I join you."

They gave him a welcoming smile, and Sergeant asked him how the government building was going. "That's what I wanted to talk to you two about. Carol says it looks like we have all the people we are going to get. Shelly, can you post a computer alert? We want to set up a community meeting. I have spoken with the computer and camera people. We will be able to broadcast the meeting to everyone's home computer. I was thinking we should also have a session for questions and answers at the end. So we want each category of workers to send two representatives to be present at the live meeting, and all the educators should be present too."

"Are you going to hold the meeting in the theater?" Shelly asked.

"That was our first thought, but we decided fewer people on site is easier, so we'll hold it here in the restaurant. If you will stop by the government offices, Velda Biggs will give you a printout of what we have discussed here."

"When do you want to hold this meeting?" she asked.

"The sooner the better," the judge answered.

Sergeant looked at Shelly and said, "I agree—the sooner the better."

The judge looked from one to the other and smiled as he rose to leave the table, saying, "Yes, well, I'd better be going. Be sure to let me know if I can be of service to the both of you."

"I guess I'm going home now," Shelly said. "Amy and Jake will be out of school soon. Will you come have dinner with us?"

"I need to see the quartermaster about issuing me another radio, then check in at the office, and yes, I'll be there for dinner," Sergeant said.

Shelly felt as if she were floating. She was glad she hadn't taken the trike, as the walk home was wonderful. While she fixed Amy and Jake an after-school snack, she tried to think of how to discuss Sergeant with them. Jessie was at her feet, eagerly awaiting any stray tidbit that might fall. Misty sat on top of the refrigerator, looking as if she were holding court. Shelly heard the pet door rattle as Golly came in, tongue hanging out, looking satisfied. As he noisily lapped water from the water dish on the floor, Shelly asked him, "So where have you been all day?"

The dog wagged his tail and nudged the food dish. Shelly shrugged and turned with plate in hand when Jake came in first, saying, "Hi, Mom. What's to eat?" He took the plate with a quick "Thanks" and dived right into the snack. Shelly wondered if he even looked at what it was he was eating.

Amy came in saying, "Momma, look at my picture. Can we put it on the refrigerator? Do we have tape? Guess what? I have a new friend, and she has a cat too. Can I go to her house? I know where she lives. Oh, yummy—toast triangles, cheese, and fruit. Thank you, Momma."

Shelly smiled at their exuberance, sat with them, and gently said, "Guys, you like Sergeant, right?"

Jake, eying Amy's plate, nodded. Amy nodded as she pulled her plate closer.

"How would you both feel if he lived here with us?" Shelly asked.

"Would he be like my brother and sleep in my room? Gosh, Mom, that would be so neat," Jake said excitedly.

"No, he would be like my husband and sleep in my room," Shelly said calmly.

Jake's face fell, and he stared at her. "Would that make him our daddy?" Amy asked hesitatingly.

Jake jumped up from the table and shouted at Amy, "No, he won't be our daddy! We already have a daddy, but he's dead. I don't want another daddy."

Jake ran to his room and slammed the door. Amy looked at Shelly, her eyes filling with tears, and said, "I didn't mean to make him mad, Momma. I know Sergeant wouldn't be our real daddy, but I would still like to have him live with us."

Shelly hugged her, telling her it was all right. She determined she would talk to Jake. Shelly knocked on Jake's door and then entered. Jake was lying on his side with his knees pulled high and his arms wrapped around a pillow hugged to his stomach. She sat on the bed and pulled Jake into her arms, saying, "Jake, you are right. You will never have another daddy, but that doesn't mean that if I married Sergeant you couldn't still be friends with him."

Shelly continued to hold him and waited for Jake to say something. When Jake stayed silent Shelly tilted his head up so she could look into his eyes and said, "Oh, Jake, I wish I could read your mind so that I would know how to help you understand this."

Jake looked at her in surprise and said, "You mean you can't read my mind? You always know when I'm thinking of daddy, and it makes you cry."

Shelly looked at him with sudden understanding and said. "No, Jake, I was never reading your mind; I was reading your heart. I didn't cry because you were thinking of your daddy; I cried because you were hurting and missing your daddy, and I couldn't make it all better for you."

"Mom, do you love Sergeant like you loved daddy?" he asked.

"No, son, I could never love anyone like I loved your daddy, but that doesn't mean that I can't learn to love Sergeant in a different way."

"Would I have to call him Dad?"

"No Jake, and if you or Amy think you would be unhappy with Sergeant living with us, then I'll tell him he can't live here. We all have to be willing to marry him, or it doesn't happen," Shelly said.

Jake was silent for several moments and then took a deep breath before saying, "Mom, I know Amy would be really happy with Sergeant here. And you smile a lot more when you're with him. I guess I won't be unhappy if he is here. You know, Mom, we talked in school about how our population needs to be really careful about how we grow. Is he part of that too?"

Shelly sighed. "Yes, Jake, I guess he is part of that too."

"So I guess we've got to marry him, huh?" he said.

"Yes, Jake, I guess we do," she answered.

Jake picked at a tiny hole in the knee of his pants and then looked at her and asked, "Are you sure he can't just be our brother?"

Shelly shook her head, doing her best to contain the smile that tugged at the corners of her mouth.

Jake shrugged. "So when is the wedding?"

"I don't know, but Sergeant will be here for dinner. We can all plan it together."

They sat on the bed, not speaking, both looking down at their feet, each lost in their own thoughts. Suddenly, Jake's head snapped up and he turned twinkling eyes to Shelly. "If we have a wedding, will there be a party? And if there is a party, there will be a cake and lots of food, right?"

Shelly laughed and said, "Yep, there will be a party with food."

"Okay, this is going to be good," he said, rubbing his hands together. "When will Sergeant be here? Can we have a say in what food is at the party? Come on; let's tell Amy. She is going to love all this." Jake sprang out the door to find his sister.

After giving Amy the good news, they made a unanimous decision to fix an extra-special celebration dinner. The walk to the plaza for groceries was more like a happy dance, with Jake and Amy walking backward most of the way and all three making plans for the wedding. Jake's suggestions were mostly about what food should be served. Amy's list included a wedding dress from Rosa, invitations from Christy, and her role as a flower girl. They were laughing and talking when they entered the grocery shop. Stuffed chicken breast was the choice for dinner with Sergeant that night. Shelly went to the meat counter and asked Alex Coleman, the shop owner, to pound out four nice-sized chicken breasts and add a quarter pound of sausage for the stuffing. She gathered ingredients to make rice with mushrooms and then chose a bunch of spinach to mix with the stuffing. Amy and Jake gathered vegetables for a salad.

While Jake and Amy stood at the sink, washing vegetables for the salad, Shelly started on the sausage stuffing. As she finely diced an onion, she wondered if Sergeant would be as easygoing about her cooking skills as Doug had been. She had long ago given up aspirations of being a gourmet chef, titling herself a "what the heck" cook. When you sat at her table, you had to say to yourself, "What the heck; it's all edible."

She scooped up a quarter of the onions and dropped them into a bowl, quickly washed her hands, grabbed a kitchen towel, and held it to her burning watery eyes. Amy had rinsed the spinach and dried it by wrapping it in a towel. Shelly bunched up the spinach and started chopping it slowly. She had tried chopping using the television chef style of knife skills but had never really gotten the hang of it. "Well, it doesn't take a speed chopper to make good food," she thought as she scraped the spinach into the bowl. She unwrapped the sausage, and the aroma of fresh sage wafted around her as she dropped it in the bowl. A shredded piece of bread went in on top of it, and then she added an egg to the bowl.

Shelly glanced at the children. Jake was showing Amy how to cut the cherry tomatoes in half. Shelly bit her tongue to stop herself from saying anything when she saw the knife in Amy's hand. Jake was being patient, and Amy was being careful. Shelly sighed. "Amy isn't a baby anymore," she thought. After adding salt and pepper, Shelly stuck a hand in the bowl to mix the stuffing mixture, letting her mind wander. She thought of all the cookbooks she used to have and had never used. Oh, she might have opened one up to get an idea of ingredients, but then she would close the book and put a dish together. She loved to cook but hated to measure. Her talent was knowing what went well together—which spices to use. She didn't call her dishes recipes; she called them experiments. Of her experimental meals, 95 percent were delicious; the other five percent—well, what the heck; it was all edible.

Shelly set the stuffing mixture aside and washed her hands. She opened up the chicken breast. The butcher had done a very nice job; they were evenly pounded and of a uniform size. She seasoned the chicken with salt and pepper; put a quarter of the sausage mixture in each, forming the stuffing into slightly elongated logs; and then carefully wrapped and rolled the chicken around it. After washing her hands again, she had a moment of flighty panic as she rummaged through the cabinets. She smiled when she saw a small box of toothpicks. The keepers never stopped amazing her with their attention to detail. She fixed a toothpick in each chicken breast, dipped each one in an egg bath, rolled them in seasoned flour, and put them in a frying pan to lightly brown them in a small amount of oil. When each breast had the color she wanted, she put them on a cookie sheet and popped them in the oven to finish cooking. Shelly was working on the rice and mushroom dish when a knock on the door signaled Sergeant's arrival.

Amy ran to open the door, waved it open, and threw herself into Sergeant's arms. "We're going to marry you!" Amy said with excitement. "And there is going to be a wedding, and food, and I get to be the flower girl. Isn't that just wonderful, Sergeant?" She finished by giving Sergeant a strangling hug.

Sergeant hugged Amy right back, and he agreed that it was wonderful as he set her back down on the floor. He looked at Jake and said, "Is it all right with you too, Jake?"

"I would rather have had you as my brother and had you sleep in my room. But Mom says you have to be her husband because of the population thing," Jake said with a sigh.

"Yeah, I would have liked having you for a little brother, but I guess your mom's right about the population thing. We all have to do our part for that," Sergeant said seriously. He then added, "Something sure smells good in here." During the meal, Jake and Amy filled Sergeant in on plans that they had been making, and exchanged other ideas with him. Shelly listened, content to go along with most of what they wanted. She drew the line at serving chili-cheese fries at the reception though. When it came to picking a day for the wedding, she reminded them they would have to talk with Rosa and Zeke first to see how much time they needed to prepare. The planning continued up until bathtime and bedtime.

After Shelly had tucked the children in, she sat on the sofa, leaning her head on Sergeant's shoulder, enjoying the warmth of his arm around her. "You're sure you are all right with this?" he asked.

"Yes, it's going to be good for all of us," she answered.

Sergeant kissed her gently and then asked, "Do you think you can grow to care for me, Shelly?"

Shelly stroked his face softly and said, "I already care for you, Tom. It may not be with the same fiery, carefree passion I had with Doug, but I'm not eighteen now, and this is no longer a carefree world we live in. What I feel for you is steady and calming, and that's a good foundation to build the strength of love and passion upon."

"That's plenty enough for me," he said, rising from the sofa and pulling her up with him for a close, prolonged hug. "You check with Rosa, Zeke, and whoever else is on the kids' list; I have a few arrangements to make on my own," he said with a parting squeeze.

CHAPTER 25

Shelly got Amy and Jake off to school the next morning, and she then rode to the government offices to pick up a copy of the alert the judge wanted her to post to everyone's computer. When she started to type the message into her computer, she noticed the government seal embossed at the top of the page. It was the same as the US seal. She smiled, knowing the seal was Christy's work. She thought about it for a moment and decided to scan the page instead and post the alert as Velda had written it. The meeting would take place in two days, allowing time for representatives to be chosen.

Shelly decided that she would start with Rosa. She figured all other plans would depend on how quickly a wedding dress could be made. She knew Rosa was busy because it seemed every other person she passed in the community was wearing a Rosa design. She parked next to the cake shop and walked through the plaza to Rosa's clothing shop. Rosa took one look at Shelly's face and clapped her hands with excitement. "Tell me you're getting married."

"Yes," Shelly said, "And I'm here to see how long it will take you to make me a wedding dress."

With a mischievous look, Rosa told her she would be right back and disappeared into the back. She returned with a long, soft cream-colored wedding gown with what looked like lace overlay. Shelly gasped. "It's beautiful! This can't be for me, though. We just decided last night to get married."

Rosa laughed as she laid the dress across Shelly's arms. "Honey, I started this when I saw the way that security man looked at you the last time you were here. Go try it on; I have to step out for a moment."

Shelly closed herself in the dressing room, taking a minute to admire the workmanship before she put on her wedding gown. She stood quietly for a moment, remembering her wedding to Doug. They had been married at the courthouse. She wore a matching white skirt and blouse. Doug wore new jeans and a sport coat. She came out to look at herself in the large three-way mirror that was next to the dressing room.

Shelly looked down at her dress, purposely not looking at herself until she was sure the gown was arranged perfectly. When she raised her head to look at her reflection in the mirror, her eyes filled with tears. At that moment, Rosa and Christy scurried through the door, both wearing big smiles. The smiles faded as Rosa and Christy saw Shelly's face. They quickly ran to her.

"Oh, Shelly, what's wrong?" Rosa asked.

"Come, dear; tell what's wrong," Christy said, patting Shelly's hand.

Shelly slowly shook her head, pointing to the mirror. "I'm pretty," Shelly said, wiping furiously at the tears.

The three women looked in the mirror. Christy stepped behind Shelly, took a pin out of her own hair, and gathered and twisted Shelly's hair, pinning it in place. "You're not pretty, my dear; you're beautiful," Christy said, looking over Shelly's shoulder at their reflection.

Rosa walked around her, pinching and pulling at the fabric of the dress. "I wasn't sure how long it would take that man to get you to the altar, so I left it a little big," she said. "I will have to take it in a little."

"Where did you get so much lace?" Shelly asked.

The two women grinned, looking at each other like co-conspirators. "Christy made it with a lace-paper punch," Rosa said.

"Ah, it's not really lace, but it was the best we could come up with. Rosa's the real genius. She's the one that sewed it on the dress," Christy said.

Shelly hugged them, telling them both how amazing they were. Christy and Shelly discussed invitations, while Rosa stuck pins in the gown and mumbled to herself. When Shelly was back in her own clothes, she and Christy went to the card shop to look at wedding invitation samples.

The variety Christy presented was astounding. There were various types of paper, many colors, borders, and script styles, and then Christy started talking about different techniques. Shelly ran her fingers through her hair, wondering how she was ever going to decide. At that moment, Sergeant poked his head in the door. "This isn't one of those secret things I'm not suppose to see is it?" he asked.

Shelly jumped up and pulled him in. "You're here just in time. Help me pick."

Sergeant pointed to a fancy French script, told Christy the flowers should be daises, and asked her to work up a couple of samples they could look at later. Shelly looked at him in amazement. "You sure made that look easy."

She gave him a speculative look, and then a gleam of mischief showed in her eyes. She jumped up, grabbed his hand, and dragged him toward the door, saying, "Come on; let's see if you can pick a cake that easily." She called back over her shoulder to Christy, saying they would talk later.

Shelly loved to take her time and browse when she was in the cake shop. The decorated cakes and cookies were truly works of art. She wasn't much of a baker. Baked goods required precise measuring. She fully appreciated and admired what the two women that ran the cake shop produced. Shelly had thought the women were sisters, but they told her that they had been friends since childhood. When Shelly and Sergeant entered the cake shop, Margie and Patty welcomed them excitedly. "You're here to order your wedding cake," Patty said knowingly.

"Now, how did you know that?" Shelly asked.

Patty giggled. "I was at the card shop when Rosa ran in to get Christy so she could see you in your wedding dress," she said.

"Come on back and sit down," Margie said. "We'll go over your options."

She showed them pictures of tiered cakes, sheet cakes, cupcakes, geometric shaped cakes, and more. Shelly and Sergeant chose a traditional three-tiered cake with bride and groom toppers.

"Now, what flavor?" Margie asked.

"Chocolate" was Shelly's immediate reply.

Sergeant winced. "Can you make a cake that tastes like chili-cheese fries?" he asked.

Margie smiled. "I'll tell you what—why don't you two come back later this afternoon for a taste test?"

Outside the cake shop, Shelly and Sergeant drifted toward Zeke's while discussing cards, cakes, and flower girls. It was Sergeant's idea to have Jake walk Shelly down the aisle and give her away, and Shelly hugged him for his thoughtfulness.

At the restaurant, Shelly and Sergeant had bowls of beef stew. Sergeant used the last bite of his bread to sop up the last of the thick gravy at the bottom of the bowl. A man Shelly didn't know walked up and sat at their table. Sergeant introduced him as Joseph Parker, head of maintenance, and asked how things were going. "Okay, but I'm having a bit of a problem," he said, taking a bite of his own stew.

"Anything I can help with?" Sergeant asked.

"Maybe," he replied. "You know this place pretty well. I'm having trouble finding the main electrical supply source. It's the same with the water and the waste treatment. We have found electrical junction boxes that service each street, farming, and the barns, but that is as far as we can trace it. It's the same way with the water supply. Our chemist and lab techs have analyzed the water. It's some of the purest they have ever seen that wasn't distilled. They found minute traces of iron, magnesium, and fluoride in it. The first two occur naturally, but the fluoride doesn't; it has to be added somewhere. Waste is the same story; we don't know where it's going. How am I supposed to perform preventative maintenance on something I can't find?"

"Is there a problem in any of these areas?" Sergeant asked as he eyed Shelly, her head bent, silently pushing a pea around the bottom of her bowl.

"Well, no, but it makes those of us in maintenance a little nervous not knowing," Joseph said.

"I'll keep an eye out in the cave for what you are looking for, and I'll have Jim Lightfoot look around outside," Sergeant said. "In the meantime, I wouldn't worry about it if I were you. It seems that when the elder group put this place together, they thought of everything."

"I guess you're right," Joseph said doubtfully as the three of them rose from the table in unison.

Sergeant walked Shelly to her tricycle, telling her he had to get in touch with Jim Lightfoot. As she mounted her trike, The sergeant said, "Shelly, about the utilities—"

Shelly interrupted him with a light kiss, quickly saying, "Thank you for not asking me something I can't discuss. Now, I'm off to tell Grace about my dress."

Sergeant watched as she turned the trike around and headed away from the plaza, noting how she would rather detour around instead of taking the direct route through the plaza.

CHAPTER 26

Shelly and Grace stood leaning their arms on the fence, admiring the big bay gelding Marty was lunging in the training pen. A young man stood on the other side, next to a western saddle sitting on the fence, waiting for Marty to call him in. Shelly told Grace all about the plans that had been made for the wedding. They both laughed about Sergeant wanting a chili-cheese-fry cake. Grace agreed to be matron of honor after being assured that Amy was looking forward to being a flower girl and would not be upset about not being maid of honor. Shelly jumped at the idea of Karla being a second flower girl, knowing Amy would love having Karla included. Shelly was giving Grace a departing hug when she thought she heard a dog bark. "That sounded like Golly," she said.

"It probably is; he comes here first thing every morning. I give him a piece of toast, and then he goes to help the sheep men with their sheep. They say having him is like having three extra workers," Grace informed her.

Shelly laughed and said, "Well, that is one mystery solved."

Shelly returned to her apartment. Amy, Jake, and Sergeant were already there, putting together an after-school snack. Golly was lying on the floor at the edge of the kitchen with his tongue hanging out, panting. Shelly wondered how he had managed to beat her home as she told the rest of them where Golly was going every day. Sergeant told Shelly that as he had passed the cake shop, Patty had reminded him to be sure to come back after dinner for their taste test.

Sergeant and Jake decided to try to catch some fish for dinner. Shelly decided that she and Amy would go to the grocery shop in case the men came back empty-handed. On the way, they stopped in the card shop to ask Christy and Karla about Karla being a flower girl. Then they stopped at Rosa's shop to order two flower girl dresses. Shelly also let Rosa know that Grace would be matron of honor and would need a dress too. They returned to the apartment just as Jake and the sergeant were turning the corner onto their street. Each carried only a fishing pole.

After dinner, they all walked to the cake shop while talking about wedding plans. When they arrived, Margie and Patty had an assortment of small cakes laid out for them to taste. They were all in agreement on the double-chocolate fudge cake with raspberry filling for the first tier, lemon cake with lemon filling for the second tier, and white vanilla cake with strawberry filling tor the top tier. They were shown a drawing of the cake. It was a simple design with yellow daisies and green leaves. Patty emerged from the back with a small cake and announced, "We thought this might work for the groom's cake."

Patty cut each of them a small piece and waited for their comments. Shelly examined the cake; it was dark with a white filling and a smooth light-orange icing. She took a bite of the still warm cake and then laughed, watching the surprised expressions on the faces of the others. Sergeant grinned, saying, "It's a chili-cheese-fry cake."

Of course it wasn't exactly a cake. It had a dense consistency that came from the beans in it. Shelly could taste the chili peppers, cumin, beans, and onions. The filling was definitely potatoes, and the icing wasn't icing; it was melted cheese. "I know the filling is potatoes," Shelly said, "but this is not exactly mashed potatoes."

Patty smiled. "You're right. Zeke helped us with this. He put the potatoes through a potato ricer instead of mashing them, for a little better consistency."

Shelly was busy for the next few days planning food with Zeke for the reception. Rosa had ordered shoes to match the dresses from the cobbler. So Shelly had to have her own, but she made sure Amy, Karla, and Grace got their feet measured at the cobbler shop too. Food, dress fittings, and shoe fittings occupied much of her days. Shelly felt joyous as she and Grace rode the fields on horseback looking for the biggest patches of wild daisies. Shelly could tell that Sergeant and Jake had a secret, but she hadn't managed to coax it out of them. She couldn't figure out how Sergeant had the time for anything. He and Jim Lightfoot had been combing the valley looking for utilities that she knew they wouldn't find. When Sergeant wasn't with Jim, he was fishing with Jake.

Thoughts of the wedding were temporarily put aside as the restaurant filled for the government meeting. Looking around, Shelly realized she knew most of the people there. She put them in two categories: people she knew before the cave, and those she met after they arrived in the cave. On the stage was a podium; Sergeant was standing to one side. Velda Biggs was sitting off to the other side at a desk with a pencil and pad. Shelly watched as the cameraman signaled Judge Barker to take his place at the podium. Judge Barker placed his notes on the podium and nodded to the cameraman. Sergeant called the meeting to order and introduced Judge Barker.

Judge Barker began his speech. "People of Cave Haven, you have been called to this meeting to discuss the circumstance that we currently find ourselves in and the future we hope to build. As most of you know, a deadly man-made virus has decimated the population of the world. In this country, besides us, only those few that found refuge in prepared shelters have escaped its rampage and death. A small group of us has met daily to discuss how to proceed from this point. The first thing we decided was to refer to our shelter as Cave Haven. It is our opinion that we should keep as written the original US Constitution of our national government. Our president and many elected lawmakers are still alive in a bunker under the White

House, so we will not concern ourselves with national government until all the people of the United States can be counted and are in communication with each other. Each of you will receive a copy of the original Constitution, and you are asked to make yourself familiar with each aspect of the document.

"My main purpose today is to go over how the government for Cave Haven shall be operated and to discuss the laws that have been written for our community. We have adopted the ten laws that each of us received upon arrival. Additionally, beginning tomorrow, for the safety of pedestrians, vehicles will no longer be permitted in the shopping plaza, except to cross at intersections. Tricycles and carts are to be parked on side streets. As everyone is aware, our workforce is shorthanded. We are going to have to call on the younger members of our community to help with this situation. We are asking that the young people work four hours a day, in addition to going to school four hours.

"Our learned professor of history has convinced us that the medieval guild system may work well for Cave Haven. Tomorrow every child age twelve and older will receive a form to fill out. This simple form will ask about your likes, dislikes, abilities, talents, school grade average, and job preferences. These forms will be turned over to the head of personnel, whose office has been relocated to the government offices. Personnel will assign each of you a profession to report to, based on this form. For those twelve to sixteen, please don't be disappointed if you aren't placed according to your first choice. You will be rotated every four months to a different profession. Citizens sixteen and older may apply for an apprenticeship. If accepted, they will be required to work at that apprenticeship for a minimum of one year. At the end of that year, they may continue in that apprenticeship or apply for a different apprenticeship position. The tests for journeymen and master craftsmen will be decided by each guild. Now, are there any questions?"

A single hand slowly rose. The judge asked the woman to stand and ask her question. "How long are we going to work without getting paid?" Roberta Black asked.

Shelly wondered fleetingly if the judge would blast her, but he didn't. The judge answered seriously. "At this time, we have no monetary system in place; right now everyone is working—let's say—on trade. Your labor is paid for by your continued life in this community. In helping the community survive, we offer you access to all we have to give: housing, food, goods, and services."

Still standing, Roberta countered with, "But how do we get ahead?"

The judge shook his head. "Ahead of what? Whom do you want to get ahead of? Until we are reconnected with the rest of the people alive in the country, our goal here is survival and building a peaceful, orderly society."

Roberta sat down. No one else raised a hand, so the judge concluded. "If anyone happens to think of a question, the computer folks tell me that they have installed addresses on everyone's computer. So feel free to contact me or the Personnel Department. Now, before we adjourn this meeting, let me reiterate the importance to each and every one of you of learning the Constitution. The near demise of humanity was not the fault of a few demented souls; it was the silent consensus of millions of now dead people permitting hate to exist, and even promoting it. Let us not repeat their mistake.

"The people in every country that did not hold their governments accountable for corruption, fraud, and terrorism have paid for it with their lives. Here in our own country, we who had the freedom to select lawmakers that would most benefit the country voted ignorantly based on looks, charisma, charm, and false promises. Many voted not with knowledge or understanding, but with only a single-minded desire to beat the opposition. When we again get the opportunity to vote, look to the person that will best serve the country. That person should be first guided by the Constitution and then guided by our list of ten laws. The Constitution is the document that held this country together for over two hundred years, and our laws are universal truths for all sentient beings to abide by. Don't vote for someone that offers some groups of citizens personal gain, because the fulfillment of a promise for one group must always come at the expense of another. Above all we must be very careful of what we allow our government to be involved in when it goes beyond what is set down in the Constitution."

The judge nodded and gathered up his notes. Shelly smiled; not once had he so much as glanced at those notes. Then Sergeant adjourned the meeting.

CHAPTER 27

Shelly took her time leaving so Sergeant could catch up with her. She was lost in her own thoughts, thinking about how thrilled Jake would be with the idea of working, since he would soon be twelve. Suddenly she heard in her mind "I need some help here. I am trapped and may be hurt."

"General, are you hurt?" she thought, knowing even as she asked that it wasn't General she had heard.

"No, it is your huntsman," General answered.

"Where is he? How badly is he hurt?" she sent as she frantically searched the crowd for the sergeant.

"Shelly, I can hear you perfectly. A tree limb broke and fell on me. I'm not sure how badly I am hurt. And who is this General you're talking to?" Jim sent.

Finally Shelly spotted Sergeant making his way toward her. He started to hurry when he saw the look on her face. "Can you tell me where you are, Jim?" Shelly thought.

"I'm at the south end of the valley, about seven miles from the mouth of the cave," he answered.

"What's wrong, Shelly?" Sergeant asked her with concern.

Shelly pulled him into the vacant dormitory. "Jim is trapped under a tree limb about seven miles south of here," Shelly said. "He's not sure how badly he is hurt."

Sergeant lifted his radio and, with a brief explanation, told Mike Strand to meet them at Shelly's apartment. Then he called Scott Cutter, asking him to pick up a cart and the doctor, giving him the directions to follow.

Sergeant grabbed Shelly's hand and started back into the still crowded restaurant. Shelly stopped and pulled him toward the narrow hall door at the other end of the dormitory, assuring him it would be faster.

They met Mike. Sergeant jumped into the front seat next to Mike; Shelly sat in the backseat, behind Mike; and the three of them sped toward the south forest. "General, can you tell me exactly where Jim is located?" Shelly thought.

"Bear a little to the right, and then travel straight through the forest," General sent.

Using hand signals, Shelly guided Sergeant, who in turn gave Mike directions.

"Why didn't you tell me there was another person here you could hear?" Shelly thought.

"We did not know," General replied.

"How could you not know?" Shelly thought to him. "I thought you mind-probed all the people that were dropped?"

"Not everyone was probed," General sent. "Many of your species have enough strength for us to hear but not enough for you to communicate with. This one was not probed."

"I don't understand; how could you not know his strength?"

"For many of our unit, this is a first mission; miscalculations were made. This human is very strong and was able to hide his strength from us during screening. He not only partially covered his broadcast but also hid the cover. He is the only human with this power we have encountered."

"Does that mean there may be more humans that have strength or power that you don't know about?" Shelly sent.

There was a pause. "Twenty minutes ago, we would have said this strength and power did not exist in your species on this world."

They both heard a chuckle, and then Jim sent, "If I may insinuate myself into this conversation, may I offer an explanation?"

"We would very much appreciate an explanation, Mr. Lightfoot," General sent.

Shelly was surprised that General had allowed Jim to even hear the conversation. "I am Native American. My father was a holy man—what some call a medicine man—as was his father and his father's father, as far back as the beginning of time. I was not to be allowed to know the secrets of our people until I exhibited the ability and power to hide those secrets. I was on my way back to my home to undergo the sacred rights ceremony when the virus hit. Now it looks as if I will never learn, or hold, the secrets of my people. They are all gone."

"Do you know how, or from whom, your people first gained this ability?" General sent.

"Our stories, handed down through the generations, tell of the Sky People that taught my people many secrets. Only the holy men hold those secrets; they are received during the sacred rites ceremony."

Both Shelly and General felt Jim's sadness.

The cart came to a stop. They had taken it as far into the woods as they could. The rest of the way would have to be traveled on foot. Sergeant ordered Mike to stay and wait for Scott and the doctor. Shelly had already started through the heavy brush, while Mike pulled a come-along and chain from the back of the cart and handed it to the sergeant. By the time Sergeant caught up with Shelly, they were close enough for Jim to use his voice to guide them to him. He was next to the barrier. The limb lay across his waist, and a huge, old pine tree towered above him. In the heavy underbrush, it would have been impossible to find him if he hadn't called for help mentally. Shelly squatted next to Jim. "Do you hurt anywhere?" she asked aloud. "Can you feel your legs?"

"I'm pretty sure I'm not hurt," Jim said. "I'm stuck."

Sergeant looked up into the tree, following the path of the limb with his eyes. Sergeant snaked the chain around the limb that had Jim pinned, and he then hooked up the come-along on a thick branch of a tree next to the one they were beneath. "Jim, how in the heck did this limb manage to catch you? It had to make a lot of noise coming down," Sergeant said as he worked.

"Oh, it certainly made a lot of noise," Jim said with a chuckle.

"Jim, did you hit your head?" Sergeant asked. "Because you aren't making a whole lot of sense."

"It was like this. Do you see how tall this tree is? Well, I thought that if I climbed high enough, I would be able to see the top of the barrier. It was a bit of a jump to reach this limb, but I had a good hold and started to swing up when the darn thing broke. It happened so fast, but it seemed to take forever to hit the ground." Jim explained.

"You mean you are in this mess because you climbed a tree to look over something you can see through?" Shelly said. "I told you the barrier will come down when it is safe to leave here."

"I wasn't trying to leave. I just want to be able to leave if it becomes necessary. I can't stand feeling like I'm in a cage—a big cage, but still a cage." Jim said, unapologetic.

Sergeant called Shelly over to the come-along and showed her how to use it. He bent down at Jim's head, placing his hands under Jim's arms. "Jim, Shelly will raise the limb; as soon as there is enough room, I'm going to pull you out."

"Shouldn't we wait for the doctor?" Shelly asked.

"His color is good, and there is no blood anywhere. I don't think he is hurt."

Sergeant nodded to Shelly, and she pulled down the handle of the come-along until she heard a click. She raised and lowered the handle two more clicks and saw the limb move a fraction of an inch. "A couple more," encouraged the sergeant.

The handle was getting hard to pull, and Shelly wasn't sure she was going to be strong enough to go much more. She was pulling with both hands when Mike's larger hand covered hers and finished the job. Shelly stood back out of Mike's way as Scott and the doctor arrived. With a sudden rush when the limb was high enough, Jim instinctively crab walk his way backward; at the same time, Sergeant pulled him. They ended up in a heap, Sergeant sitting with his legs splayed open and Jim in his lap with his head on Sergeant's shoulder. They sat that way as the doctor examined Jim. The doctor stood and looked up into the tree, seeing what Sergeant had seen. "I don't know how you managed not to break your back or neck, but it looks like you're sound. Come by the office and we'll get those cuts and scratches disinfected," the doctor said.

Mike helped Jim up. Jim stood, flexing his knees to be sure they worked right. He wasn't hurt, but he was a bit wobbly, so Mike and Sergeant helped him back to the cart. As Shelly climbed into the cart next to Jim, she heard General say, "Show this one how to open the barrier before he injures himself."

Jim, with a look of surprise, thought at her, "You know how to open the barrier?"

"Yes, but please don't ask me any other questions; only General can decide what he wants you to know," Shelly thought to Jim.

Jim sat back and thought, "Do you think this General knows the secrets of my father?"

They both heard General: "We do not know what secrets your father would have passed on to you. Were there others among your people that had your abilities?"

Jim shook his head and sent, "I was only taught what all my people learn. I was instructed from an early age that my ability must be hidden from others at all cost."

"But you exposed your abilities to me—why?" Shelly sent.

"For one, I had no idea anyone would answer my call. Had my people survived, I would have died before I called for help. The reason for hiding my ability was to be sure I had the power to protect the secrets."

"So your ability has nothing to do with the fact that you are a Native American," sent Shelly.

"We are taught that our spiritual leaders can communicate with the spirits. I was not taught what others may know. From a very young age I could mind-speak with my father and grandfather as long as we were close. It was distance I was working on when the virus took them."

Shelly thought for a moment and sent, "You said you were on your way back. Does that mean you can speak over distances?"

"My father answered my questions from fifteen hundred miles away," he answered.

Shelly glanced at Sergeant, and he cocked an eyebrow and looked at Jim. Shelly gave him a barely perceptible nod. Jim returned with Sergeant to Shelly's apartment. When Shelly offered him food and drink, he requested water and stated that he could use a bite to eat. Shelly quickly provided Jim with a glass of water. She returned to the kitchen. Sergeant and Jim sat at the table and watched Shelly as she sliced bread and ham. Sergeant turned to Jim, asking, "Where is the radio I gave you?"

"It was in my pocket, but I couldn't get to it," Jim answered.

"So how did Shelly know you were in trouble?"

Jim took a long drink of water, studying Sergeant over the rim of his glass. As he slowly lowered the glass, he said, "I guess you'll just have to ask her that question."

"He can mind-speak," Shelly said as she handed Jim a plate with a ham sandwich on it.

Jim straightened and started to say something, but Shelly held up her hand to stop him. "Sergeant already knew the answer when he asked you, Jim," Shelly said. "He was watching us on the way back."

Jim shook his head. "All my life, this is something I have hidden. Now, all of a sudden, it seems to be common knowledge."

"No, it's not," Shelly said. "Sergeant is the only one that knows."

"We would prefer to keep it that way," Sergeant said.

Jim nodded and rose to leave. "I'm going to run by the doctor's office right quick. When he is done with me, you can show me how to get through the barrier."

CHAPTER 28

Sergeant turned to Shelly, stunned, "You know how to take down the barrier?"

"No, I can't take it down, but I can get through it. I told you once that if you wanted out, you would be let out."

"Well, why all of a sudden have you decided Jim should learn how to get out, but I wasn't even given the information that you knew?" Sergeant asked.

"I'm not the one that decided he should know," Shelly said. "That was General's decision. He didn't want Jim getting hurt trying to get out, and I am not certain how he will feel about you knowing how to get out too."

"You're going to show me how to get out," Sergeant stated forcefully.

"Unless General forbids it, and so far he hasn't." Shelly replied.

Jim was edging toward the door, watching the conversation go back and forth, when the door opened. Amy and Jake rushed in excitedly. "The play is opening tomorrow night," Jake reported.

"Can we go, Momma?" Amy asked, bouncing up and down in front of Shelly.

Before Shelly could reply, Sergeant said, "Hey kids, I know you want to go to the opening, but I've been looking forward to this being your mom's and my first real date."

Jake and Amy looked at each other and then looked back at Sergeant. "We understand, and it's okay," Jake said, but the disappointment in his voice was plainly evident.

"If the grannies go, can we go with them?" Amy asked.

"Why don't you go ask them?" Shelly said with a smile. "We have an errand to run. I want you to stay with Granny Christy until we come for you."

Both children shot through the door without a backward glance. "You're going to show us now?" Sergeant asked.

"If Jim is up to it after he sees the doctor, and if you can get a cart to take to the barrier," Shelly answered.

While Sergeant contacted Mike to bring a cart, Shelly contacted General. "You have a question," General stated.

"Sergeant knows about Jim. It seems best to show Sergeant how to open the barrier when I show Jim. Do you have a problem with that?"

"Both are men of integrity and will not divulge the knowledge to others. We do not object," General sent.

When Sergeant had driven them out of the cave, he asked Shelly which way to go. "Any part of the barrier is fine, as long as we can't be seen, Shelly said.

Jim directed Sergeant through the woods to a place not far from where Shelly and her children had entered the barrier. The three of them walked up to the barrier, and Shelly confidently placed her finger above her head and slid it firmly to the ground. The barrier split open. She motioned the two men to step outside the barrier and then back inside. The exercise completed, she raised her finger and closed the slit. Shelly looked at the two men. "You should be able to open and close the barrier the same way."

Sergeant tried first and was able to easily open and close the barrier. When Jim opened the barrier, he stepped outside and started walking away. "Don't, Jim; the virus is airborne, and we are already taking a gamble by opening the barrier this much," Shelly warned him.

Jim nodded, came back inside, and closed the barrier. "Sorry, but when I was up in that tree, I saw a bare line running down the side of a mountain. I think it might be a road of some sort. When it's safe, I want a closer look at that."

Shelly turned back to the cart. She didn't want Sergeant to guess she knew about the place Jim wanted a closer look at. She sighed deeply, running her fingers through her hair. She hated keeping things from the man she would soon marry. "General," she sent.

"You have a question." General responded.

"When the barrier is down, they are going to find my car."

"Why should that be a problem?" General sent.

"They will know I haven't been totally forthcoming with them."

"Only those that will not ask questions will see the significance," he assured her.

Shelly wasn't so sure, but there wasn't much she could do about it. "Later," she thought, "I'll worry about it later."

Sergeant pulled up to Shelly's apartment. "Jim and I are going to do a little more searching for the power source, he said. "Do you mind if I just drop you off?"

"Of course not," Shelly replied, stepping out of the cart. She watched as they turned around and drove off.

"General," she sent as she went through the door.

"You have a question," General replied.

"Is there a possibility they will find the power source for the cave?" she asked.

"Not as long as you keep them out of the hidden room," General answered.

"That's where the power source is?" Shelly asked skeptically, "How can that be? That room isn't big enough to hold the amount of machinery needed to power this entire cave."

"We explained to you on the first day that everything needed to run your system is in that room. The power source we have installed is not of your world," General said.

"But I thought we were using simple electricity," Shelly said.

"You are correct," General said. "We have adapted the source to covert its power to a form that you are familiar with."

"But how can that be?" Shelly asked.

"You are—" General began.

Shelly finished his thought with a sigh. "Forbidden this information."

Shelly heard her computer ping. She answered it to find Rosa smiling at her. "Glad I finally caught you, Shelly. I have dresses for Amy and Karla, and a suit for Jake to wear to the theater opening."

"Oh, Rosa, that is so kind of you," Shelly said. "I don't know how I am ever going to thank you for all you have done for us."

"No big deal," Rosa laughed. "You and your family are perfect models for my work."

"I'll round up the children and be right there," Shelly said.

She ended the call with Rosa and called the card shop to be sure Amy, Karla, and Jake were there. Christy laughed, saying that they were there but she wasn't sure how much longer she was going to be able to keep Jake from escaping. Shelly told her to tell the children to wait for her. She had a surprise for them. "That should keep Jake in one spot until I get there," she thought as she left. She was reaching for her trike when she heard the pet door rattle. Jessie was at her feet, wagging her tail so hard the whole back end of her body was wiggling. Shelly reached down and picked her up. "You poor thing," she said, scratching the little dog behind the ears. "I know you're lonely, but you can't go with me."

Shelly put the dog back in the apartment and told her to stay. Jessie hung her head, looking up with eyes that plainly said she was pitifully hurt. As Shelly rode to the plaza, she kept glancing back. Golly could be trusted to stay when told, but Jessie, on the other hand, often had selective memory.

When Shelly entered the card shop, all three children ganged around her, demanding their surprise. "I didn't say I was bringing you a surprise," she laughed. "We have to go down the street a ways for you to see what it is."

Shelly thanked Christy for watching her children as they scooted out the door. She led the way down the plaza, the children bouncing with excitement behind her. Jake's face fell when she turned into Rosa's shop. "Aww, Mom," he grumbled with disappointment. "I thought this was going to be something good."

The girls were ecstatic over the prospect of a new outfit. Rosa saw them come in, and she had a light powder-blue dress, a soft lavender dress, and a black suit laid out when they got to the counter. Rosa noted Jake's slightly sour demeanor, and sent the girls to the dressing room. She put her arm around Jake, and suggested he take the suit to the back room to try on. Amy and Karla rushed from the dressing room to stand before the three-way mirror. Amy was wearing the blue dress, and Karla was wearing the lavender dress. They were all smiles and giggles, and did dainty pirouettes, making their dresses flare out. Jake came shuffling from the back room, shoulders slumped and head hanging. Rosa asked the girls to move as she placed Jake in front of the mirror. "Now, you tell me what you see," Rosa demanded gently.

Jake looked at his reflection, cocked his head, and stood up straight, squaring his shoulders. Shelly felt a lump in her throat as Jake said exactly what she saw: "I kind of look like a man."

"Good, that's just what I wanted. Now, you remember to walk tall because that's my handiwork you're wearing," Rosa said as she straightened the black handkerchief in the breast pocket.

Then Rosa turned her attention back to the girls, "Now look here; I had the knitting and yarn shop make these coverings to put over your shoes," Rosa said, displaying two pairs of knitted bottomless booties in colors to match what each girl was wearing. "There was no way the cobbler's shop could make new shoes to match, so I hope these will work."

The girls stretched the booties over their shoes and went back to admiring themselves in front of the mirror. "Thank you, Rosa. You are so kind to make opening night a memorable one for all of us," Shelly said sincerely.

"Yes, thank you, Rosa," Amy said, giving Rosa a hug.

"Thank you for the pretty dress, Rosa," Karla said shyly.

"Me too," Jake said. "I mean thank you; I really do like it."

Rosa patted Jake's shoulder. "You're going to have to have to beat the girls off with a stick in that suit," she said.

Jake's face turned bright red as he stammered, "Gosh, I hope not."

CHAPTER 29

The next day, all Amy and Jake could talk about was the opening. Amy thought she should start getting dressed right after breakfast. Shelly finally suggested they take Jessie and Misty for a walk by the stream and maybe bring back some fresh flowers. She didn't want to admit to the children that she, too, couldn't wait to get dressed up. She had been to the bathroom half a dozen times, looking in the mirror at her hair, pulling it back, and then up, and then sideways, trying to figure out how she wanted to fix it. She finally gave up and called Carol. "Are you ready for the opening?" Carol asked immediately when she saw her.

"I don't know what to do with my hair," Shelly said with a touch of desperation. "Do you know if there are any curling irons in this place?"

"Sure, the beauty shop has them," Carol answered with a touch of humor. "Do you want me to pick one up and come do your hair for you?"

"Only if you're sure you have the time," Shelly replied. "You would be a lifesaver."

"Not to worry," Carol said with a laugh. "I'll be there in a couple of hours."

Shelly fixed herself a cup of tea and sat down, trying to relax. She thought about all the things other women could do that she had never even thought of. She thought of her life growing up. Her father had crippling arthritis. He had tried filing for Social Security disability, but he had been rejected. The agent told him he could find a sit-down job—a job he was never able to find. Shelly never knew if it was pride that kept him from filing again as his condition worsened, or if it simply didn't occur to him. He was a kind man whose attention never wavered when she talked with him.

Her mother had kept the family going with waitress jobs. Shelly learned in first grade that she didn't live in the right part of town. But it was in junior high school that she finally understood her family was poor. In high school, she wasn't exactly bullied; it was more like she was ignored. She never had a close friend and was never asked to a dance. Mother always made sure she had Christmas and birthday gifts; they were mostly clothes from secondhand thrift stores. The walls in their home were never repainted. It was enough that they were warm in the winter. New furniture consisted of a newly purchased blanket from the thrift store thrown over the sofa or chair. Nevertheless, hers were loving parents. They had done the best they could. They may not have showered her with material things, but they imparted love, sound values, and common sense to her while she was growing up.

Shelly was jerked out of her revelry as Jake and Amy came barreling into the room.

"Can we get ready now?" Amy begged.

Shelly smiled and hugged her little girl. "Why don't you two take your baths, and I'll call Granny Christy to see when she wants you."

As Amy and Jake ran to their room, Shelly went to the computer. "Are the kids ready to come to my place yet?" Christy asked as soon as she answered Shelly's call.

"They are taking their baths now," Shelly said.

"Why don't you have them come over here to get dressed?" Christy said. "Karla is driving me crazy, asking every other minute when they are going to be here. They can help entertain Kerry while I get dressed."

"If you're sure it won't be too much trouble," Shelly said.

"Heck no, won't be half the trouble I'm having at the moment, and Grace will be here to help," Christy assured her.

Shelly told Amy and Jake they were going to get dressed at Granny Christy's when she heard them get out of their tubs. She combed Amy's hair while Jake put their clothes together. It wasn't long before they were dashing out the door. Shelly had just finished her shower and slipped her nightshirt on when there was a knock at the door. Carol arrived with a full cloth shopping bag. "The first thing I need to see is your dress," she stated in a businesslike manner. "Wow," she said when Shelly held up the dress. A slow smile spread over Carol's face, "Oh, we are going to have fun here."

Carol sat Shelly in a chair and emptied her bag on the table. Shelly's eyes widened as she took in the array of products Carol dumped from her bag. She picked up a ceramic jar, unscrewed the lid, and peered at the light tan goo inside. "What's this?" she asked.

Carol looked at what Shelly was holding. "Setting gel for your hair. The lady that runs the beauty shop makes it with honey and lemon juice. Now sit still while I preform my magic."

Shelly sat patiently while Carol combed the goo through her damp hair. Then she started on her face.

"I didn't know you were going to do my makeup," Shelly said as Carol patted, brushed and painted. "Are you sure all this is necessary?"

"You want to live up to that gorgeous dress, don't you?" Carol stated. "Be quiet or I'll smudge."

Shelly sighed, thinking to herself, "I can always just wash it off." When Carol was finished with the face, she went back to the hair. She pulled, twisted, and brushed the hair into place before using the curling iron. Carol then stepped back and studied Shelly from all sides. "You're done," she announced. "Go look in the mirror."

Shelly went to the bathroom, and with some trepidation, she looked in the mirror and stared, dumbstruck. Her hair was slicked up side, back, and front, while one long, thick coiled curl cascaded down the left side just past her shoulder. Carol had made her face smooth; her eyes had been given the illusion of a slight slant and now had a catlike shape. A smoky coloring enhanced the look. Her lips looked fuller, her cheekbones higher. "That doesn't even look like me," Shelly said in awe. "I look—"

"Beautiful," Carol finished, standing behind Shelly, looking at their reflection in the mirror.

"I never knew makeup could change me like this," Shelly said, turning her face to see it at different angles.

"Are you serious?" Carol laughed. Then she saw the childlike amazement in Shelly's eyes reflecting back at her. "You are serious. Didn't you ever play with makeup when you were a kid, or wear it to work?"

"No," Shelly said softly. "I never had access to it growing up, and all I ever wore to work was a little lip gloss and maybe a brush of mascara."

"You really don't know how pretty you are, do you?" Carol said.

"I always thought of myself as sort of plain," Shelly said in a matter-of-fact tone. "Doug used to tell me I was beautiful, and I loved that he thought so."

"Sounds to me as if your Doug was just being honest with you," Carol replied. "Now, I've got to run or I'll be late for the opening act."

Shelly had just slipped on the soft yellow slippers Rosa had made for her when there was a knock at the door. She opened the door to find Sergeant outside. For a moment they stood frozen, appraising each other appreciatively. Without taking his eyes off of her, Sergeant stepped inside and waved the door closed. He had seen her in the dress before, but, with her hair and makeup done, tonight Shelly was stunningly beautiful. He swallowed dryly as Shelly walked slowly around him. She had previously seen him only in his dark blue security uniform. Rosa had designed a black suit with a white shirt and black tie, and the corner of a yellow handkerchief showed in the pocket of the suit jacket. The suit was a perfect fit, accenting his wide shoulders and narrow hips. Shelly faced him. Looking up, she said in a sultry voice, "You look yummy."

Sergeant arched one brow and grinned. "I was going for dashing, but I'll take yummy."

After a light kiss, Sergeant steered her to the door, reminding himself of the need to control the hunger that had risen within him.

The play was a comedy, with the audience laughing loudly, clapping, and giving the actors a standing ovation at the end. Shelly was surprised at how busy Rosa had been. Many of the women were in gowns she had designed. The men were wearing black suits too, though only a few were as smartly done as Sergeant's suit. The premier party had been set up in the plaza. Tables were set along both sides of the street, with the area around the fountain left for dancing. A twelve-piece orchestra was playing. Zeke had recruited teenagers for the waitstaff. Sergeant stayed next to Shelly as they mingled up and down the plaza. They were relaxed and speculated on the pairing of others. Marcus was with Carol, which they agreed was expected, but both were surprised to see Rosa and Larry obviously enjoying each other's company. Larry no longer looked like a shy younger version of his brother. Shelly hadn't realized how tall and well-built Larry was. As they talked with the younger couple, Shelly noticed the way Larry looked at Rosa.

"That man has a thing for you," she whispered to Rosa.

"Umm, you think?" Rosa whispered back, her eyes sparkling.

"Yep, and you have a thing for him too," Shelly said.

"He is the kindest person I have ever met," Rosa replied dreamily.

Shelly changed the subject, asking, "How did you get so many gowns and suits ready by the opening?"

"The teenagers, both boys and girls. And many of the women know their way around a sewing room. The men weren't too hard, because I used the same color and pattern for most of them."

Shelly studied the suits the men wore. Rosa hadn't done much to the trousers. The jackets had been made from the tunics and were long-sleeved; the two front pockets had been replaced with a single breast pocket, with the corner of a handkerchief showing. The only differences among them were the colors of the handkerchiefs. Shelly asked Rosa if there was any significance to the colored handkerchiefs. Rosa smiled, "Those that are colored match the colors of the dresses of the women they are with. The men with black handkerchiefs are available. If you will notice, many of the women are wearing black. They are available also."

Shelly looked around, picking out the women in black, talking to the men with black handkerchiefs. "Do they know about the black?" Shelly asked.

"No, I thought it would be fun to see if anyone notices," Rosa said.

Shelly laughed, agreeing, as Sergeant captured her and guided her into a waltz. Later they were in no hurry as Sergeant walked Shelly home from the party while discussing the wedding plans. "Everything is pretty much done," Shelly said. "I've had the last fitting for the dress, the shoes are done, and the invitations are ready to hand out. Zeke and the cake ladies just need a couple days' notice."

"Rosa has made me another suit," Sergeant said. "I thought this one was fine, but she insisted. I'm pretty sure I have everything on my end covered."

"What is it you had to cover on your end?" Shelly asked.

"Well, I talked to the judge and things," he replied, wide-eyed.

"Right," Shelly laughed as she waved the short-hall door open.

The wedding took place a week after the premiere. Judge Barker presided over the late-morning outdoor ceremony. Shelly and Sergeant had agreed nothing could compare to the beauty of the valley for a backdrop as they said their vows. Shelly was surprised when a four-year-old boy walked down the aisle carrying a pillow with two gold wedding bands on it. The reception was held in the dormitory. Daisies decorated the tables. Shelly found out later that the Drapery Shop had made the white tablecloths and chair covers. Zeke had outdone himself with food, and the cake was as delicious as it was beautiful. The groom's cake was a hit too, especially with the men. One end of the room had been reserved for dancing. Many of the people that had arrived in the first drop had been invited. Shelly couldn't think of a thing that could have made the day more perfect. At the end of the afternoon, Sergeant stood and thanked everyone for attending. He pulled Shelly to his side as Grace appeared with a large cloth tote bag and handed it to Shelly. "What's this for?" she asked Grace.

"Your honeymoon," she answered with a smile and a wink.

"One of those things I've been working on," Sergeant said as he gently pushed Shelly ahead of him through the narrow hall door.

They stopped by the apartment to pick up cloth bags that had been packed without Shelly's knowledge. She kept asking what was going on, but Sergeant would only smile secretively and say she would have to wait and see. By the time Sergeant led her outside the cave, the wedding guests were assembled in two long lines. At the ends of the lines was a cart decorated with flowers and ribbons; a Just Married sign hung from the back. Shelly laughed as they ran, hand in hand, down the middle of the lines of guests amid a shower of daisies and best wishes. They drove past the outdoor barn, and Shelly couldn't contain herself; she had to ask where they were going. Sergeant smiled, saying only that they were heading somewhere they could finally be alone.

They were driving through the north woods, on a path that obviously had been recently cut to accommodate the cart, when they suddenly drove into a small clearing, where a small log cabin had been built. Shelly looked at the sergeant in amazement. "When did you have the time to do this?"

"It wasn't just me. Did you really think Jim and I were hunting for a power source I know will never be found?" Sergeant said, grinning. "Actually, almost every single guy in the cave helped build this. Wait until you see the inside. Most of the single women had a hand in decorating this place."

CHAPTER 30

As Sergeant helped her out of the cart, Shelly looked around, trying to see everything at once. It was a true rustic log cabin. There was a covered porch, and attached to the rafters was a swing built for two. Sergeant waited patiently while Shelly tested the swing, listening to the bubbling of the stream close by. When Sergeant held his hand out to her, she took it readily. She gasped as he swept her into his arms, nuzzling her neck as he opened the door, and carried her across the threshold. After a long, lingering kiss that Shelly didn't want to end, Sergeant gently set her on her feet. "We have to light candles before it gets too dark to find them," Sergeant said. "Joe Parker didn't want to run electricity out here without finding the main source."

"We believe it is your custom to give a newly married couple a wedding gift," Shelly heard Grandfather say in her mind. "You will find a light switch next to the door."

Shelly turned and flipped the switch as Sergeant started to light a candle. She laughed at the look of surprise on his face and said, "Courtesy of the elder group—a wedding present."

"How, and when, did they do that?" Sergeant asked.

"I can't count the number of times I've asked myself those same questions," Shelly said. Her eyes glittered when she said silkily, "Why don't you light the candles, and I'll turn off the lights." Silently she sent, "General, you are forbidden to listen while we are here."

"Understood" was all that he replied.

They spent a week at the cabin, doing all the things newlyweds do on a honeymoon. They spent long hours first ardently, then lazily, getting to know each other intimately. They played, laughed, fished, strolled in the moonlight, and talked endlessly about everything. Late on their last night, they were sitting outside on the porch swing. The music of the forest surrounded them: the rustle of breeze-blown leaves; the bubbling, splashing stream; the crescendo of the crickets, which would suddenly stop and then start to build again; the call of an owl. Shelly softly told Sergeant about how the baby she carried was from Doug's DNA. It hadn't really seemed that it mattered before, since all the women were pregnant, but now, after the week they had spent together and the unexpected closeness she felt with him, it felt like a secret. She had so many secrets that she couldn't share. However, this secret was about her and her baby, not the keepers. She just didn't feel right about keeping this secret from him. He listened, stroking her hair while she spoke. When she grew quiet, he asked, "If they have the technology to do this, do you think they may have changed the DNA of the babies in any way?"

"No, I don't think so," Shelly said.

"Did you ask? It seems there is a lot they don't tell you unless you ask directly."

She looked at him thoughtfully, closed her eyes, and mentally called, "General."

"You have a question?" General answered.

"About these babies—is it possible for you to do anything to their DNA that makes them different ... enhanced somehow?"

"It is possible, but it is forbidden. We are permitted to remove or repair gene flaws that may be the cause of inherited illnesses, such as cystic fibrosis, polycystic kidney disease, hemophilia, and others," General explained.

"Thank you," Shelly sent as she opened her eyes. She said to Sergeant, "They are not allowed to change or enhance, but they are permitted to remove or repair genes that may cause inherited diseases."

"Do they answer all your questions?" Sergeant asked.

"Oh sure, but if the question is about the past or technology, they usually tell me that information is not permitted, or forbidden," Shelly said. "They also won't help us in our daily living. They are here only to see that humanity survives as a species."

"You say they are here," he said. "Where exactly are they from?"

"I really don't know, and that is probably a question that would get the 'That information is not permitted' answer."

He shook his head, saying, "At first, it mattered a great deal to me to know about them in detail, but it has gotten to where it doesn't bother me so much anymore."

"Same here, but I've learned to trust and respect them," she said.

Sergeant nodded in understanding. "I guess that is my problem with them; I don't trust them."

Shelly was a little nervous with where the conversation was leading, but she had to ask. "Why don't you trust them?"

He took a moment to answer, trying to pick the right words. "Because he is no more a general than I am. I doubt any of them have even been in the military."

Shelly asked carefully, "What brought you to that conclusion?"

"Because he asked Scott to go get Amy that day in the conference room." Sergeant said.

"I don't understand. What was wrong with that?" Shelly asked.

"Military don't ask; they order—especially generals," Sergeant stated firmly.

Shelly finally understood Sergeant's distrust. He was, after all, a marine, and proud of it. "Well, I have a feeling he may have taken that route to expedite the dismissal of Roberta. I mean, would you have even begun to listen to a man in a suit?"

Sergeant nodded in agreement. "I guess the fact that he wasn't wearing a uniform from any branch of the service I recognized should be a plus in his favor. And he never did claim to be from any one certain country. Like I said before, it just doesn't seem to matter as much anymore."

Shelly squeezed his hand and changed the subject. "You know, I have loved being here with you, but I miss Jake and Amy. It will be nice to get home and have my family together."

Sergeant ran his finger down her cheek, and just before kissing her, he said, "You have no idea how much I am looking forward to being a part of your family. And one important thing I want you to know," he said, laying his hand on Shelly's stomach. "I don't care whose DNA this baby carries; he is mine."

The next morning, they went through the cabin, making sure everything was clean and ready for the next occupant. The used candles were replaced with new ones, the refrigerator was emptied, the bed was stripped, and the wood box next to the fireplace was refilled. The ride back through the woods and fields was leisurely. They were going home, to safety, contentment, and happiness. As they started across the open valley, Shelly noticed a group of workers fencing off a large area. "Wonder how come they are doing that?" she said, pointing.

Sergeant looked and said to her, "They are going to use that as a hay field. The animals will need to eat this winter."

Shelly smiled; she liked the feeling of permanence, knowing plans were being made for the coming winter.

In the months that followed, others were married. Among them were, Carol and Marcus, and Rosa and Larry. Roberta married Quartermaster James Fielding, to the surprise of everyone. Though not everyone could take time off for a honeymoon, many couples planned their wedding dates around when the little cabin would have an opening.

Life in the cave was simple. Parties became the main distraction to ward off boredom. The reasons for parties were various: engagements, weddings, birthdays, anniversaries, and holidays. And sometimes they were held just as an excuse to get together. Oddly enough, it was the parties that contributed to the sense of dissatisfaction that seemed to permeate through the society. People wanted a new, more labor intensive outfit for each party. Since the gold wedding bands were automatic for those that were married, other pieces of jewelry were desired. Elaborate party decorations were expected, and more exotic foods and pastries were demanded.

Shelly got the first inkling of the discontent from Rosa. She had stopped in at the clothes shop for new pants and tunics to replace the ones her growing children needed. Rosa asked her what design she wanted on them, and when Shelly told her none, Rosa snapped at her, saying, "Well, you're the only one that doesn't want something special."

Shelly went to several of the shops and found the same irritation in each owner. She didn't understand why people, knowing supplies were limited, could make so many unreasonable demands. She decided it was something she needed to speak to the judge about. Shelly was surprised when she discovered Judge Barker knew about the discontent. She was disturbed when he told her just how deep it ran. Carol had already told him of complaints she received from shop owners, tradesmen, farmers, and laborers. Some residents felt they worked harder than others and deserved more. Others felt some were asking for more than they deserved. The number of residents not even bothering to show up for work was growing. And to top it off, the seed Roberta had planted for people to be paid had taken root. Judge Barker shook his head, admitting he was at a loss as to what to do about it.

A few nights after her talk with the judge, Sergeant was playing checkers with Amy, Jake was working on homework, and Shelly was mending a tear in the new pants she had just gotten for Jake. The light on the radio suddenly started blinking. Shelly flipped the switch, and a voice stated it was Washington and demanded an answer. She depressed the mike button and said, "This is Shelly Bradford; who is calling?"

"Hold for an announcement from the president," was the reply.

While they waited, Sergeant called Judge Barker and requested he come to hear the announcement. The judge arrived and took a seat next to Shelly. Sergeant sat in a chair on the other side of her. Shelly noticed that the children were sitting on the sofa, and she quickly sent them off to Grace's apartment.

CHAPTER 31

The children were gone when John Drummond's voice clearly spoke out of the radio speaker. "The president has given an executive order that all women between the ages of twelve and forty, and all men between the ages of twelve and twenty-one, will be counted at this time. Furthermore, when the danger of infection has passed, those in the age groups indicated will report to the White House."

Shelly flipped the switch off and looked at the two men. "What does he want with little boys?"

"If I were to guess, I'd say he means to build an army," Sergeant said.

"Surely you don't really think he intends to put twelve-year-old boys in an army," Judge Barker said in disbelief.

"Not right away," Sergeant said. "But if he gets them that young, he can school them, corrupt their minds, and make their loyalties lie with him and not their families. And if there is opposition that involves weapons, you can be guaranteed those are the very ones he will put on the front lines. What man—or woman for that matter—would take the chance of firing on his own flesh and blood?"

Shelly shivered at the thought of Jake in the hands of such a monster. "It's not hard to figure out what he wants with the women and girls," Shelly said. "He intends to pass them out to those men that are loyal to him already, or to buy the loyalties of others."

Both men looked at her, and the judge finally said, "Shelly, you're the communication expert. We trust you will give the correct response."

Shelly took a deep breath, flipped the switch, and depressed the mike button. "Mr. Drummond, we respectfully decline to answer your questions, unless the request comes directly from the president."

"Shelly Bradford," Drummond growled, "is that you making yet another demand? You are skating very close to treason with your constant defiance. It will take a few moments for the president to be summoned."

Shelly made sure the mike was off but left the radio on to be sure to hear the president speak. "Why do you want to speak with the president?" Judge Barker asked.

"She wants to be sure he is still alive," Sergeant answered for her.

They sat quietly, each not wanting to speculate on the future. "General," Shelly called mentally.

"You have a question?" the general sent.

"Can the barrier be left up after the danger from the virus has passed?"

"The danger from the virus no longer exists. The danger now is infection and diseases related to decomposing bodies. The barrier will not be permitted much longer," General answered.

"This is the president," the radio speaker sounded.

Shelly depressed the mike button and spoke. "Sorry to bother you again, Mr. President, but we would like your personal assurance that you gave the order for the gathering of the men and women in Washington."

There was a long pause. The muffled cry of a woman clearly sounded in the background, and the president said, "Yes, the order was issued."

"Thank you, Mr. President. And by the way, you have a girl with a birthday coming up, don't you?"

The strained voice of the president replied, "My oldest will be twelve in sixty-two days."

"Well, tell her we will light a candle to celebrate and will be wishing her a happy birthday," Shelly replied perkily.

"She is a bit under the weather right now; I'm sure it will cheer her up to know you are thinking of her," the president said quickly.

"You will give us your count now, Shelly Bradford," Drummond demanded.

"One woman, age thirty-two," Shelly said.

"You lie! You said before that there were four women and three children," Drummond screamed.

"I did not lie. You said women under forty. The other women here are my and my husband's mothers, and my grandparents. The children here are three, five, and seven," she stated.

"I look forward to meeting you, Shelly Bradford," Drummond said.

To Shelly and the men sitting with her, Drummond's words sounded like an evil threat. Shelly flipped the switch on the radio to Off. "How did you know he had a girl with a birthday coming up?" Judge Barker asked, impressed.

Shelly ran her fingers through her hair. "I didn't. It was a shot in the dark. But he has three children, so one of them surely had a birthday coming up. But if we don't get them out of there soon, that monster is going to take the president's daughter as soon as she is twelve."

"You know your numbers didn't add up," Sergeant said thoughtfully.

"What numbers?" Shelly asked, confused.

"You told Drummond before that there were elven people in the shelter; just now you only mentioned ten."

With her fingers in her hair, she said, "That just goes to show why people seldom get away with lying. You can never keep your stories straight; there will always be a loose thread somewhere—and someone like you, Sergeant, to pull that loose thread."

"If there were only a way we could talk with NORAD without Drummond or his people hearing," Judge Barker said offhandedly.

Shelly sat up straight, caught the sergeant's eye, and knew that they had the same thought. "General," Shelly called.

"You have a question?" General replied.

"Could Jim Lightfoot mind-speak to the one with the ability at NORAD?" she asked.

"He has the power," General said. "Getting the other person to listen may be a problem."

"If the president and his family leave the White House, can you pick them up?" she asked.

"We are permitted to pick up any not in shelters before the barrier drops," General sent.

Shelly grinned, rubbed her hands together, set the radio frequency to NORAD, and depressed the mike button. Sergeant was in the kitchen on his radio. "NORAD, this is Shelly Bradford calling. Please come in, NORAD."

"NORAD here, Shelly," a male voice stated back through the speaker. "How may we help you?"

"We assume you picked up the broadcast from the president," she said.

"Affirmative, Shelly," the voice answered.

"We wanted to celebrate his daughter's upcoming birthday by lighting a candle and listening to music. We have a CD player, but we don't have my mother's favorite song here. It's called "The Sound of Silence." Mother says it is from the sixties by a duo called Simon and Garfunkel."

"One moment, Shelly, while we check to see if we have it," the voice said.

Shelly made sure the mike was off and then turned to the men. Judge Barker sat staring at her, obviously confused. Looking directly at the judge, she said, "Judge Barker, I hope you will understand, but some things here have to stay confidential."

He nodded slowly. "You're going to ask me to leave, aren't you?"

"Yes, sir, I am."

"Will the president's freedom result from the things I am not privy to?" the judge asked.

"We can only hope. There are so many things that have to go right, and it must be done quickly."

The judge rose and said, "You will let me know the outcome."

Shelly assured him he would be the first to know. As the judge waved the door open to leave, he came face-to-face with Jim Lightfoot. Nodding to one another, they passed without speaking.

"You got lucky," Jim said. "I was here picking up supplies. So what's up?"

Sergeant and Shelly quickly filled him in on what was going on. Jim sat in the chair vacated by the judge and doubtfully shook his head. "I don't think I know how to contact someone I've never met."

"General, can you help Jim with the contact?" Shelly sent.

"No, that is not permitted," General answered.

Shelly ran her fingers through her hair in frustration. "Can you at least give him a name or show him what the person looks like?" Shelly sent.

After a short pause, General sent, "That is permitted."

"Oh, it's a woman. Nice-looking woman too," Jim said suddenly. "Her name is Katrina Prescott; she has people around her."

"Wait; don't contact her yet," Shelly said.

"Why not? I think I'm in love," Jim said.

"General helped you locate her; can you do it again without his help?" Shelly asked.

"Yes, I will be able to find her again," Jim stated positively.

"We're waiting for an answer from NORAD; it may make contact easier if she is alerted to expect something."

Shelly fixed them a snack and something to drink while they waited. "What could possibly be taking them so long?" Sergeant said, pacing anxiously. "Surely there is someone there that knows that song."

The radio came to life. "Cave Haven, this is NORAD calling. Come in, Shelly," the now familiar voice called.

"Shelly here. Have you got the song?" Shelly said into the mike.

"We have the song. Do you want us to play it for you?" he asked.

"Not now. I'm not sure I know how to record. Can you keep it close and play it when I figure out how to work this machine?" Shelly said.

"Can do, Shelly. Is there anything else?" the voice said.

"Yes, NORAD, my grandfather thinks he may have a grandniece there with you. Her name is Katrina Prescott. Is there some way you can quickly check on that?"

After several squirming moments, the voice answered, "Katrina Prescott is in residence."

"That is wonderful news. Please let her know that she will be hearing from her great-uncle Jim soon," Shelly said.

"Will do, Shelly," the voice promised.

"Thank you, NORAD. And don't forget the song. Shelly signing off."

"NORAD signing off," the voice said.

CHAPTER 32

Jim sat with a glazed look on his face. "Are you watching her," Shelly asked.

"Yes. She just got an order to report to the commanding general's office. She is worried she has done something wrong."

They waited patiently for Katrina to make her way through a maze of corridors. "They are leading her into a conference room. Good heavens, from the brass in here, it looks more like a war room. They are grilling her about her uncle and the song. She doesn't know what they are talking about. She is very scared."

The sound of anguish in Jim's voice was a direct reflection of Katrina's feelings. "Contact her now. Tell her to say 'Shelly Bradford.'"

"Katrina, don't be afraid. My name is Jim Lightfoot. I am using ESP to contact you. Tell them that, and then say 'Shelly Bradford.'"

Katrina clutched her head. "What do you want?" she said aloud. "How are you in my head?"

A man at the table started to question Katrina, and another held up his hand and motioned for silence. "Katrina, the men at the table need information," Jim sent. You and I are the only ones with the power to communicate with ESP. Please, Kat, just say 'Shelly Bradford.'"

"Shelly Bradford," Katrina said, with tears running down her face.

"Good girl, Kat. Now, can you just repeat word for word what I say?" Jim sent.

"Yes," she said aloud.

The men watched Katrina silently as she brought her panic under control. "Now you must tell them 'I am communicating through ESP with Shelly Bradford. Do you understand?'"

Katrina repeated Jim's words.

The commanding general said, "We are trying to understand. At least now the title of that song makes a little sense."

Jim nodded and said, "You're doing great, Kat. Say 'The words I speak will be Shelly Bradford's words. Find this girl a chair.'"

Katrina gasped. "I can't say that."

The commanding general said gently, "Katrina, whatever it is, please say what you are hearing."

Katrina sobbed once and then, in a rush, said, "The words I speak will be Shelly Bradford's words. Get this girl a chair."

A chair was immediately provided. Katrina sank into it, her eyes staring down toward the floor. Jim soothingly sent, "Kat, I know this is new and scary for you, but if you didn't have the strength to handle it, you wouldn't have been blessed with this ability. Shelly Bradford is here with me. I am going to try to bring her in with us. Just to let you know, we are new at this also, so don't get upset if it doesn't work. If you are with me, just think yes; don't say it aloud."

"Yes," Katrina thought, and she then begged, "Tell me how is this happening to me. I don't understand."

Jim was patient but firm. "Kat, we don't have time right now for explanations, but I promise I will tell you all I know after this meeting."

Jim explained to Shelly what he was going to try to do. "Just a minute, Jim," she said, "General, can I do this? Is there any danger?"

"Your Jim Lightfoot has already accomplished more that we would have said he has the ability to do. To put it simply, we do not know if he can do this, but there is no danger in trying."

Shelly glanced at Sergeant; he was sitting on the edge of his chair with both hands clamped around a glass. She stood up briefly, grabbed a throw pillow from the sofa, and tossed it to him. He caught it and gave her a look of irritation. "If you need to hold on tight to something, use that. You're going to break that glass you're strangling."

He grinned at her sheepishly, holding the pillow in his lap, and put the glass on the floor beside his chair. She turned and nodded to Jim.

"Come with me and meet Katrina," he thought to her.

Jim's mind guided Shelly's mind into the conference room where Katrina was sitting. Then Shelly felt herself guided into Katrina's mind. "Try to say something to her," he instructed Shelly.

"Hello, Katrina, my name is Shelly Bradford," she said. "If you can hear me, think your answer."

"It's nice to meet you, Shelly. Gosh, this is awkward."

Jim and Shelly smiled as they heard Katrina's thoughts. "Do you know anything about the president and his family being held captive?" Shelly asked Katrina.

"No," Katrina said aloud in a startled voice.

"Tell them I just explained to you about the president," Shelly sent.

Katrina relayed what Shelly had sent.

"That is top secret classified information," exploded one of the men at the table.

Katrina cringed, whimpering. Shelly and Jim felt her try to remove her mind from them. Jim held her, sending, "Kat it's all right. That man is a boob."

"But I'm not cleared for top secret. What will they do to me?" Katrina sent.

The commander sent the man from the room, saying forcefully, "This young woman may be our only hope of keeping the president alive. One more outburst and I will have this room cleared."

Shelly and Jim spent a moment calming and reassuring Katrina before continuing. Katrina gathered herself, regaining her composure. "I'm ready to continue," she thought.

Jim suggested to her it might be easier for her if she closed her eyes while she spoke Shelly's words, and that she should explain why she was doing so to the men at the table. When everyone understood the procedure, Katrina closed her eyes and spoke the words Shelly sent to her. "I think we are all in agreement that it is imperative the president and his family must get out of the White House shelter. It is not possible for us to go in and get him, and highly unlikely he can escape, so we are going to have to make Drummond throw them out."

Shelly outlined their plan, assuring the men the virus was no longer a danger and that if the president were out of the shelter, he would be picked up. She stressed the urgency of time limitation. "We will consider all you have said. Can Miss Prescott contact you when we have a decision?" the commander asked.

"We are all new to this; we are not sure if she has the strength to initiate contact" was the answer.

After a farewell to Katrina, Jim brought Shelly back and released her mind. Both sat back in their chairs, exhausted.

"Well, what did they say?" Sergeant asked anxiously.

"They said they would consider it," Shelly said. "Can you please get us a drink of water?"

"Consider it!" Sergeant blasted as he hurried to get them a drink. "Don't they realize there isn't time for them to have some long, drawn-out roundtable discussion on this?" He handed them each a glass of water.

Shelly took a long drink and then said, "We tried to make them understand, but I have the feeling the ultimate decision rests with the commanding general. It's late; I should probably call Grace and let her know we are coming for Jake and Amy."

When Shelly had Grace on the screen, Grace told her not to bother, as the children were already asleep. She said she would send them home in the morning in time to get ready for school. Shelly told her how grateful she was and closed out. When she stood, the light started blinking on the radio. She sat down quickly, flipping the switch, and the radio sounded with "Can you come in, please?" Without turning around, she told the men it was NORAD. She depressed the mike button. "This is Shelly," she said.

"Just wanted to give you a message from Miss Prescott," the voice said. "Quote: Hoping to get in touch with Uncle Jim soon. End quote."

"Thank you, NORAD. He is sleeping now. I will give him the message in the morning. Signing off."

"NORAD out," the voice said.

Shelly switched off the radio and breathed a sigh of relief. When she turned around, she could tell Jim was already in contact with Katrina. "Kat says they are going for it. They will put the plan into action the day after tomorrow."

Jim stood and walked to the door. "I'll stay around the cave until this is over. Call if you need me."

After he was gone, Shelly sat in Sergeant's lap, saying, "I'm tired; who would have thought thinking could wear you out like this. Will you let Judge Barker know we hope to have the president free on the day after tomorrow?"

Sergeant held her close with one arm, resting his free hand on her belly. "I'll fill in the judge tomorrow. Shall I carry you to bed?" he asked.

"No, I want to grab a quick shower first," she said. "It will help me sleep better."

CHAPTER 33

The next day, minutes seemed like hours. Shelly wandered the streets aimlessly, admiring door paintings, until she happened on a cleaning crew. She joined with them, picking up a broom and sweeping the streets, washing the outsides of apartment windows, and cleaning public bathrooms. She listened and joined in the conversations and banter that went on while they worked. Before she knew it, the crew said they were done for the day and thanked her for the help. As she walked home, she realized how much she had enjoyed the peaceful working camaraderie of the crew and the idle chat they shared.

Shelly was fixing after-school snacks when Jake and Amy came in. Amy was bubbling over with news of classmates, friends, and teachers. After they had eaten, Amy went to her room to do homework. Jake sat sullenly at the table, not speaking, staring at his homework. Shelly sat across from him and said, "Okay, what gives?"

He looked up at her and said, "I talked to Mr. Lightfoot on the way home. I told him I was going to be twelve next week and I was going to sign up to work with him. He said I wasn't acceptable."

Shelly knew Jim wouldn't have said Jake wasn't acceptable, so she prodded carefully. "Mr. Lightfoot said those exact words?"

"Well, not those words exactly," Jake said, "but about the same thing."

"Jake, if I am to understand what is going on, you need to tell me exactly what Mr. Lightfoot said—not your interpretation of his words," she said.

Jake gave a long, exaggerated sigh, "I told him I was going to sign up with him. He said his job was mainly to provide extra protein and that he wouldn't accept me until I had first worked with farm animals and with the butcher. Now, that sounds to me like he said I wasn't acceptable."

"Did he tell you the reason he wanted you to work the other jobs first?" she asked.

"Yes," Jake replied.

"Well, what was the reason?" Shelly pushed.

After another long sigh, Jake said, "He said I needed to learn to love and care for animals so that I would never enjoy killing them. And he said I needed to learn to butcher them properly so that none of any animal I kill is wasted. But Mom, I already love animals. And why can't *he* show me how to butcher them?"

Shelly leaned back, crossed her arms, and stared at Jake until he started to squirm. "What?" he said with a touch of defiance. "I told you what he said."

"Jake, you look me in the eyes and tell me if you truly believe Mr. Lightfoot finds you unacceptable," Shelly said firmly.

Jake glared at her for a moment and then dropped his eyes and said, "No, I know he doesn't really mean that."

Shelly said gently, "I know that too. I also know that the real reason you are upset is because you hoped you were going to run the woods half the day for the next four months."

Jake grinned, saying, "And you claim you don't read my mind."

"That has nothing to do with reading your mind," Shelly said playfully. "But it has everything to do with being your mother." Then she said seriously, "Jake, the reason for allowing a twelve-year-old to work is not only because the community needs your help; it is also so you can apply yourself to as many different jobs as possible. It is our hope that when you are old enough to choose an apprenticeship, you will know where your interests lie and will be ready to make the decision."

"I know all that, Mom," he replied. "But heck, it sure would have been fun running the woods for the next four months."

The next morning, Sergeant left Shelly with an extra radio. Shelly promised to call him if she heard anything from NORAD. She made him promise to contact Judge Barker and Jim. Sergeant hadn't been gone five minutes before she started to fidget. She went into the kitchen and cleaned the refrigerator and the stove. She went through the cupboards, scrubbed the floor, and then moved to the bathrooms. After the bathrooms were clean, she stripped the beds and put the sheets in the washer. She continued going through the apartment until everything was scrubbed, polished, and swept, and it still wasn't quite lunchtime yet.

Shelly was sitting at the table, drinking coffee and wondering what she would do for the rest of the day, vowing to herself she was going to learn to knit. A knock at the door brought her quickly to her feet. She waved the door open to find Judge Barker carrying a tray holding two bowls of stew. "I got tired of pacing the office. I hope you haven't eaten lunch yet," he said, setting the tray on the table.

"Frankly, I hadn't even thought of lunch. Is lemonade all right?" she asked, getting silverware, napkins, and drinks.

"Zeke made stew again," Judge Barker said, nodding to the offer of lemonade. "He said if the parties don't slow down, we will be lucky to get that."

"I don't think the food will give out, but Zeke may," Shelly said as she poured the drinks. "They are working him pretty hard."

The door opened. Sergeant entered, carrying a tray holding a bowl of stew, three bowls of salad, and a loaf of warm sliced bread. Shelly grabbed another glass from the cupboard, and more silverware.

"Stopped by Zeke's place," Sergeant said to the judge. "He told me you were heading here, and what you were bringing."

They had just settled around the table to eat when there was a knock at the door. "Now, who could that be?" Shelly said as she stood.

"It's me, Shelly," Jim sent.

"Well, come on in," she thought, sitting back down.

Jim entered carrying a tray holding a bowl of stew, a bowl of salad, three pieces of cherry pie, and a huge slice of chocolate cake. "I went to Zeke's," Jim said. "He said you guys forgot dessert."

They all laughed, agreeing Zeke was underappreciated.

They ate slowly, lingering over the meal, talking about everything except what was really on their minds. Shelly and Sergeant were clearing the table when the judge commented, "I wish there was some way we could just ask them when they are going to call Washington."

Jim stood up, going to the kitchen. He rolled his eyes at Shelly and said, "Do you have a cup of coffee you can spare?"

"Sure, but let me make a fresh pot," she said, and she quickly rinsed the pot to start a fresh batch.

"They were waiting for us to contact Kat before they contacted Washington," Jim sent to her.

Sergeant wrapped his arms around Shelly, giving her a hug as he whispered in her ear, "The judge is watching you two, and he is a very intuitive man."

All three stood in the kitchen, staring at the coffee pot. Sergeant and Jim went to sit at the table with the judge while Shelly fixed a tray for coffee.

Shelly had just set the tray on the table when Sergeant said, almost casually, "Light's blinking on the radio."

The men moved their chairs around Shelly as she sat at the radio. Sergeant and Judge Barker were on either side of her. Jim placed his chair behind the judge. Immediately after sitting down, Jim's eyes became glassy. Shelly flipped the switch, and the radio came to life. "This is Washington; what do you want, NORAD?"

"We have an urgent message for the president," NORAD stated.

"One moment, NORAD," Washington said.

"Do you know what they are going to say?" the judge asked.

"Not exactly," Sergeant answered.

"This is John Drummond. Go ahead, NORAD; we will relay your message," Drummond said.

"Negative, Washington. Message is top secret for the president's ears only."

"We will get the president," Drummond said tightly.

They heard a bang as if something had been thrown. "That man sounds more demented every time I hear him," Sergeant said.

"Demonic is what he sounds like to me," Shelly countered with a shiver.

"This is the president," the weak voice of the president echoed from the speaker.

"Mr. President, this message is for your ears only. Are you alone?" NORAD asked.

"Yes, I am alone," the president said.

"Mr. President, have you had any deaths from illness in your shelter?"

"None that I am aware of," the president replied.

"Mr. President, the virus has mutated. If you have people there that are showing any signs of sickness, you must expel them from the shelter now. This mutated virus is spread through direct contact, until the infected person dies, at which point it becomes airborne as the body releases decomposition gasses. People that become sick must be expelled before they die. Shelters are run on filtered air, and the mutated airborne virus survives through the filtration process. Do you understand, Mr. President?"

"NORAD, if we expel people from the shelter, they will die."

"Mr. President, if you don't expel those that are sick, along with anyone that has had direct contact with them, the entire shelter will die. Mr. President, over half the population here at NORAD is dead. None of us expect to be alive three days from now."

"NORAD, how did this mutated virus get into your shelter?"

"Our scientists lived long enough to find it. They were sure it came in with an apparently healthy person in its mutated form. The incubation process in the mutated strain is months, but once it becomes airborne, it reverts back to its original form. Mr. President, is there any sickness in your shelter at this time?"

"My oldest daughter has had the flu for over a week."

"Mr. President, it is not the flu. I am sorry for you and your family."

"Thank you …"

"Mr. President, are you still there?" NORAD asked.

There was only silence from the radio.

"The president's radio was turned off," Jim sent to Shelly.

"Do you think that Drummond will buy this hogwash?" Judge Barker asked.

"We can only hope that his megalomania will prevent him from looking at the facts too closely, and that whoever was in the room with the president will only hear 'mutated virus, expel before death,'" Sergeant answered.

"If someone thought to write the message down and goes over it, we may be in trouble," Shelly said, "But I don't think Drummond will think of that."

"So when will we know if it worked?" the judge asked.

"We are hoping our next contact will be from General, telling us they have picked up the president and his family," Shelly said.

"But I thought you said the elder group wouldn't pick up the president," Judge Barker said.

"Not as long as he is in a shelter; that's why we are hoping Drummond will kick them out," Shelly explained.

The men moved their chairs back to the table. Shelly started a new pot of coffee and then sat down with the men. "Will General Elder take the president to NORAD?" Judge Barker asked.

"We don't know," Shelly answered.

CHAPTER 34

"The light is blinking on the radio," Jim commented.

Shelly went to the radio and turned it on. It was Washington. John Drummond's voice spewed forth. "Citizens of the United States, I regret to inform you that our beloved president, our vice president, and their entire families are dead."

Shelly cried out, "Surely that madman isn't evil enough to have killed them!"

"Before his demise," Drummond continued, "our president named me, John Drummond, as interim president until an election for a new president is held. As the acting president, I am now issuing the following executive order: Any man or woman that wishes to run in this presidential election and become the next president of the United States must fill out and submit the proper forms to Washington, DC, by midnight tonight. Voting for the election will be held tomorrow in Washington, DC. You must present a valid voter registration card to vote in this election. Voting will begin at eight a.m. and end at noon. Be assured, citizens, that I, President John Drummond, am here to serve the people of the United States. I promise to make everyone's life better. Washington signing off."

"Lord help us; what have we done?" Judge Barker said.

"General," Shelly sent frantically.

"You have a question?" General replied.

"Is the president dead?" Shelly asked.

"Of course not; his entire party is safe," General sent.

"Well, why haven't you informed us?" Shelly demanded.

"We have been busy picking up others," General said.

"What others?" Shelly asked.

"Washington wasn't the only ones who heard the NORAD broadcast regarding a mutant form of the virus. We have picked up nine that were expelled from another shelter. They have been ill-used. Especially bad-off is a young female."

"What do you mean by 'ill-used'?" Shelly asked.

"It seems they have been used as slaves. They received little nourishment. A young female is with child."

"How old is she?" Shelly asked.

"She is thirteen. The healers are worried not only for her physical well-being but for her mental health as well. We will drop those from Washington in your dormitory tonight. The healers need more time with those that were slaves."

"Thank you, General," Shelly said. "I know you will do everything in your power to help those people. They couldn't be in better hands."

"We will do our best for them," General replied.

Shelly sat back with a relieved sigh.

"So the president and his family are safe?" Judge Barker asked.

"Yes, the president and vice ..." Shelly clapped her hand over her mouth.

Jim stared at her, shaking his head slowly back and forth.

"How long have you known?" Sergeant asked the judge.

"What, that she could contact General Elder?" Judge Barker said. "I've known almost since I first arrived."

Shelly's eyes widened in disbelief as she uttered, "How?"

"Remember that little ruckus between the two men over Rosa in the restaurant?" the judge said. "You were watching the fight, and I was watching you. Your eyes were odd. You were nodding and shaking your head as if you were talking to someone, but your lips weren't moving. I thought at first you had some kind of communication device on you. Also, your profession as a communication expert suggested a proficiency in technology that you simply don't have—no offense. I wasn't absolutely sure until today that it was ESP."

"Told you this man is very astute," Sergeant said drolly.

"You did not," Shelly said petulantly. "You said he was intuitive."

Sergeant laughed. "Either way, you're found out."

"So, now, though I'm not sure why, it's Jim's job to contact NORAD and tell them the president is safe," stated the judge.

Shelly looked at Judge Barker in amazement. "How on earth do you know that?"

Judge Barker chuckled. "Did you really think I wouldn't wonder about Jim's presence in this? It would have made sense to have Harold Vickers for his knowledge of political science, or Calvin Johnson for history, but the master huntsmen—he just doesn't fit in. Then, earlier today at lunch, there was a knock at the door. You started to answer it, but your eyes got that odd look, you sat back down, and Jim came in. When Jim went into the kitchen for coffee, your eyes went odd for a moment, and Jim stood still for no apparent reason. Though his back was to me, I would have bet his eyes were odd as well. It was soon after that when NORAD started the broadcast to Washington. And Jim, you may have sat behind me during the broadcast, but I did glance back at you a few times."

"Well, you are the most observant man I have ever met," Shelly said.

"I was a sitting trial judge for many years. I learned to watch my courtroom without seeming to, and to read body language."

Shelly looked at Jim and said, "Some secret keepers we are. I wonder how many other people suspect."

"Well, for what it's worth," the judge said, "the only thing I have heard is some offhanded speculation of what you do in your position as communications expert."

Shelly nodded thoughtfully. "That is something I have been thinking about. I really haven't contributed a lot to the community. I think I should have another job."

Sergeant looked at her, his eyes narrowed and jaw clenched. "Haven't contributed? The first day, you rescued us from that tyrant Roberta. You probably saved Jim's life. And it was your plan that has freed the president of the United States. Don't you realize how remarkable all of that is?"

"But only the people in this room know any of that," Shelly said reasonably.

"You saved Jim's life?" Judge Barker asked.

Jim nodded. "Tell you about it later."

"Anyway, I worked with the cleaning crew yesterday, and I enjoyed it," Shelly said. "I liked working. I like the sense of fulfillment I get from standing back, looking over my work, and knowing I have done a good job. Whether it is cleaning a toilet or saving a president, if you've done the best you can do, and you know the job has been done right, it brings a sort of peace to your soul. In every job—be it doctor, teacher, or janitor—if the person is trained for it as a professional, then the person holding that job should be treated as a professional. Each is vital to a smoothly running society. Does any of this make any sense?"

Sergeant leaned over and kissed her lightly. "Yes, Shelly, it makes perfect sense. It's just a shame that more people don't look at their jobs, or other people's jobs, with the same perspective."

Shelly waved her hand at Sergeant and asked Jim if he had contacted Katrina. Jim said that he had informed them the president was safe, but he'd said nothing else. "Good. I'm not sure we should tell them about the slaves," Shelly said.

"What slaves?" all three men said in unison.

Shelly looked at them, her eyes settling on Jim. "You didn't hear what General told me?" she asked.

Jim shook his head slowly and said, "The general doesn't often include me in the conversations between the two of you."

"Oh, I just assumed you heard what I heard. There is still so much of this I don't understand."

Shelly went on to quickly fill them in on the information General had given her concerning those from Washington and those that had been used as slaves. When she was done, she told Jim it might be a good idea to let NORAD know everything about the people picked up in Washington. Jim's eyes turned glassy, and a moment later he said, "They are celebrating and want to know what we think of making a radio broadcast saying the president is safe."

Shelly smiled savagely and said, "It might be more fun to let the president make that broadcast at eleven fifty-nine tomorrow morning."

Sergeant grinned. "You have such a wicked sense of humor."

Jim smiled. "The people at NORAD have just said the same thing, Sergeant.

Shelly just smiled, thinking how much Funny was going to enjoy the broadcast.

The four of them sat relaxed at the table, discussing all that had transpired. "So the Washington people will be dropped sometime tonight. I guess we won't be allowed to welcome them on their arrival," Judge Barker said.

Shelly shook her head. "Do you know how the drops are made, Shelly?" he asked.

Shelly looked at him innocently, saying, "The only thing I am permitted to say about that is that they won't suddenly appear in the middle of sparkly, shimmering air."

Judge Barker cleared his throat. "Yes, well, I guess I already know more than I'm supposed to. Now, I'd better get back to the office, since I didn't let anyone know where I would be."

Jim rose to leave with the judge but turned back, saying aloud, "I'm going to marry that girl."

"But how? She lives in Colorado," Shelly said.

"She isn't always going to be in Colorado," Jim stated firmly.

Sergeant left just after the others. Shelly sat thinking about the coming of the new arrivals. She wondered about their accommodations. "This is something Carol needs to handle," she thought as she left the apartment, wheeled her trike out of the short-hall door, and headed for the government offices.

CHAPTER 35

Carol was in her office going over applications from twelve- to sixteen-year-old students as Shelly entered and made sure the door was closed. "I needed a break from this," she said smiling gratefully. "Most of these kids want to work for the master huntsmen or the equine administrator."

Shelly laughed as she sat, saying, "Jake wanted Jim too. But Jim has already told him he wouldn't be accepted. He steered Jake in another direction."

"This must be something important if you want to discuss it behind a closed door," Carol said.

Shelly went over most everything that had transpired concerning the president, leaving out only the parts that were to be kept secret. She ended by saying, "The upshot is that the president, vice president, and their families will wake up in the dormitory tomorrow morning."

"For heaven's sake, Shelly," Carol said, shooting up out of her chair. "How am I ever supposed to handle that? I haven't the slightest idea what the protocol is for them. Do we have extra-big apartments? Where's my map?"

Carol pulled the map out of a file cabinet, opened a desk drawer, and started shoving papers into it. Shelly grabbed a half-full cup of coffee from the desktop before it too followed the papers. Carol opened the map and stared at it. "The occupied apartments have red circles around them," Carol said as a look of dismay shadowed her face. "This doesn't give any indication how large these apartments are."

While Carol agonized over her map, Shelly ducked her head so Carol couldn't see her eyes. "General," she called silently.

"You have a question?" General answered.

"Are any of the apartments extra-big, or nicer, where our president may be housed?" she asked.

"No. Other than more bedrooms and slightly larger rooms to accommodate larger families, all the apartments are basically the same."

"Are maybe a couple of the larger apartments close to the government offices?" Shelly thought.

"The closest empty ones are on the corner of South First Avenue and East Fourth Street. They are across the street from each other," General replied.

"Thank you, General," Shelly sent.

Carol was going through the file cabinet, groaning.

"What are you looking for?" Shelly asked.

"I'm trying to find the file of someone with a bunch of kids," Carol said, not looking up. "Maybe if I see the apartment they are in, and what it looks like on the map, I'll spot something that will help me."

"Carol, sit down a minute," Shelly said. "I think I may see something."

Carol whirled around. She looked at Shelly calmly sitting in her chair. Grinning sheepishly, Carol said, "I guess I lost it, didn't I."

As Carol sat, Shelly pointed to the corner apartments, "It looks like maybe all the corner apartments are bigger, and these two seem to be the closest empty ones."

Carol studied the map for a moment, jumped up, and said, "Come with me to check them out."

Carol and Shelly parked their trikes next to an empty corner apartment and waved themselves in. It was as General had said; the layout was basically the same as that of the other apartments. There was a bathroom in each of the four bedrooms, and the kitchen, dining room, and living room were bigger. Shelly leaned against the wall next to the door as Carol walked through every room. Then Carol walked down the hall toward Shelly, saying, "It should be more opulent, bigger."

"Carol, after what they have been through, I think just having a safe place to live is going to make them happy," Shelly said.

Carol stood looking around, frowning. "I know you're right, but the least we can do is to get their windows covered, and we need to stock this place. Come with me to the curtain shop and help me pick them out."

Before setting off on the shopping spree, they both checked the apartment across the street. The furniture was darker, richer looking, and both agreed that it was the one for the president.

They rode to the plaza, parked their trikes on the side street, and walked the rest of the way. Shelly smiled to herself as she noticed the name of the curtain shop had been changed to Custom Curtains and Drapery Shop. When Shelly and Carol entered the shop, they looked around at the myriad colored and patterned drapes hanging on wooden rods along the walls of both sides of the room. Carol pulled the corner of a drape out and was admiring the pattern when a woman stomped out of the back. "If you two expect me to make you something special, you can just forget it," she said testily. "You'll just have to settle for what's hanging."

"Excuse me?" Carol said primly, dropping the curtain.

The woman studied Carol for a quick moment and then, in a friendlier tone, said, "You're the head of personnel, aren't you?"

Carol nodded. "We are expecting a couple of new arrivals and want to hang curtains before they get here."

"Well, like I said, what you see is all that I can offer. The quartermaster refuses to give me more material, thank heavens."

"I don't understand. Why would the quartermaster refuse you supplies?" Carol asked.

"Because these women order a set of custom drapes, and a week after the drapes are hung, they are back in here wanting something different," the curtain shop owner replied. "At first it was fun. I enjoy working with new patterns, but it has steadily become more women wanting something different. The quartermaster finally cut me off, and I am glad he did; there aren't enough people to hire to keep up with what was being ordered. I started demanding they return the drapes and curtains they didn't want."

Shelly and Carol looked at each other. "What do you think?" Carol asked, holding out flowery patterned drape.

"I think we should just get plain white drapes. If the ladies want something different, they have a very nice selection to choose from," Shelly said, gesturing at the hanging drapes.

"You're right, Shelly," Carol said decisively. "The more we can give them to do, the shorter their adjustment period will be."

They stood back, looking at the drapes they had just hung in the president's apartment, making sure the folds were hanging straight. Carol wished again that she could do more for the newcomers.

"Well, we can make sure these places are well stocked," Shelly commented. "They are going to need personal supplies as well as food."

Carol gave Shelly a spontaneous hug, grabbed her hand, and pulled her out the door, saying happily, "Oh boy, let's go do some serious shopping."

They rode back to the plaza, again leaving the trikes on the street. Then they walked onto the plaza, stopping at different shops, saving the grocery store for last. What they thought was going to be a fun adventure turned into a depressing ordeal. Many of the shopkeepers were surly, though most were placated when they found out Shelly and Carol were stocking apartments for new arrivals. They were discussing the unhappiness of the shopkeepers as they passed by the toy shop. Shelly stopped suddenly. "Let's get the president's children a toy."

"See, Shelly; this is why I needed your help. I would have never thought of getting something for the kids," Carol said.

They turned back and entered the toy shop. Isaac was setting up a wooden train on a shelf, and he smiled when he recognized Shelly. They exchanged greetings, and Shelly told him they were looking for something for a boy who was about four years old and two girls aged seven and eleven.

"Bethy," Isaac called to the back room. "Come out here and help Shelly find some toys."

Elizabeth came out of the back, and Shelly told her what she was looking for. "I have just the thing for the girls; Isaac can hunt up something for the boy," she said, walking over and taking a ten-inch porcelain teen fashion doll off the shelf. "This may be right for the eleven-year-old. She has two outfits to go with her." Reaching for a baby doll on a higher shelf, she said, "This is perfect for the younger one."

Shelly and Carol agreed to both choices, and while Elizabeth wrapped the dolls in scrap cloth, Isaac brought over a three-piece train set. He proudly showed off the details of the engine and each car. The women were impressed with the intricate carvings and were delighted when he opened the cattle car to reveal four removable cows. Pleased with the acquisitions, Shelly and Carol thanked the Taggarts and reached for the cloth bags that held the toys. Isaac stepped forward with the bags and took a bundle from each of them. "We need shopping carts for the plaza," he said.

Isaac walked them to their bikes. Shelly and Carol thanked him for the help. He told Shelly to tell Amy that he and Elizabeth missed her help. With no room left in the trike baskets, the two women had to haul their bulging bundles back to the apartments and return for groceries. It was late by the time they were done, and they agreed to meet the next morning at Zeke's place.

CHAPTER 36

Shelly left early the next morning, leaving Sergeant to see Amy and Jake off to school. She had already made plans the night before for Sergeant and Judge Barker to meet her and Carol at Zeke's restaurant. She found Carol at a table that had been set up in the dormitory. The president, vice president, their families, and another young man were still sleeping. Shelly walked over to check on the sleepers. She stopped at cots holding the seventeen-year-old twin boys that belonged to the vice president. Her heart ached as she took in the pale thin faces; they were so alike—so young and innocent in sleep. She walked back to the table where Carol sat patiently. Speaking in whispers over coffee and cinnamon rolls, they waited. The president was the first to wake. Shelly and Carol hurried to him, kneeling down to eye level as he sat up. He rubbed his head and looked at Shelly, saying groggily, "Who are you? Where am I?"

"I'm Shelly Bradford," Shelly said.

"You and your family are at Cave Haven," Carol added, "somewhere in the mountains and safe."

The president sat for a moment, processing what he had been told. As a slow grin crossed his face, he looked at Shelly and said, "If you're Shelly Bradford, she must be Dorothy, and I guess I'm to believe we're not in Kansas anymore."

Carol, looking confused, said, "No, I'm Carol White, and I've never been to Kansas."

The president and Shelly laughed quietly, and at Carol's deepening confusion, Shelly simply said, "Wizard of Oz."

"Oh," Carol said, trying to laugh with them. "Well, who expected him to wake up making jokes?" She turned her attention to the president. "Why don't you come sit at the table, Mr. President? We'll get you something to eat and wait for the rest of your party to wake up."

"What can I get you for breakfast, Mr. President?" Shelly asked, trying her best to sound like a normal waitress.

"If I could have anything I wanted for breakfast, I'd wish for three eggs sunny side up, sausage, and a huge glass of cold milk," he answered dreamily.

"Would you like your sausage as links or patties? Toast, biscuits, or pancakes? And would you like some fresh fruit with that?" she asked.

"You really have all of that?" he asked in disbelief. When Shelly nodded, he shook his head, saying, "I must be in heaven."

It was his turn to look confused when Shelly and Carol laughed. "Links, biscuits, and yes to the fruit," he quickly said.

Shelly departed to the kitchen to fill the president's order, leaving Carol to explain about Amy and heaven.

When the president finished his breakfast, Sergeant and Judge Barker had arrived, and the others were still asleep. The president had twice walked to the other members of his party to check on them. When he returned and sat the second time, Sergeant asked, "Mr. President, we know your family and the vice president's family, but who is the young man?"

"He is a marine corporal that was trapped in John Drummond's madness. He is a good man. He would have died for us, had I let him. Each time I was called to the radio, a guard loyal to Drummond, the brute of an animal, brought my wife along at knifepoint to make sure

I only said what I was instructed to say. We were in the radio room when that brute realized Drummond was planning to throw him out of the shelter because he was the only one that had any direct contact with us. It got ugly. Drummond used a stun gun on him. Then he opened the door to the radio room and called the corporal and another guard to drag him out to the main door. Drummond and a guard went personally to get the vice president and our families. The guards and corporal didn't realize what was happening until the door closed, locking them out with us.

"The last thing I remember is all of us standing in front of the White House. The brute was sitting on the ground sweating, one of the guards was yelling at him, and the other guard was cussing and crying. This marine was asking me if I had any orders for him." The president looked at his hands and sadly said, "I guess we have pretty much destroyed our civilization."

"I guess we will have to rebuild it then, won't we," Shelly said with quiet determination.

The president appraised her and said, "Your name should have been Hope. That is what you do—inspire hope in others."

The other members of his party began to wake. The president went to them, comforting, explaining, and guiding them to restrooms.

Shelly stood up and signaled Zeke from the door. Moments later, teenagers were bringing in more tables and setting them up a discreet distance from the one already there. Zeke wheeled in a steam table filled with hot breakfast foods. More staff followed, setting down shallow tubs of ice and placing smaller tubs filled with fresh fruits and vegetables on top of the ice. A table holding drinks, both hot and cold, was rolled in. A waiter and waitress stood by the food, ready to fill warm plates. A staff member from the nursery was on hand to take over the four-year-old son of the president. It didn't take her long to win him over with a plate of pancakes. The first lady turned to her husband and said, "Oh, this is a heavenly sight."

Sergeant rolled his eyes. Carol and Shelly turned their faces away, trying to hold on to their laughter, and the judge looked at them quizzically. Sergeant gestured to the corporal, inviting him to sit with them. A waiter provided an extra chair before the corporal reached the table. "Corporal Robert Peters, US Marine Corps. The food and service are a whole lot better here than where we just came from," he said, sitting down with a plate that was piled high.

Shelly, Carol, Sergeant, and Judge Barker surreptitiously watched as the newcomers ate. It was obvious to all four that these people had been on short rations. Even the president ordered a cinnamon roll and another glass of milk. When everyone finished eating, Carol went over and asked them if they would like to see their quarters.

Sergeant led the way through the restaurant. Belatedly, Shelly realized they should have taken the back way through the narrow hall. Several people in the restaurant recognized the presidential party, and Shelly knew that the entire community would be privy to their presence before the day was done. When they started across the plaza, the procession stopped and the new arrivals stared around them in amazement. "Who built all this?" the president asked.

"We don't really know. We call them the elder group," Judge Barker answered. "They are the ones that brought all of us here in the same manner they brought you here."

"I'd like to know more about the elders," the president said.

"As would we all," Judge Barker chuckled.

Sergeant guided them to a row of carts with drivers parked next to the cake shop. When all were comfortably seated, they drove quickly to the appointed apartments. All the men waited in the street while Shelly took the vice president's wife and boys, showed them how to wave open the door, and escorted them inside the apartment. Carol guided the first lady and children in the same manner. Shelly and Carol made sure the women were settled and then silently left both families to explore their new surroundings.

As Shelly and Carol headed toward the circle of men in quiet conversation, Shelly noticed that Sergeant had dismissed the cab carts. Carol suddenly grabbed Shelly's arm and said, "We didn't select and stock an apartment for the corporal."

"Weren't the apartments on both sides of the corner apartments empty?" Shelly whispered. "Why not put him in one of them."

"We're going to the conference room, Shelly," Sergeant said as he cut his eyes to Carol.

"Carol is going to show Corporal Peters his apartment," Shelly said smoothly, walking up and standing next to him. "Then she's going to take him to the plaza for supplies."

"Excellent idea. And we should have Jim in on this meeting," Judge Barker said.

Sergeant nodded and turned to Carol. "You might want to make the quartermaster your first stop and pick up three radios. I'll call Mr. Fielding now and let him know to release them to Corporal Peters. Also show Corporal Peters where to get his tricycle."

The corporal looked to the president, who said, "You go with Miss White. When you are finished, please stay close to the women; they trust you."

"Yes, sir," Corporal Peters said with a sharp salute.

As they walked the street, heading for the conference room, the president commented on the door paintings. "They started out simple," Shelly said. "Now, some are rather intricate, covering the entire door. You can spend a whole day looking at doors and not see them all. It's like walking through an art gallery."

They settled around the conference table, and the president asked if he and the VP might have paper and pencil to take notes. Shelly had gone to her apartment and gathered up writing pads and pens, and loaded a tray with glasses and a pitcher of ice water. Jim entered the conference room as Shelly was handing out supplies and water. Introductions were made, and the president began speaking. "The first thing I want to do is to thank all of you for getting us out of

Washington. But especially you, Shelly, for providing a ray of hope where there was none. The last thing John Drummond said to me was 'Now you can go find your kitty cat.' Okay. Now I want to know all the details about these people you call the elder group."

Judge Barker cleared his throat. "I can only tell you what General Elder revealed to me. General Elder is a member of a centuries-old secret elite paramilitary group of scientists, engineers, inventors, chemists, and other highly educated people. They have never aligned themselves with any government. They have often released various inventions or products that would benefit the public. Their technology far surpasses what the rest of us have known. Their main purpose is to guarantee the continued existence of humanity."

"That's it?" the president asked. Judge Barker nodded. "Would it be possible to meet with General Elder?" the president asked.

The judge looked at Shelly. "You would have to ask our communications expert that question."

CHAPTER 37

All eyes turned to Shelly, who ducked her head, thinking to herself, "Gee, thanks, Judge, for throwing the monkey on my back." Shelly lifted her head and faced the president. "As the judge said, they won't align themselves with any government. They don't look at us as individuals, but as a species."

"But you can contact him and make the request?" the president pushed.

"General," Shelly sent.

"You have a question?" General replied.

"Will you meet with the president?" she asked.

"No," General answered, and Shelly knew he was gone.

"He won't meet with you, Mr. President," Shelly said.

"But you can ask him, right?" the president asked again.

"I just asked him, sir. His answer is no," Shelly stated calmly.

The president looked closely at Shelly. "Do you have a communication device on you somewhere?" he asked.

"No, sir. I have ESP," she replied.

The president and vice president looked around at the sober faces of those seated at the table. All were slowly nodding affirmatively. "This isn't a joke, is it?" the president said, his eyes riveted on Shelly. "We will need more details to understand what is going on here."

Judge Barker looked at his watch and said, "Mr. President, Shelly will be happy to fill you in, but right now we have a more important matter to discuss."

"What could be more important than what we are discussing right now?" the president asked with a touch of irritation.

"The presidential election that is being held at this moment, and the acceptance speech of John Drummond when he announces himself the winner and next president of the United States of America," Judge Barker answered.

The president's eyes darkened, and for the first time Shelly saw the true strength of the man. Then she heard it when the president leaned forward and replied, "You are right, Judge Barker; that is a much more pressing matter."

The president furiously took notes as the judge relayed what Drummond had announced the day before. "You're saying you discussed this with NORAD? Then Drummond probably knows I'm alive. He has several radios set up and has them constantly monitored."

The judge cleared his throat. "We didn't use the radio, Mr. President. That's where Jim comes into this equation."

The president turned his steely eyes toward Jim and said, "The master huntsman? I wondered why he was summoned."

Shelly spoke calmly. "Mr. President, there are a handful of people that have the ability of ESP. Jim is much stronger than I. He has the power to reach one with our ability that is at NORAD. One more thing: our ability is not common knowledge, and we would like to keep it that way for now."

The president sat back, crossing one hand across his chest. He stared at the table and rubbed his bottom lip with his index finger for a moment. He then straightened up in his chair and said, "I still have a lot of questions, but they can wait. Judge Barker, how much time do we have?"

"We have about ten minutes, Mr. President," the judge answered, pushing himself from the table. "The radio is in Shelly's apartment."

They all stood, and Shelly was thankful for her cleaning spree the day before. The light was blinking on the radio when they entered the apartment. Sergeant and Jim set chairs around the radio and then made themselves comfortable on the sofa. Jim's eyes immediately turned glassy. "That's Washington on the radio calling for everyone to stay tuned to hear the results of the election, and an announcement from the new president," Jim said.

"How much time, Judge?" the president asked.

"By my watch, three minutes," he answered.

"We'll go on the air now; your watch may be off," the president stated.

Shelly turned on the radio and put the microphone in front of the president. The president waited for a brief pause in the repeating broadcast and then spoke firmly. "This is President Gregory James Williamson. The information of my death, the death of Vice President Duncan, and our families' deaths is fraudulent. The criminal Colonel John Drummond spread this lie. When the virus drove us into shelters, Colonel Drummond, along with other military personnel loyal to him, took over the shelter at gunpoint. I, along with the vice president and our families, was held prisoner by these men. Yesterday, Colonel Drummond evicted us from the shelter to what he expected was certain death, but we didn't die. With the help of brave and loyal citizens of these United States, we found sanctuary in another shelter.

"People of America, I make you this solemn promise: When the crisis caused by the virus has ended, and when we again walk the land we love, Colonel Drummond and those associated with him will be hunted down and made to pay for their crimes. And rest assured that in three years, when my term ends on the first Tuesday in November, you will have the freedom to participate in a legal election for your next president.

"I wish to make one last comment to those currently surrounding Colonel Drummond. It would behoove you, if you harbor any hope of clemency, to place him and his associates under arrest. This is President Williamson, signing off."

Immediately the radio roared to life with the screaming of Drummond. "You liar! President Williamson is dead. I am the president. I won the election today with one hundred percent of the vote. I am the leader now. You have to obey me now, whoever you are. I will have you shot; your head will be put on a pole. I will kill everybody in this shelter if you don't tell me right now where you are. I am the president now, and—"

They all heard the rapid popping of shots being fired, followed by a few moments of silence. "Mr. President, this is Private Michael O'Brien. I just murdered my commanding officer and ten others. Mr. President, they celebrated last night. They brutalized women and girls. Two civilians were killed."

They heard the private sobbing. The president said with quiet sadness, almost to himself, "He is only eighteen. He just got out of basic training." The president picked up the mike and barked fiercely, "Private O'Brien, I am your commanding officer. You are to consider the actions you have just taken as carried out under my direct orders. Is that clear, Private?"

"Yes, sir," the private said in a breaking voice.

"Now, soldier, I want you to tell me if you are in any immediate danger."

"No, sir. The door is locked. Those that were in this room were the ones that held the rank and power. Most of the soldiers that took orders from them didn't know you were in trouble. We that knew didn't know who to trust," the private answered.

"Is there anyone with a higher rank than you that you trust?" the president asked.

"There's Corporal Peters, but I haven't been able to find him since yesterday," the private answered.

"Corporal Peters is here with me," the president said, looking around the room.

Sergeant was already on his radio when he saw the president look at him. He handed the radio to him, saying, "It's Corporal Peters, sir."

The president had a quick conversation with Corporal Peters and then went back to talking with the private. "Private, can you get Corporal Kirth to the radio room?" the president asked.

"Yes, sir," the private said, his voice sounding stronger.

They heard Private O'Brien make the call to Kirth.

"Private, do you know if the attorney general made it into the shelter?"

"Sir, I don't know, sir."

The president had Sergeant get Corporal Peters back on this radio. Corporal Peters confirmed that the attorney general had indeed made it to the shelter. "Private O'Brien, the attorney general is in the shelter. Have him brought to the radio room."

"Sir, yes, sir."

Again they heard the private make the call. The president leaned back in the chair, rubbing his bottom lip. No one spoke.

"Corporal Kirth here, Mr. President," a new voice said over the speaker.

The president grabbed the mike. "Who is the highest-ranking officer there now, Corporal Kirth?"

"Sir, that would be me, sir."

Shelly saw the president's knuckles turn white as his hand gripped the microphone tighter. "Corporal Kirth, you have just been promoted to sergeant, and you are now in charge of military personnel. You are to detain anyone you think may have been loyal to Colonel Drummond. The attorney general will be responsible for civilians and the running of the shelter. Do you understand your orders, Sergeant Kirth?"

"Sir, yes, sir," the newly promoted sergeant said.

"And Sergeant Kirth, if you have any questions or problems, you are to contact me. Understood?"

"Sir, understood, sir" was the sergeant's snappy reply.

When the attorney general's voice came on the radio, the president apprised him of the situation, put him in charge of the shelter, and assured him of the stability of the current military personnel. When the president finally pushed away from the radio, his exhaustion was obvious. "Can I get you something to eat or drink, Mr. President?" Shelly asked.

"Coffee would sure hit the spot right about now," the president said. "Would you mind if we sat at the table?"

CHAPTER 38

Sergeant and Jim jumped up and repositioned the chairs to the table as Shelly made coffee. When they had all taken seats, Sergeant asked, "Mr. President, how did Drummond ever get in the position to do what he did?"

The president sat looking at his hands, which lay folded on the table. He appeared to be trying to organize his thoughts. He spoke slowly. "He held that duty post several years before I was sworn in. We ran a check on him, and he looked good on paper. He was from a long line of career military officers. He rose in the ranks quickly, though now I believe that was due more to the name and reputation of his father and forefathers than to his own achievements. He had control of the placement and transfer of all military personnel stationed at the White House. It wasn't hard for him to keep those officers who were loyal to him and transfer those that weren't. All the low-ranking soldiers that made it into the shelter are young. He took control as soon as we entered the shelter, and he separated us from the rest of the civilians. I and my family, like sheep, followed an officer that led us to a room, and then locked us inside. The same procedure was followed with the vice president. It was days before Drummond informed us of our situation.

"Often he would come in, taunt us, and tell us how powerful he was. If I tried to talk sense to him, or stand up to him, my family suffered and food and water were withheld. Then he started on Brooke. He would make her stand in the middle of the room while he walked around her, looking her up and down. Brooke is only eleven years old. He told her in very graphic detail exactly what he was going to give her for her twelfth birthday. Always he would have that brute holding the rest of us in the corner at gunpoint. Do you understand now, Shelly, how much your reference to a kitten meant to us? I was finally able to let someone know we were in trouble.

"Drummond became worse—more cruel. He started telling Brooke he might not wait until her birthday. That's when we had Brooke pretend she was sick. Corporal Peters was able to slip us a pepper shaker. Any time we heard the door being unlocked, she would get in bed, sniff some pepper, and then rub some in her eyes. When the transmission came in from NORAD about the mutated virus, I knew we were dead, but by that time, eviction from the shelter was a preferable choice. Had I had my wits about me, I would have seen the discrepancies of the report. It all happened so fast."

The president stopped talking as he sipped some of the coffee Shelly had set in front of him during his narrative. Sergeant had so many more questions: Where had the Secret Service been when Drummond was taking over? How did Drummond manage to get the president and vice president in the same shelter? In times of crisis, they were supposed to be separated. Just as he started to speak, Shelly caught his eye and gave a barely perceptible shake of her head. She laid her hand on the president's wrist, saying gently, "You're tired. Why not go home, comfort and reassure your family, and rest."

"There's so much to do—so much I need to understand," the president replied.

"There is nothing that won't wait twenty-four hours. You need to rest. You can start again tomorrow with a clear mind," Shelly said.

"You are probably right," the president replied. "Though I should at least contact NORAD."

"I have already informed them of your need for rest," Jim interjected. "Your experiences in Washington were relayed to them verbatim. They are not expecting to hear from you until tomorrow."

"Thank you, Jim. Judge Barker, do all the people here work together as well as this group?" the president asked as he headed toward the door.

"So far we haven't had a problem with people working together," the judge hedged. "But we are not going to discuss anything more about the people today. Mr. President, do you like to fish?"

The next day, Shelly readied the conference room, making sure there were notepads and pencils at all the chairs. The night before, she had sent everyone in the community a brief synopsis of why and how the president was now to reside at Cave Haven. Very quickly after sending the communications, it became necessary for her to set her computer up, with Jake's help, as an answering machine telling callers she couldn't take their calls and details would come soon. At the president's request, Judge Barker had gathered, along with Velda Biggs to take official notes, a small group in the conference room that included Calvin Johnson, Harold Vickers, James Fielding, Dr. Murphy, Carol White, and Sergeant Williams. When the president and vice president arrived, the group was already there waiting. The president asked for Shelly and Jim Lightfoot to be in attendance. When all were assembled, Judge Barker gave a presentation of the short history of Cave Haven to the two men.

"So the problems you are experiencing now are overuse of supplies, and the desire of people to be paid for their work," President Williamson summarized. When all had nodded in agreement, the president continued. "You say everyone agreed to abide by the US Constitution and to keep the form of government as a democratic republic, yet you have set up no government and no republic, and you have not voted for a leader. What you are doing here is treating people as if they all are the same. By the act of making people the same, you deny them their freedom of individuality. After the short time you have been here, your system is already breaking down. The more you give people everything for free, the more they want because they are instinctively trying to make themselves unique in some way. They will happily deplete their surpluses, and then they will revolt when asked to make do with less.

"Who owns the apartments, businesses, farms, barns, and the very livestock used to feed the populace?" President Williamson looked at each of them around the table, and shook his head sadly, saying, "Ladies and gentlemen, I would suggest you take a close look at the type of government you are practicing in actuality. Human beings are not the same. We can be equal but never identical. We are individuals. We strive not just for what we need but also for the freedom to obtain what we want. Few of us settle for one goal in our lives; once we reach a goal, we look for the next one to achieve. You will need a monetary system. If people have to pay for their necessities and save for what they desire, the depletion will slow. The flagrant waste of supplies will stop."

Shelly knew the president was right. She thought of the first time she had seen Rosa in her belly dancer outfit. Rosa had used her creativity to be seen as unique, as an individual. It was the same with the door paintings. Shelly realized that when something beyond basic needs was given to one group, then something was taken away from another group. Worse, when the people were freely given what they wanted, those people had their own individual creativity, dreams, and drive taken from them. She shook her head and brought her attention back to what the president was saying.

The president looked around the table and said, "I am ready for suggestions."

"We have gold in the stream that runs through the valley," Sergeant said. "Jim thinks he has spotted a vein in the side of the mountain east of here but is waiting for the barrier to drop before he can investigate further."

Carol raised her hand and said, "Samuel Ginsburg is a jeweler; I'm sure he could make some coins."

Sergeant radioed his office to have one of his men bring Samuel to the conference room. Shelly dropped her head. "General."

You have a question?" General answered immediately.

"Do we have the equipment here to smelt gold and mint coins?" she asked.

"It will be in place in the morning beyond the citrus greenhouse," General responded. "We will also restock the supplies for the quartermaster. Remember: once the barrier is down, we can no longer be of assistance."

"Thank you, General," Shelly sent. "General?"

"You have a question." General stated.

"All the new technology here—did the keepers invent it?"

There was a slight pause before the general sent, "No, our species does not invent technology; we adapt it to its best use."

"Then who invented all of this?" Shelly asked.

"A species we know as the makers," General answered.

Samuel Ginsburg was escorted into the conference room. Shelly stood, asked to be excused for a few minutes, and left the room. She knew where the discussion was going, and not everyone in the room could know she had contacted General. Judge Barker smiled at Mr. Ginsburg and said, "Samuel, you have been asked to join us because we would like you to make coins for Cave Haven."

Samuel blinked in surprise and said, "My equipment is limited. I make jewelry."

"But can you design coins?" the president asked.

"Of course I can design coins, but I simply don't have the equipment to do what you are proposing. Even if I had the gold necessary, it would require a furnace to smelt the gold, a machine to make blanks, another machine to stamp the blanks, and still another machine to cut the ridging on them."

"Any other thoughts on this subject?" the president asked.

"If I may," James Fielding said. "If you give a salary to every worker, and they all pay for what they need or want, then there are a few of us that will end up with most of the coins—those at the beginning of the chain of supply."

"Right you are, Mr. Fielding," the president replied. "And when those supplies run short, you are going to have to buy from others that scour the cities to replace what is needed. Those working in the areas of farming and ranching will have to pay for labor. It will be up to those at the beginning of the chains to be sure the supplies continue to be available and the populace is treated fairly. Also, taxes will have to be paid by all to be sure maintenance personnel, teachers, security personnel, and government workers are paid. Now, why don't we close this meeting and convene again tomorrow. The vice president and I would like a tour of this facility."

Shelly entered the conference room as the others were standing up to leave. Sergeant told her she had missed the last of the meeting but said he would catch her up on the details after he gave the president and vice president a tour of Cave Haven.

President Williamson asked that Shelly show the first lady and Mrs. Duncan around the plaza.

Shelly led the women through the different shops. Each picked up different drapes, but it wasn't until they reached Rosa's clothes shop that they became animated. Rosa agreed to design each woman a pantsuit and a dress. In the course of conversation, while taking measurements, Rosa commented she would leave extra-wide seams so they could be let out in a couple of months. Mrs. Duncan laughed, saying she had never had to worry about her weight. Rosa stopped and looked at Shelly.

Shelly ducked her head. "General, are these women pregnant?"

"Of course," General answered.

Shelly raised her head. "Rosa, why don't you fix us some tea. Ladies, we need to sit down. There is something you need to know immediately."

"Oh, for heaven's sake. If you have something to tell us, just be done with it," the first lady said impatiently. "After what we have been through these past few months, there is little you can say that will upset us."

"If I told you that nine months from now you will be delivering a child, would that upset you?" Shelly said bluntly.

Mrs. Duncan started laughing while Mrs. Williamson glared at her. Shelly pulled out a chair from the small table. "Please, sit down."

The ladies sat.

Shelly waited until Mrs. Duncan had stopped laughing. "What I'm about to tell you is what every person in this community already knows. The world's human population was being decimated to the point of extinction. The group that provided us with this shelter has technology and knowledge that is beyond anything we can imagine, and they're interested in only one thing—the continuation of the human species. All the women over the age of twenty-three were impregnated to assure the continuation of humanity. You are both with child."

Mrs. Duncan shook her head. "You don't understand. My husband and I tried for years to have a child. When the doctors finally discovered I could not become pregnant, we adopted our twin boys. Also, my childbearing years are behind me."

"Mrs. Duncan, what you don't understand is that right now we have women up to the age of sixty-five that are going to have children. If there was a medical reason you were barren, the elder group fixed it."

"Is there, by chance, a good nanny available?" the first lady asked flippantly.

"Probably not, but we have an excellent nursery here," Shelly answered.

"You are positive about what you have just told us?" Mrs. Duncan asked, with longing in her voice and tears in her eyes.

Shelly silently nodded.

CHAPTER 39

The same group convened in the conference room the next morning. The vice president was wearing a smile and looked to be walking on cloud nine. The president first called on Mr. Ginsburg for any updates. "I looked at my equipment and thought about it all night. I even thought of somehow utilizing the forge the blacksmith uses down at the horse barns. We just don't have the facilities to mass produce the coinage we are going to need."

"Excuse me, Mr. Ginsburg, but would a foundry help?" Shelly asked innocently.

Everyone in the room turned and stared at her. "As I said yesterday, we need to smelt the gold and will need other machinery for production," Mr. Ginsburg said impatiently.

"Oh, I guess you mentioned that while I was out of the room," Shelly said. "But we do have a foundry and other machinery on the other side of the citrus greenhouse."

"Why wouldn't this foundry be common knowledge?" the president asked, studying her closely.

"Probably because no one was assigned to work there," Shelly said, nervous at the speculative look Sergeant was giving her. "A communications expert isn't called upon that often, so I have had a lot of extra time to explore. Heck, what do I know; it may not even be a foundry." She knew she was talking too fast and too much. "Why don't I take Mr. Ginsburg and show him the place," Shelly said. "It may not have the right kind of machinery that he needs."

"As head of security, I think I should ride along with them to see this place I knew nothing of," Sergeant said lazily.

"Have a nice time explaining this one," Jim Lightfoot chuckled in her mind.

"If you don't start ducking your head when you mind-speak, your glassy eyes are going to get us caught by more people then we need," she sent back, mentally visualizing sticking out her tongue at him.

Shelly and Sergeant had taken the backseats in the cart. As they rode, he leaned over, and they spoke in low voices so the driver and Ginsburg wouldn't hear them. "So when did you ask the elder group for a foundry?" Sergeant asked.

"Yesterday, when I saw where the discussion was going," Shelly said.

"Is that why you left the meeting yesterday?"

"Yes, I couldn't very well say the foundry would be set up overnight, and if I had stayed, they would have asked why I hadn't said something. There would have been too many questions."

Sergeant nodded. "Did you ask for anything else?"

"No, but General said they would restock the quartermaster one more time."

Sergeant sighed. "Is there a reason you didn't tell me all of this yesterday?"

Shelly ran her fingertips through her hair. "I guess I got wrapped up with telling Mrs. Williamson and Mrs. Duncan about the babies, and it was late when I got home. I just forgot all about it until we got to the meeting and I saw Mr. Ginsburg."

Sergeant took her hand as she started to rake her hair again. "It doesn't really matter. But you sure are full of surprises."

They rode in silence until they arrived at the citrus greenhouse. They followed a path Sergeant knew had not been there yesterday, moving along the front of the greenhouse until they came to a single door. Sergeant pushed it open, and Mr. Ginsburg hurried in. He moved from one machine to another, nodding his head, until he came to what looked like a huge furnace, only more. Scratching his head, he slowly moved around it. He found an instruction manual. After flipping through the book, stopping occasionally to read carefully, he finally turned to them with a look of awe. "This machine will not only smelt gold; it separates different metals, such as copper, silver, and iron. It also removes all toxic gases and byproducts, and disposes of them safely. It says here that as long as we don't try to take it apart, it should work until it is no longer needed. I have never heard of this technology."

When they were settled back in the conference room, Mr. Ginsburg gave an overview of the foundry and assured them all that not only gold but also silver coins could be minted. He had started to explain the wonders of the new furnace when they heard a disturbance coming from the hall. Then there was a light rap on the door. Corporal Peters stuck his head in, saying, "Mrs. Fielding wishes to speak with her husband."

The president nodded, and Roberta entered, going straight to James. She leaned down and whispered to him.

"Are you sure?" he asked.

Roberta nodded emphatically. James turned to the president. "It seems the warehouse was restocked sometime last night."

"Mrs. Fielding, won't you take a chair and tell us exactly what you found." the president said respectfully.

Shelly, Sergeant, and Judge Barker looked at each other with consternation. "The president caught that look you guys just gave each other." Jim sent to Shelly.

Roberta sat with all her former arrogance and told the president how she had found stacks of new crates at the back of the warehouse. "I didn't go through all of them, but it looks like we received everything we were short of," she reported.

"So when we have the monetary system in place, you should be ready to go," the president said to James.

"Are you saying there is going to be money?" Roberta said, butting in. "That means I can charge anything I want for my supplies."

"It means the quartermaster will set a fair price on the goods under his supervision," the president said firmly. "Thank you for this information, Mrs. Fielding; you may be excused now."

They could all see the angry set of her shoulders as she stalked from the room, and none missed the stabbing glare James aimed at her back. The rest of the meeting dealt with going over what was already in place in Cave Haven. President Williamson agreed that since there were no colleges, the guild system was an ideal way to educate the young. He was assured that the children would be like interns and not involved with anything dangerous.

Shelly's mind wandered while the men went on about mundane matters she had no interest in. She thought about how Roberta had looked huge compared to the rest of the other women, and she wondered if the twins would change Roberta's attitude. With a start, she realized most of the men were getting up; the president, the vice president, and Judge Barker stayed seated. Shelly and Sergeant went to their apartment for lunch. "I wasn't paying attention; how come the judge stayed behind with the president and vice president?" she asked.

"They are going over the speech the president is going to make, and about the election for mayor of Cave Haven."

After Sergeant and Shelly had eaten lunch, neither having anything pressing to do, Sergeant suggested they had plenty of time for a nice nap, to which Shelly eagerly agreed. They had just gotten comfortable when Shelly heard "Those that were kept as slaves will be dropped tonight."

Sergeant, watching Shelly's eyes turn glassy, laid back with a sigh.

"General, do you do this on purpose?" Shelly sent, exasperated.

"Explain," General demanded.

"Never mind," Shelly sent quickly. "I'll let Carol know. How is the little girl?"

"Her mind is troubled," General said. "She will need patience."

"Can't you just erase the bad memories?" Shelly asked.

"We can, but we feel it is more important that she remember her condition is not voluntary and that she fought, and that her mother, and others, fought for her also."

"She will have it hard," Shelly thought sadly.

"Combating evil is never easy," General stated. "We will do all we can to help her."

"As expected," Shelly sent.

"Is he gone?" Sergeant asked when Shelly relaxed against him.

Shelly nodded and told him all General had relayed to her. Then she started to get up. "Where are you going?" Sergeant asked.

"I need to tell Carol about the drop in the morning," Shelly said.

"You can call her on the computer after dinner," he said, pulling her to him.

She agreed.

The next morning, Shelly helped Carol with the new arrivals. They were given a meal in the dormitory. "They're scared and nervous," Carol said. "I think we should take them to their apartments and let them settle down in a homier atmosphere."

"You're right," Shelly agreed. "We can show them how to call, give them a few days to acclimate to their surroundings, and keep a close check on them."

When the newcomers had finished eating, Carol approached the group as they eyed her with suspicion. "This is a large shelter," Carol said. "We have apartments for you that are already stocked with most of what you need. You are free to come and go whenever you are ready."

Carol looked at the little girl, "Your name is Danielle, isn't it? We have a nice school with many other children for you to get to know."

"I won't go to school," Danielle stated flatly, without looking up.

"But everyone needs an education," Carol said gently.

"I can read, write, and figure out when someone is trying to cheat me out of money. I will not go to school," she said in monotone, and she finally looked up.

Carol thought her heart would break when she saw Danielle's eyes. They weren't the eyes of a pretty little teenage girl; they had the look one would expect in a hardened warrior—cold, fierce, and knowing. "Well, we will give you all a few days to settle in, and then you can decide what you would like to do," Carol said. "If you will follow us, we will show you to your new home."

"Look, lady; we aren't going anywhere with you until we know exactly where we are and what you want with us," one of the three men said insolently.

"What he is saying is that whatever games you are playing here, we aren't playing; you can just turn us loose," another of the men said sarcastically.

All of them—the three men and six women—glared at Carol with hate and defiance. Carol stepped back in confusion, and Shelly exploded. "What do we want with you?" she said, stepping closer to the table, her eyes glittering, her hands on her hips, and her chin slightly jutting out. "I'll tell you what we want with you. The human race is close to extinction; we want your sperm." She jabbed her finger at the men. "And we want your eggs." She jabbed her finger at the women. "We want you to blend in with this society and work for yourselves. We know how hard you have had it the past six months, and we know of the hideous conditions you were forced to survive in. You are out of that now. However, if you want to wallow in the depravities and evils of the past, that is your choice. Or you can choose to take advantage of the opportunities offered here and rise above what you have been through."

"Where are we? Your guess is as good as the guesses of the rest of the people here. No one knows exactly where we are. Everyone was brought here in the same manner as you were. You want turned loose? Well, don't we all. This entire valley is enclosed within a barrier that was erected to keep out the virus. The barrier won't come down until the danger of infection has passed. What we won't allow is disrespect and surliness from a group of people we are trying to help."

Sergeant and Scott Cutter stepped into the dormitory. "What?" Shelly yelled at them.

"It sounded like you might need some assistance," Sergeant said.

Shelly looked at those still sitting at the table. "Do we need the help of security here?" she asked.

A woman stood. "I'm Lucy, Danielle's mother," the woman said. "The last time people took us in claiming they only wanted to help us, they made us prisoners and used us. Monica's baby died when one of them shook him too hard because he was crying. See what they did to my baby." She barely caught the sob that escaped as she stroked Danielle's hair.

Shelly gathered Lucy in her arms, her voice softening, and said gently, "We know. We wish to God we could have gotten you out of there sooner. However, you are safe here. No one will force you to do anything. Those two guys over there are here for your protection. Please give us a few days and see for yourselves that we are everything we say we are."

Lucy looked at the others, and all lowered their heads. Then she looked back at Shelly, her eyes still full of wariness. "We will go with you."

Carol stepped forward. "We thought to take you the back way, but we can go through the restaurant, and you can see a little bit of what is here. There will be more people if we go through the restaurant, and it's only natural that they will stare at you. It's your choice."

CHAPTER 40

Lucy squared her shoulders. "If we are going to be part of this place, we might as well see what we are in for."

They departed the dormitory, going into the restaurant. Carol took the lead, with Shelly bringing up the rear. Sergeant fell in next to Shelly. "Do you want me to call for carts?" he asked.

"No. If they walk to their apartments, they may feel easier walking away from them."

They both stood back as Carol explained the plaza, the shops, the kiosk, and the tricycles next to the cake shop. "She's in her element," Sergeant commented.

"She's good at it," Shelly agreed.

Carol put two of the men in a two-bedroom apartment; one man and one woman got another two-bedroom apartment. The rest of the women wanted to stay together and were given a large corner apartment. They were shown how to access the computers and were urged to make calls if they had any questions or needed anything. Sergeant was waiting in the street for Shelly and Carol. When the two emerged from the last apartment, Shelly went to him and put her arm around his waist. The door to the apartment she and Carol had just left opened. The five women stood staring at them. "Is there something more we can help you with?" Carol asked.

Lucy took a step forward. "It doesn't lock."

"I don't think there are locks anywhere in Cave Haven," Carol said, looking to Sergeant for confirmation. Sergeant shook his head. "The only thing close to a lock is on the tricycles," Carol continued. "And I think that is mainly to keep the children from riding them."

"Then can we have a gun?" Lucy asked.

"There are no guns here," Sergeant replied.

Lucy looked at him skeptically.

"Would you feel better if I brought someone from Maintenance to look and see if he can install some kind of lock?" he asked gently.

"I don't think any of us will be able to sleep knowing that someone can walk right in at any time and that we have no way to protect ourselves," Lucy said earnestly.

Sergeant nodded. "I will bring him by in a couple of hours," he promised.

The next few months went smoothly. The winter was brutally cold. The cave was warm and snug. Weavers made use of sheep and llama wool. Rosa made use of the rolls of woolen fabric. Cattle found shelter next to the mountain. A sled had been fashioned out of one of the big wagons, and four of Grace's draft horses were used to transport hay out to the cattle. The work was hard, but few complained. The president gave an inspiring speech, and Judge Barker was elected mayor. Gold was mined, and coins were minted. With the people earning wages and paying for what was needed, parties became simple affairs rarely using more space than provided in the dormitory. The pregnant women were close to having their babies, and the doctor marveled at how well the pregnancies were going. Jake had decided to serve his first four months with the shepherds, figuring that since Golly was already working with the sheep, he might as well join him. Despite their age difference, Amy and Karla were best friends and received the first of the Taggart dolls.

The slave group accepted the jobs they were offered without complaint. They worked hard and were always polite when spoken to, but they kept themselves apart from the community. They also refused speak or answer questions about who had held them captive. The women hadn't gotten a lock on their door, but they settled for large hunting knives. Danielle continued to adamantly refuse to attend school. The judge finally declared her an emancipated minor. She showed an interest in and talent for art, and Mary Sanders grudgingly agreed to take her as an assistant. The first project Mary gave her required a knowledge of geometry. To keep her job with Mary, Danielle had agreed to go to school, stipulating she would only go half a day, not knowing when she demanded the stipulation that starting at the age of twelve, children went to school for only half the day.

It was just after 2:00 a.m. when Shelly woke Sergeant, telling him it was time to go to the clinic. Sergeant calmly called for a cab and checked on Jake and Amy. Just as he was thinking about calling Grace, Shelly called from the bedroom. He went to see what she needed. "You'd better get help; this baby is coming," she said tightly, her eyes frantic.

Sergeant leaned down and pushed a tangle of hair off her sweaty brow, saying condescendingly, "You're all right, sweetie; babies take a while to get born. We have plenty of time."

Shelly's eyes turned wild. She reached up and grabbed the front of his nightshirt, pulling him down so his face was inches from hers, and yelled. "Listen, you blasted dimwitted man; I've had two other babies, and I'm telling you this baby is coming! Scrub your hands and get some towels. Now!"

"Now?" Sergeant said, baffled.

"Now," Shelly said, trying to stifle a groan as she lay back in the bed.

Sergeant ran straight to the computer and called Grace. As soon as she came on the line, Sergeant yelled, "Help!"

When Grace waddled into Shelly's bedroom, she found Sergeant holding his newborn son and staring at him with a look of wonder on his face. Grace went to Shelly. "I've called the doctor," she said. "He will be here any minute."

Sergeant looked at the woman, saying with disbelief, "He came so fast."

Grace took the baby, laid him on Shelly's breast, and covered him with a clean towel. "I'll fix a warm bath for the baby. Sergeant, why don't you go wash up and wait for the doctor. You might also tell the cabdriver he won't be needed."

Sergeant nodded and backed toward the door. "Should I wake Jake and Amy?"

Shelly was counting fingers and toes on her new baby and didn't look up when she said, "No, let them sleep. They can meet their new brother in the morning."

The doctor had just finished examining Shelly when Grace handed him the clean baby to check. When Shelly had the baby wrapped and back in her arms, the doctor asked, "How do you feel?"

"Tired, but I really feel pretty good," she replied.

The doctor nodded. "Shelly, you are the fourth of the implanted woman to deliver. Roberta's twin girls came a couple weeks early. The babies were a little small, but we had time to get her to the clinic. The other two births were like yours; one barely made it to the clinic, and the other was delivered in the cab cart. As soon as you feel up to it, will you send the other implanted women an alert on the computer? Tell them not to try to make it to the clinic. They are to call me as soon as they feel the first labor pain if they want any chance of having a doctor attend the birth. Also, I will have the nurses put together birthing kits they are to keep handy in case I can't get to them in time."

Sergeant and Grace came back into the bedroom after the doctor had left. Shelly lay admiring the tiny baby tucked into the crook of her arm.

Sergeant sat on the edge of the bed, gently stroking the tuft of hair on top of the baby's head. "Have you got a name for him?" Grace whispered.

"Trey Douglas, if that's all right with Sergeant," Shelly said.

"I think it fits him perfectly because we sure scored here tonight," Sergeant said without looking up.

"Scored?" Shelly asked, confused.

"You know, Trey Douglas—initials T. D., as in 'touchdown.'"

When the women remained silent, Sergeant looked up to see blank expressions on their faces.

"Like in football," he said.

Shelly and Grace rolled their eyes at each other as comprehension finally dawned on them.

Three nights after Trey's birth, Shelly sat in the dim light that filtered through the drapes from the streetlights. She was sitting in the rocking chair that Sergeant had brought home and placed in the living room. The baby had just finished his meal. This was the first night Sergeant hadn't woken instantly when the baby cried. Shelly was about to take the satisfied baby back to his crib when she heard a soft melodious voice in her mind. "Shelly, may we come and see the baby?"

"Patience," Shelly sent. "Of course. When?"

"Now," Funny sent as the door slid open.

Patience, Strong, Funny, Curious, General, and Dr. Grouch entered the living room. They were dressed as they had been the day she first met them, but none were glowing. The six of them gathered around the chair, each gently touching the baby. "Would you like to hold him?" Shelly asked, handing Trey to Patience.

Patience cradled the baby carefully, turned to the others, and moved to the center of the room. They gathered around her, each laying a hand on the baby. Shelly watched as tiny motes of light swirled around them. The tiny lights didn't increase in size, but their numbers continued to multiply. The keepers seemed to meld together. The lights became so numerous that, as they spun and danced, the group blurred, appearing to be one bright star. Shelly realized she was witnessing the visual manifestation of the beauty of love in its purest form. She understood for the first time just how far her species had yet to evolve. Slowly, the tiny lights diminished. When they were gone completely, Patience handed the baby back to Shelly.

"You have no idea what this has meant to us," Patience sent to Shelly. "Thank you."

Shelly smiled and then gasped at the dark figure of Sergeant, who was standing just inside the living room doorway. He strode quickly to her side and then turned, looking at the six keepers. "Who are you?" he demanded, stepping in front of Shelly.

CHAPTER 41

"We are the keepers; you should not be awake," Grandfather said as force fields began to glow.

"Better known to you as the elder group," Shelly said, with a resigned sigh. "This one you know as General Elder." Shelly indicated Grandfather.

Sergeant stepped over and turned on a lamp. Then he grabbed the back of the rocker to steady himself. "You are not human," he said in a shaky voice.

Shelly heard Funny's familiar chuckle as he and Strong methodically set dining room chairs around the rocker and gave one to Sergeant. When they were all seated, Misty jumped into Curious's lap, and Jessie into Funny's lap. Golly lay with his head resting on Strong's feet. "Did you honestly believe humans could build all of this?" Grandfather asked peacefully.

Sergeant thought for a moment. "I had a hard time believing this entire place could be built in secret," he answered. "I had a harder time understanding why Shelly was so secretive about you. Now that I think back on it, she never said you were human. I should have figured it out. It all falls into place now. Though I would like to know how you built all of this in such a short amount of time."

Grandfather was silent for a time before answering carefully. "Most of the inner structure was completed hundreds of years ago. We mainly converted and stocked it for your use."

"So who used this place hundreds of years ago?" Sergeant asked.

"You are forbidden that information," Grandfather said immediately.

"Grandfather," Shelly asked aloud. "How is it that Sergeant was able to wake up tonight?"

"He should not have," Grandfather said. "Your species continues to surprise us. We are coming to the realization that much of what we do not understand about your species concerns your primordial instincts. Your individual survival depends on your emotions—anger and fear being primary. We also do not understand this obsession that drives you to assert your individuality. We survive as a unit. We have assiduously worked as a unit over tens of thousands of years to contain emotions."

"Grandfather, it is obvious that you love babies," Shelly said. "Why don't you have them?"

"We have babies," Grandfather said. "Because of our longevity, our reproduction is much different than yours. It is not until a part of our unit dies that another is conceived."

"Then your population never grows?" Shelly asked.

"If our unit has a need, more babies are conceived. However, this is a very rare occurrence."

Shelly thought of Grace and Roberta, and how they had longed for a child. She remembered the pain of that longing in Grace's face from the first time she saw Jake and Amy. She thought of that pain multiplied in the keepers and felt a surge of pity for them.

"How long have you watched over our planet?" Sergeant asked.

"We are not permitted to give you that information," Grandfather replied.

"Do you always have someone here?" the sergeant asked.

"Your planet is under constant surveillance," Grandfather said.

Sergeant rubbed the back of his neck and then said, "I don't see why you have to keep so much secret."

Grandfather answered slowly. "In the past, your species was given information you were not ready for. Much of that information was misused and lost. We will only tell you what you are ready to know."

"Grandfather, are you going to allow him to remember this meeting?" Shelly sent.

"Yes, we have felt the pain you feel in keeping us secret from him. You are advanced among your species. We trust you, and we trust his discretion," Grandfather sent.

As the keepers rose from their chairs, Grandfather said aloud, "The ability your baby possessed was already strong, but our combined bonding with him has had the unexpected side effect of adding strength to his abilities. This bonding was not our intention. In fact, it is forbidden. However, we did not foresee what occurred between the baby and us. We were unaware it was even possible. This is another first for us, it seems, where your species is concerned. Since the bonding was not intentional, we are not permitted to remove consequences. It will be up to the two of you to nurture his abilities and prepare Amy and Jake. Soon they will begin to hear him. As he grows older, he will also develop the ability of telekinesis. Your master huntsman will be able to instruct him in its use."

"Jim Lightfoot can use telekinesis?" Sergeant asked.

"Of course," Grandfather said. "That is how he avoided injury when the tree limb broke and fell on him"

Force fields were dropped, and Shelly received hugs from each of the keepers. Sergeant received gentle handshakes. The keepers left silently. Sergeant glanced at Shelly and then ran to the door. He got it open just in time to see Funny pass through what looked to him to be a solid wall. He quickly walked to the wall where the keepers had disappeared. As he felt the wall for some sign of a doorway, Shelly came and stood next to him.

"They just walked through solid rock," he said in amazement.

"No they didn't," Shelly said. "There is a door there."

Sergeant started to argue, but Shelly held up her hand. "Trust me, there is a door there, and it's not the only door in Cave Haven that can't be distinguished."

Sergeant shook his head. "How do they do that?"

Shelly smiled, shrugged, and said, imitating General, "We are not permitted to disclose that information." She heard Funny chuckle.

"Do you think he tried to mislead us?" Sergeant asked when they had returned to the apartment.

"About what?" she asked.

"When I asked if they always have someone here, he could have just said yes, but he said we were always under surveillance."

"First you have to try to stop seeing them as individuals," she said. "They are part of a whole, with subtle differing traits. I don't think they have it in their makeup to mislead, but sometimes when they speak, the entire meaning isn't conveyed. I call it a cross-species thing."

Shelly went on to tell him about the misunderstanding there had been concerning the babies, and how angry she had been because they hadn't told her ahead of time. She also explained how confused they were at her anger because they were sure they had taken the proper action to multiply the numbers of the survivors.

"What were they talking about when he said their combined bonding had strengthened Trey?" the sergeant asked.

"How long were you standing there before you came over to me?" she asked.

"Just a second or two," he answered.

Shelly described, as best she could, the light show he had missed.

"I wish now I had seen it, but at the time, I may have done something really stupid."

Shelly shuddered at the thought of what Sergeant might have done, and what might have happened to him and the baby the they were holding if all the keepers had activated their force fields at the same moment.

"What I don't understand is why they even made contact with you," Sergeant said. "They could have picked you up and dropped you like they did the rest of us."

"I think because they desperately wanted this community to be started in a certain way," she said thoughtfully. "And they want to understand us. They knew Roberta had problems, but they couldn't conceive of greed, class envy, or deceit. They truly want us to evolve, but they are very limited in their knowledge of how that evolution takes place."

"Well, Mrs. Williams," he said, planting a light kiss on her forehead. "It sounds as if they have had thousands of years to figure us out but haven't managed it, so we sure aren't going to figure them out in one night. Shall we put this little guy to bed and try to catch a couple hours of sleep?"

"Sounds like a plan to me," she agreed as they moved toward their bedroom.

Sergeant let Shelly sleep in the next morning, getting Jake and Amy off to school himself. He had already left by the time Trey woke her with a demanding cry for breakfast. When Trey had been fed and bathed and was back to sleep, she contemplated a short nap, but her craving was interrupted when the computer pinged. Shelly sat at the computer and was pleased to see Grace smiling calmly from the screen. "Hi, what are you up to?" Shelly asked.

"Oh, not much. I just called Doctor Murphy, and I'm pretty sure my baby is coming."

"I'll be right there!" Shelly said, excitedly jumping up.

She ran to the counter and quickly scribbled a short note as to where she was going. She gathered up some diapers and clean baby gowns, stuffing them in a large tote bag. She swaddled Trey in a baby blanket, and they were out the door.

Dr. Murphy was just climbing out of a cab cart as Shelly and Trey arrived. "Nice outfit," he said offhandedly as he waved open Grace's door.

Shelly looked down at what she was wearing as she followed him in. "Oh, I guess I forgot to get dressed," she giggled in embarrassment, realizing she was still in her nightgown. It was the one Sergeant was partial to. Rosa has designed it to make nursing easier.

"If you guys will quit your jabbering, I could maybe use a little help in here!" Grace yelled.

Dr. Murphy didn't slow on his way to the bedroom, while Shelly had to stop to deposit the tote and carefully lay Trey in the crib that Grace had readied for her own coming baby. She scrubbed her hands and went into Grace's bedroom. The doctor handed her a squirming baby boy with orders to clean him. Shelly had the baby ready to hand to Grace as the doctor snapped his bag closed. "You're leaving already?" Grace asked.

Dr. Murphy looked at her tiredly. "You're healthy; he's healthy," he said. "All I am at these births is a catcher. Call if you have a problem. If I hurry, I may get a couple hours' sleep before I have to race to catch the next one. He's a good-looking boy. Biggest baby I have ever delivered. You got a name for him yet?"

Grace smiled tenderly at her baby. "His name is Heath Jarred Foley."

The doctor nodded as he left, mumbling, "A good name ... sounds familiar."

"Can I get anything for you, Momma?" Shelly asked softly.

Grace grinned. "I am a momma now, aren't I."

Shelly smiled, nodding. "I know I'm supposed to be tired," Grace said, "But I'm about starved to death."

Shelly laughed. "I know exactly what you mean."

CHAPTER 42

Shelly went to the kitchen where she found next to nothing in the way of fresh food. "Her stable kitchen is probably better stocked that this one," Shelly thought as she called Zeke. Then she called Christy, giving her the news of the new baby. Shelly busied herself around the apartment while waiting for the food to arrive. She knew how important it was for Grace to have some alone time to bond with her baby. She looked at some folders lying open on the table that Grace had been working on. The name of a horse was printed across the top of each folder. They included drawings of the horses that detailed markings and scars. There were also lists of dietary needs, training routines, habits, and rider preferences. A light tap on the door signaled food delivery.

Shelly waved the door open and found Zeke carrying a tray piled with so much food he could barely see over it. He set the tray on the counter and turned to go but took the time to look Shelly up and down. "That Sergeant is one lucky man," Zeke said, and he hurried out the door.

Shelly's face was still burning red from embarrassment when she carried a tray of food to Grace. "Do you have an extra nightshirt I can borrow? Shelly asked.

Grace laughed at her. "What are you so embarrassed about? That nightgown covers every bit of you."

"Oh, come on, Grace; you know perfectly well that a see-through negligee wouldn't reveal as much as a Rosa original design hints at," Shelly responded.

"Oh, stop worrying; it probably did Zeke some good. After all, he's not attached. Is he?"

"No, he's so busy with the restaurant, I doubt he has had time to even think in that direction," Shelly said, eying Grace carefully.

"Yes, busy like me," Grace cooed to her sleeping baby as her own eyelids drooped.

Shelly eased Heath out of Grace's arms and tiptoed out of the room. "So Grace has a thing for Zeke," she thought.

Shelly was backing out of the nursery, where she had put Heath in the crib with Trey, when Christy lumbered into the apartment. She was wearing the extra-long tunic that Rosa had designed for the very pregnant women. Shelly noticed Christy rubbing her back.

"Sorry it took me so long," Christy said, still rubbing her back, "but I had to take Kerry to the nursery."

"What's wrong with your back?" Shelly asked, concerned.

"I don't know; it started aching when I was about halfway here," Christy said, now rubbing her back with both hands.

"Christy, you're in labor," Shelly said, frantically trying to remember where she had seen the birthing kit the doctor had sent to all the pregnant women.

"Oh, I'm not in labor. I was in labor for over sixteen hours with my last baby. Believe me; I know what labor …"

Christy stopped talking mid-sentence. She groaned and grabbed her swollen belly. Her eyes widened in sudden panic as she doubled over. "Shelly, I think this baby is coming!" she said as she lowered herself into a chair.

"Get your underwear off," Shelly ordered, coming back from Grace's bathroom with the birthing kit.

A knock at the door caused Shelly to say a word she thought she had erased from her vocabulary. "Come in!" she yelled.

Sergeant came in the apartment and stopped as he took in the scene before him. Christy was sitting on the edge of a chair with her tunic hiked up to her waist, and Shelly's shaking hands were trying to get the birthing kit open. He calmly took the birthing kit, untied it, and told Shelly to get the biggest bowl or pan she could find. He squatted down to check the baby's progress and nearly dropped the slippery baby that shot at him along with birthing fluids that rained on his tunic, his pants, his shoes, and the floor. He looked up to see Shelly standing next to him with a large roasting pan, biting her bottom lip. "Some towels would be good right now," he said, glancing from the wiggling gooey baby to the roasting pan.

Shelly quickly handed him some kitchen towels and then ran to fetch more from Grace's bathroom. As she tiptoed through the bedroom with the towels, Grace rose up and propped herself on one elbow. "What's going on?" she asked sleepily.

"Christy is here," Shelly answered.

"And she needs towels because?" Grace asked as her eyes fluttered closed.

"She just had her baby all over Sergeant," Shelly said, repressing the urge to giggle aloud.

"Sounds like y'all are having fun," Grace muttered as she snuggled down into the blankets.

Grace came fully awake when Shelly shook her gently, telling her to move over so Christy and her baby could lie down. Grace looked at Christy and the baby and asked, "Did you really have that baby all over Sergeant? I thought I was dreaming."

"Oh, shut up," Christy said testily. "I don't think I will ever be able to look at Sergeant in the eyes again."

Shelly quickly told Grace about Christy's delivery, and by the time she was done, even Christy could see the humor in it and was laughing. Sergeant stepped into the room, and all three women stopped laughing, but their eyes glittered with humor. "I'm never going to live this down, am I?" Sergeant asked. The three women shook their heads slowly. "I don't suppose any of you would promise not to tell anybody about it." Again the three women shook their heads. Sergeant sighed and hung his head.

"There's one thing I want to know," Grace said. "What was going through your mind when you looked at the baby and then looked at the roasting pan Shelly was holding?"

"I don't know; I think I was just looking for a place to put the baby while I cut the cord," he answered, confused by the question.

Suddenly his eyes widened in disgust. "You girls are sick," he said.

Peals of laughter followed him as he turned and left the room.

Shelly and Grace focused their attention on Christy's new baby. "What's his name?" Shelly asked.

"I always liked the name of Conner for a boy," Christy said.

"So when are you going to turn Conner over to the nursery?" Grace asked.

"What, are you nuts!" Christy said as she held the baby protectively close.

"I thought you said you didn't want a baby," Grace stated.

"Lordy, when did you ever listen to drivel? Nobody is going to get my little Conny." Christy babbled in baby talk as she brushed a kiss across Conner's forehead.

"Be careful what you nickname him," Grace cautioned. "What might be cute for a baby may not fit a growing boy."

Shelly stayed with Grace and Christy until another woman arrived to relieve her. She made a mental note to thank the doctor for being conscientious enough to think of her. She hadn't minded staying with them, but she was sleepy herself after missing so much sleep the night before.

The first thing she noticed when she walked into her apartment was the red light blinking on the radio. Jessie wiggled and whined, following her across the room to the radio. Still holding the baby, she reached down and flipped it on.

"Anybody out there listening? We have women and children here that need food. Can anybody hear me? We need help. Our food supplies are almost gone. This is Raven Compound. Is anybody out there listening? We have women and children here that need food. Can anybody hear me?"

Shelly turned the radio off. It was obviously a recorded message. She nursed Trey, changed his diaper, and then laid him in the cradle in her bedroom before she sat down at the computer to call the sergeant. Jim Anders answered and told her he would have Sergeant contact her. A few moments later, the computer pinged.

"Everything all right?" Sergeant asked as soon as he saw her.

Shelly assured him everything was fine, and she then filled him in on the recorded message. He offered to come home, but Shelly told him there was no hurry, as she was going to take a nap.

Shelly woke refreshed a couple hours later. She decided on a quick shower after she checked Trey and found him still asleep. She had just finished dressing when Trey started fussing.

Sergeant found her sitting cross-legged on the bed, feeding the baby. Misty was lying at the foot of the bed, observing the mother and baby. "Mayor Barker and the president are waiting," Sergeant said as he brushed fingertips across Trey's head. "I told them about the broadcast, and they are interested."

"I'll be out as soon as this little guy gets his belly full," she said. "Where are Jake, Amy, and the dogs?"

"Christy sent Karla over for the night. She and Amy went to tell the Taggarts about the new babies. Jake and Golly haven't come in from work yet, and Jessie is sitting in the president's lap," he answered, kissing her forehead before he left the room.

When Trey had finished eating, had been burped, and had had his diaper changed, Shelly went to join the men. She handed Trey to Sergeant, sat at the radio, and flipped it on. "Shelly Williams at Cave Haven. We hear you, Raven Compound; come back."

They waited a few minutes, and then Shelly sent out the call again. "Cave Haven, this is Raven Compound; can you help us somehow?"

"What is your location, Raven Compound?"

"We are in northern Wyoming."

"How many in your compound?"

"We have close to seventy-five."

"We will have to try to figure out logistics and get back with you, Raven."

"If you have food, we can send men to pick it up."

"We will have to get back with you, Raven."

"Do you have food, Cave Haven?"

"We have food, Raven. Getting it to you safely may be the problem."

"Where are you? We will come and pick it up."

"Raven, we have to figure out how to get it to you and stay away from the cities."

"We will stay out of cities."

"Sorry, Raven, we have to be assured diseases are not carried to us."

"Cave Haven, we have women and children here that are hungry."

"Acknowledged, Raven. Cave Haven, signing off."

Shelly turned the radio off and sat back.

"They sound desperate," the president said, rubbing his lower lip.

"Something's off," Mayor Barker said.

"What's your opinion, Shelly?" the president asked.

"I guess it's like the mayor says," she answered. "Something feels off."

"There is something to be said for listening to your instincts," Sergeant commented. "I'd like to hear what Lightfoot thinks about this group."

"Here, nine o'clock tomorrow morning," the president said.

CHAPTER 43

"So how was your day?" Shelly asked Sergeant as she went to the kitchen to start dinner.

"Pretty good. I delivered another baby."

"You're kidding," she said.

"Nope; the lady was in Zeke's place. We barely got her into the dormitory. Now, I know I'm just a dimwitted man, and I don't know a lot about this stuff, but shouldn't babies take longer to get born?"

Shelly leaned against the counter, watching the huge man and tiny baby bond. Trey had a hold on Sergeant's finger. Sergeant was smiling down at Trey, talking quiet nonsense.

"General," Shelly thought.

"You have a question?" General responded.

"I'd like to ask the healer something," Shelly thought.

"You have a question?" the healer sent snappily.

"The babies are being born," Shelly sent. "Once labor starts, they are coming very quickly. Did you change something in us?"

"Nothing was changed," the healer replied. "Slight adjustments were made."

"But I understand you are forbidden to change us," Shelly sent.

"Adjustments were made, not changes," the healer thought back. "You would prefer to have your sixty-year-old women endure hours of labor? We made slight adjustments; that is all," the healer stated testily.

"Thank you, healer," Shelly sent, but she knew she was already gone.

"So what did he say?" Sergeant asked.

"I talked to Dr. Grouch, and she said slight adjustments were made."

Sergeant frowned. "I thought they weren't supposed to change us."

"You would prefer to have your sixty-year-old women endure hours of labor?" Shelly said, imitating the grouchy attitude of the healer. Sergeant's eyes widened at her tone of voice. Shelly laughed. "That's how Dr. Grouch sounded when I said the same thing you just said."

"Well, it sounds to me like they are breaking some rules for us," Sergeant said.

"I think they are more bending than breaking," Shelly replied. "And it's only on things that won't have an impact on our evolution as a species."

Jake and Golly burst through the door. Jake announced that he was starved as he headed for a shower. Golly went straight to the water bowl, paying no attention to Jessie bouncing her front feet off of him, whining and wiggling her welcome as he drank. Amy and Karla came in talking and giggling. "Mrs. Taggart sent baby Trey a toy," Amy said, holding up a small stuffed elephant.

Shelly examined the toy closely. The body was soft and squeezable, but the legs and trunk were fairly hard. It didn't have a tail. It was a perfect baby toy, and Shelly wondered if the Taggarts were ready for the hoard of new mothers and fathers that would soon be descending on them.

The men arrived promptly at nine o'clock the next morning. They sat at the table and went back over the call from Raven Compound, mainly for Jim Lightfoot's benefit.

"Any thoughts?" Mayor Barker asked Jim.

"Mayor, how many citizens do we have at Cave Haven?"

"Twelve thousand eight hundred sixty-two, not counting the president's party, the nine former slaves, and the new babies that are popping out everywhere."

Jim nodded. "Most people in Cave Haven know our population number is twelve thousand eight hundred sixty-two, but they say their population is close to seventy-five. And they don't say 'shelter'; they say 'compound.' That sounds like militia to me."

President Williamson rubbed his bottom lip, considering Jim's answer. "Can't really blame them for not being completely honest; after all, we weren't. But I don't see how we can get food to them over mountains in the dead of winter."

"I think I could make it with llamas," Jim said.

"Sergeant, can you get whoever it is that handles the llamas here?" the president said. "And maybe we should ask Zeke his opinion on what foods will travel best."

"General," Shelly sent.

"You have a question?" General responded.

"Can you help us get food to people north of here?" she sent.

"No," General answered. "You have information on your computer that will assist you."

Shelly went to the computer and started looking through the files. "What did he say?" Jim sent.

"They won't help, but General said there is information on here that will. I just don't know what I should be looking for."

"Maps would help," he sent.

"Got them. We have some pretty good maps here," she said aloud.

She gave Jim her seat, and the other men gathered around. She checked Trey, who was awake in the cradle Sergeant had brought to the living room. She took Trey to her bedroom to feed him and change his diaper, leaving the men to work out the logistics.

Zeke and the ovine administrator, Eric Dalton, were there when Shelly came back into the living room. She sat on the sofa with the baby, listening quietly to their discussion. "We need to know exactly where they are if we are going to plan this," Jim said, studying the map.

Shelly moved to the radio. "Raven Compound, this is Cave Haven calling. Are you there?"

"We are here, Cave Haven," the speaker barked. "Are you bringing food?"

"We need to know where you are to be able to plan the trip, Raven."

There was silence for a few moments. "We are just west of Cody, Wyoming," the male voice on the radio said.

"Thank you, Raven," Shelly said. "We will get back to you when plans have been finalized."

"Tell us where you are, Cave Haven. We can pick up the supplies."

"We will get back to you, Raven. Signing off."

Shelly turned off the radio, hiding the shiver of foreboding that ran through her. Jim studied the map. "It looks like the hardest part of the trip will be getting out of this valley. They want to pick up the supplies. We could take them to Thermopolis. It makes our trip a bit closer, but it's still far enough away to keep them from stumbling upon us anytime soon."

"The llamas shouldn't have a problem, although it's still hard to figure out how long it will take us to get there," Eric said.

Jim's head jerked up as he said, "What do you mean 'us'?"

"Well, you don't think you can handle three or four llamas by yourself, do you? Besides, there is no way I would let them go without me," Eric answered firmly.

"I won't be alone; I was planning on taking Larry with me."

"Well, it looks like there will be three of us then," Eric stated.

"Make that four; I'm going with you," Sergeant interjected.

Shelly sat, biting her tongue, while the president asked Zeke about the food supplies. "I have plenty of dehydrated fruits and vegetables, flour, and dried beans. There's quite a bit of powdered milk we don't use. Frozen meat would be heavy, but I have some jerky. That should get them through the winter," Zeke said. He scratched his head before adding, "Shame we couldn't take them a cow. Those kids could use the butterfat."

"Why couldn't we take them a cow? A Guernsey is a docile and hardy breed and can go about anywhere a llama can," Eric said.

Jim shook his head. "I don't know. If this party gets any bigger, we will have a problem feeding everybody on the way there and back. And how would they feed a cow once they had her?"

Eric shrugged. "It was a thought. Maybe we can give them a cow in the spring."

"So you want to just meet them in Thermopolis?" Mayor Barker asked.

Sergeant had been studying the satellite map. Pointing, he said, "Here is a house with outbuildings just before you get to Thermopolis on Highway Twenty. We can drop off the supplies there and then call Raven to pick them up. We should be well gone by the time Raven's people get there."

President Williamson looked around at them. "Do we have a consensus on this plan?" They all nodded their agreement. "Then let's do it," he said, clapping and then rubbing his hands together.

The next morning, the men gathered at the sheep barn. Four llamas had been loaded with food. The men wore leather parkas, leather pants, mittens, and knee-high boots. All the clothes were lined with a blend of sheep and llama wool. They waited patiently while Eric made a final check of the packs on the llamas, making sure straps were tight and packs were well balanced. Shelly looked up at Sergeant and whispered, "I wish you weren't going."

"We all wish we weren't going," he said softly as he hugged her close.

Shelly pulled Jim aside. "Contact me often, and let me know when you get there. I'm counting on you to bring him back."

Jim nodded. "You know I'll do my best."

Rosa walked up to them and touched Jim's arm, saying, "Larry thought you wanted to go through everyone's pack once more before you headed out."

When Jim had walked off, Rosa put her arm around Shelly. "They are going to be all right."

Shelly gave her a strained smile. "I know, but I sure will feel a whole lot better when they get back."

After almost a week, Shelly felt as if she wanted to scream. Jim had contacted her daily, which had been some comfort, but she couldn't shake the uneasiness that hung over her like a black cloud. Shelly was in the laundry room, unloading the dryer, when Jim sent, "Shelly, we are here at the house."

"Is everyone all right?" she sent back.

"Yes. We are going to spend the night here, warm up, and leave tomorrow."

"Warm up? Does the house have a fireplace?" Shelly sent.

"No, propane," he replied. "We have the burners on the stove lit; it's already starting to heat up. I just hope the llamas don't make too much of a mess on the floor."

"Are you saying you have the llamas in the house?" Shelly asked, trying not to laugh.

"Eric insisted. It's not too bad; we put them in the dining room. I'll let you know when we leave. Talk to you tomorrow."

"Okay, give Sergeant a hug for me," she sent, not wanting to break the contact.

"I absolutely will not," Jim replied, and then he was gone.

Shelly wrapped her arms around herself, trying not to cry, and wondered when her feelings for Sergeant had grown so strong.

Jim contacted her the next morning, letting her know they were leaving. They had tied a blue-and-yellow striped scarf to a telephone pole across the highway from the house. She could contact Raven and let them know where the food could be picked up. "Raven Compound, this is Cave Haven. Come in, please."

"This is Raven," the male voice on the radio said. "Are you bringing food?"

"Raven, the food has been left in a house a couple miles south of Thermopolis on Highway Twenty," Shelly said. "A blue-and-yellow scarf has been tied to a pole to mark the house."

"Thank you, Cave Haven. We are leaving immediately. See you soon. Raven out."

Shelly sat and stared at the radio. She had a bad feeling about the "See you soon" comment. She wished she could contact Jim, but she wasn't strong enough; she was going to have to wait for him to contact her.

CHAPTER 44

Shelly was slicing bread for dinner, but she stopped when she heard Jim's voice in her mind say, "Shelly, we are being tracked."

"By who?" Shelly sent.

"We're pretty sure it's the Ravens," Jim answered.

"But how could they get there so quickly from Cody?" she asked.

"They probably lied about their location," he responded.

"Can't you lose them?"

"That would be a piece of cake. It's the dogs we can't shake."

"Dogs?" she asked, not sure she understood.

"Sounds like a dozen or more," he sent. "They are getting close."

"General," Shelly called.

"You have a question?" General answered.

"They went to deliver food, and there are dogs after them. Help them, please," Shelly begged.

"We cannot help the men," General sent. "Tell them to let the dogs catch them."

"What!" Shelly thought, in panic.

"The dogs are not sentient. We are permitted to use persuasion on the dogs."

"Jim, are you still there?" Shelly sent, praying he was there.

"Yes," Jim sent. "I know you talked to the general, but I could only hear your end of the conversation."

"He said to let the dogs catch you," Shelly sent. "They can't help you, but they can work with the dogs."

"Are you sure about this?" Jim sent.

"Have you got a choice?" she responded.

"No, and the dogs have quit barking," he sent back.

"Jim," Shelly replied, but she knew Jim had left her. She realized Jake, Amy, and Karla were staring at her. She smiled tightly. "Just some disturbing thoughts running through my mind."

It was over three hours before Jim contacted her again. "We're all right. There are fourteen German shepherds that are now our best friends. It's snowing pretty heavy. Sergeant and the others have gone on ahead. The Ravens kept some dogs on leashes; I used some beef jerky to lay a false trail, and circled around behind them. They have a small army out here—must be at least twenty-five, all well armed. They have stopped and made camp for the night. They're not as good in the woods as they think they are. The bonfires they have built are not going to keep them warm. They were not expecting to spend the night in the woods and didn't come prepared. They didn't bring food or proper equipment, and they are arguing with each other."

"Jim, how close are you to them?" Shelly sent.

"Very close. The dogs know I'm here, but they are being quiet about it. The Ravens beat a couple of them because they didn't find us."

"Jim, you need to leave now," Shelly sent. "We can't afford to lose you."

"They are pretty much settled in," Jim sent. "They tied the dogs away from the camp; I'm not going to leave them behind."

"Jim, are you crazy? Why risk getting caught for some dogs?" Shelly sent.

"Because they may use them tomorrow to come after us. It's the only way I can be sure they can't follow us. But before I go near them, do you think you could ask the general if these dogs will come with me?" Jim requested.

"General," Shelly called.

"You have a question?" General replied.

"Do you know where Jim is and what he is contemplating?" she asked.

"We have been following his choices," General answered.

"The dogs in the camp—have you used persuasion on them? Will the dogs go quietly with Jim?" she asked.

"Yes," General answered simply.

"Thank you, General," she sent. "Jim, the dogs will go with you."

Shelly felt Jim leave. She went and checked on Trey; he was sleeping. She started to the kitchen to fix a cup of tea.

"Shelly, you aren't going to believe this," Jim sent. "I crawled over to the dogs, unclasped them from their chains, and then started crawling away. I looked back, and all six dogs were crawling in line behind me. I nearly laughed out loud. We're away from the camp now; these dogs are moving like shadows. Go to bed, Shelly, and rest easy; there is no way these guys are going to catch us now."

"Just be careful, Jim," she replied. "Let me know when you catch up with Sergeant." Shelly sat at the table, wondering how big the Raven compound was.

The days and nights that followed were torturous for Shelly. She spent much of her time with Grace and Christy, comparing baby progress. Though she had daily contact with Jim, who assured her they were managing, she still wanted them home safe. The snow that had covered their escape had continued, turning into a major storm. Jim let her know when they had constructed a lean-to under a deep outcrop to wait out the storm. It was three days before they could leave the lean-to, and they were running out of food. The men and dogs were subsisting mainly on beef broth made from jerky, with small amounts of dehydrated vegetables mixed in. The llamas were having a harder time. Eric worried over them, but he knew there wasn't anything to do but get them home as soon as possible.

Shelly and Rosa had been pacing in the horse barn for a couple of hours. Jim had contacted Shelly that morning to let her know they were finally in the valley. When they came through the door, she could see the exhaustion in every move of the men and animals. There were workers that immediately took over the llamas and dogs, rubbing them down with towels and blankets. The llamas were led to stalls, where racks of hay waited, and the dogs ate ravenously of a warm meat-and-vegetable mash. The men wrapped their hands gratefully around large mugs of steaming hot cocoa. Sergeant hugged Shelly next to his side with one arm. "I never want to make another trip like that again. And by the way, the barrier is down."

Shelly looked at him, stunned, and then shook her head, saying, "If we had just waited a couple of weeks, none of this would have been necessary."

The next morning, the president, Mayor Barker, and Jim Lightfoot arrived together for a recap of what had transpired on the trip. Shelly sat on the sofa with Trey and listened to their report. The president paid close attention as Jim described the weaponry of the men. When Jim and Sergeant had finished, Mayor Barker asked, "You're sure they were tracking you with harmful intentions in mind?"

Jim nodded. "I was close enough to hear what they were saying. They were determined to find where we came from and had some interesting ideas on how to convince us to tell them once we were caught."

The president shook his head sadly. "So much death caused by comparatively few evil people. You would think the survivors would want nothing more than to live in peace with the few of us left. But evil exists to disrupt peace. It thrives on the power to inflict pain and suffering on others. We have tried fighting evil. We have proudly sent our finest into wars to defeat evil. We have defeated evil, but there are always those willing to invite evil into their souls. We have to figure out a way to eradicate evil without the use of violence because violence begets violence. To fight evil, our young must first learn to fight it within themselves. Evil cannot be allowed to live among us. We can confine lawbreakers until they are rehabilitated, but evil can never be rehabilitated. Even confined, evil will insidiously spread evil. They must be removed, and this must be done without violence."

"Do you think it can be done?" the mayor asked softly.

President Williamson looked each man in the eye before saying firmly, "We have nothing to lose by trying." The president turned to Shelly and asked, "Have we heard from the Ravens since the food was dropped?"

"No," she answered.

"Why don't we call them. Let's see what they have to say," he said.

Shelly handed Trey to Sergeant and went to the radio. "Raven Compound, this is Cave Haven calling," Shelly said into the mike. They waited. Trey started fussing. Shelly rose to take him, but Sergeant told her to stay, stating that he knew how to change a wet diaper. She had just sent out the call again when Sergeant called her to the bedroom. As soon as she walked into the room, Sergeant said, "This one's yours," and fled back to the men.

Shelly laughed as she cleaned up the baby and put a fresh diaper on him. She snuggled him and said in that voice all people use with babies, "Don't you worry, sweet pea; we will get that big, tough marine trained yet."

She handed a sweet-smelling Trey to Sergeant as she sat down and sent out the call again. This time she got an answer. "Raven Compound here, Cave Haven. We want to thank you for the food, but we are going to need more soon. Do you have more you can spare? We will be more than happy to come get it."

"Glad you got the food, Raven, but by the time you need more, the cities will be safe to enter."

"That's real good information, Cave Haven. We heard a broadcast a while back, and we understand that President Williamson is there with you. I would like you to let him know I voted for him."

"I will surely do that, Raven," Shelly said, rolling her eyes at the president.

"You folks haven't by chance come across some people out on their own, have you?"

"In this weather?" she asked.

"No. A few months back a group of our folks went berry picking. Nine of them never came back. We sent out our search-and-rescue dogs to find them, but they lost the trail."

Shelly felt herself grow cold with revulsion. These were the slavers. "Sergeant and the others risked their lives to feed this bunch," she thought. Shelly ran her fingers through her hair but said in a friendly manner, "If we happen onto your people, you have our guarantee they will be treated well, Raven. Cave Haven, signing off."

Shelly turned off the radio with a shaking hand. "I'm sorry," she said to Sergeant. "I couldn't talk to them anymore. Do you know who they are? Do you?"

CHAPTER 45

Sergeant laid his hand on Shelly's shoulder. "We know exactly who they are, Shelly. You did wonderfully not letting on you knew what they were about."

"I don't understand; do you know something about the Ravens?" the president asked.

"The nine people they say were lost—we have them here at Cave Haven," Mayor Barker informed him.

"Well how is it you didn't know about this Raven compound? Didn't you question those nine when they first arrived?" President Williamson demanded.

Shelly took a deep breath, "You must understand, Mr. President, that those people were in a bad way when they arrived here. The Ravens used them as slaves. They had been tortured, beaten, starved, and raped. We have a thirteen-year-old girl that is pregnant, and one woman's baby was murdered because he cried. They haven't integrated into the community as we had hoped they would. And all have adamantly refused to speak of their ordeal. No, we didn't push them for answers."

The president nodded, rubbing his lower lip with his index finger. "The first thing we need to do is interview them. We have to find out everything they know about the Raven Compound."

"Not Danielle," Shelly insisted protectively. "She has just started to feel safe here. Talk all you want to the others, but not Danielle."

"We can question her mother," Mayor Barker said, "and then let her mother tell her what we need to know. At least give her the option. It may upset her if she isn't given a chance to help stop this bunch. She may not be as fragile as you think."

"You may be right," Shelly conceded.

President Williamson turned to Jim. "Can you contact NORAD? I've been thinking it would be best if I and my family relocated there."

Jim's eyes glassed over for a bit. "Kat is contacting the commander."

"Sergeant, do you think you can lead a ground reconnaissance mission if it is needed?" the president asked.

"I can," Sergeant said. "But we are going to have to find them first, and that may not be easy."

"I'm hoping one of the nine will give us some clues to the location," the president said.

"Kat is with the commander," Jim spoke.

The president turned his attention to Jim. "Is there a way for them to get my family and me to NORAD?"

"A Black Hawk helicopter is available," Jim said, "but it will have to be serviced to make sure it is flight ready."

"There's no hurry. The VP has elected to remain at this location. They may use the radio to let us know when the Black Hawk is ready to fly."

"They will contact us as soon as the helicopter is made ready. They have quarters for you and your family already prepared," Jim said. Then he looked at the president with clear eyes and asked, "Mr. President, is it possible for Katrina Prescott to make the flight with them? We would sure like to meet in person."

President Williamson smiled. "Of course, Jim. The two of you deserve it."

Jim went to the kitchen and stood with his back to them.

The president continued. "Once I get to NORAD, we can use the satellite technology to try to pinpoint the exact location of the Raven Compound."

"Then what?" Shelly asked.

"Then we watch them until we can figure out a peaceful way to bring them in."

"That may take a while," Sergeant said.

"As long as they are not a direct threat to others, we will not use force," the president said. "I feel it is imperative to show our remaining population that evil can be dealt without deadly force."

Over the next few weeks, plans were finalized to fly the president and his family to NORAD. Two Black Hawk helicopters flew into the valley. Members of the military, scientists, and Katrina Prescott arrived in the first one. Jim went to help Kat out of the helicopter and immediately disappeared with her into the cave. The other visitors spent the next few days going through the cave and asking questions. Military personnel sat down with the nine former slaves. Danielle had agreed to go to the meeting, and she sat wedged between her mother and one of the other women of the group.

Sergeant, the only one from Cave Haven, sat and quietly took notes. He held his temper in check as the group, one by one, described their capture and treatment. He was heartened by the mention of a few exceptions in which members of the Ravens had done what they could to help. Though Danielle didn't speak, her mother told them of one man in particular. He took his turns with Danielle but never touched her. He had told the girl that giving her a night of reprieve from the others was the best he could do for her. When the meeting finally ended, Sergeant left without speaking. He was feeling sick when he entered his home.

Shelly immediately read his mood. "Was it that bad?" she asked.

"Yes, it was more than that bad; I think I need a shower," his trembling voice answered as he gave her a gentle hug.

It was early April, and the air was still cold as a light wind blew down through the valley. Shelly was standing alone, comfortable in her llama-wool-lined parka, viewing the helicopter that had landed in the field outside the cave. One helicopter was parked by the cave's entrance. Another helicopter she couldn't see, but knew was there, was parked close to the horse barn, being loaded with fresh fruits, vegetables, and canisters of milk. She heard footsteps behind her and wasn't surprised when President Williamson stepped beside her. "I want to thank you personally for what you did for my family and me."

"I had plenty of help, sir," she replied.

"I know," the president said. "Just before we went into the bunker, I was advised of several spaceships, each the size of a small city, hovering above our atmosphere."

Shelly felt her heart start to beat faster as she said, "That's interesting."

President Williamson nodded. "More interesting was when one ship entered our atmosphere and hovered over a mountain in Wyoming. Shelly, we know the elder group are not from this planet."

Shelly felt as if her throat were closing, and she said in a whispery voice, "I never said they were."

The president smiled. "I know it has been hard on you holding on to your secrets and still trying to be honest with me."

"Did you know all along?" she asked, struggling to make her voice sound normal.

"Pretty much from the time I took my first tour of the cave. There is just too much advanced technology involved here for it to be of human origin. There are those that want to do reverse technology on this entire place. What are your thoughts on the idea?"

"My thoughts are that it will be a waste of time," she said. "If they try, it will only disintegrate in their hands. This whole thing was built to ensure the survival of the human race. We have been given another chance to evolve into a peaceful species. But we have not been given this technology. Call it a loan, but they will destroy it before we can secure access to it."

"So do you believe these aliens are totally peaceful?" he asked.

"Yes. I don't think they have it in them to be any other way."

"Do you think we will ever be like them?" he asked.

Shelly thought for a moment before answering. "No, they are a completely different species, but we can endeavor to evolve our behavior to be more like theirs."

"That may never happen," President Williamson said skeptically.

"Maybe not," Shelly said, turning and smiling up at him, "But we have nothing to lose by trying."

Printed in the United States
By Bookmasters